SABRINA'S MAN

WESTERN JUSTICE
- BOOK 2 -

SABRINA'S MAN

GILBERT MORRIS

BARBOUR
PUBLISHING

© 2013 by Gilbert Morris

Print ISBN 978-1-61626-759-9

eBook Editions:
Adobe Digital Edition (.epub) 978-1-62836-321-0
Kindle and MobiPocket Edition (.prc) 978-1-62836-322-7

All scripture quotations are taken from the King James Version of the Bible.

This book is a work of fiction. Names, characters, places, and incidents are either products of the author's imagination or used fictitiously. Any similarity to actual people, organizations, and/or events is purely coincidental.

Cover design: Kirk DouPonce, DogEared Design

Published by Barbour Publishing, Inc., P.O. Box 719, Uhrichsville, Ohio 44683, www.barbourbooks.com

Our mission is to publish and distribute inspirational products offering exceptional value and biblical encouragement to the masses.

Member of the
Evangelical Christian
Publishers Association

Printed in the United States of America.

PART ONE

CHAPTER 1

Little Rock, Arkansas, 1864

The late summer sun, which had been hiding behind a silver cumulus cloud, illuminated the face of Waco Smith as he stood staring up at a large sign glistening with fresh paint. Here at the north end of Little Rock, the businesses framing Main Street were, for the most part, framed structures, but others made a more permanent statement with their façade of brick and marble. Waco turned and looked down to his left to the Arkansas River that dissected the town and lent its own dark odors to the sense of the southern part of Arkansas.

Waco noticed with a degree of sadness that many of the men walking the street to his right wore parts of the Confederate uniform. Many of them were missing arms, and others hobbled along on crutches or on one leg. *This war is going to ruin the South.* The thought was bitter in his mouth, for he was tired of the war as were most people in the South.

He thought with bitterness of the year that he had served in the Confederate Army. He had joined up in a fit of patriotism when Fort Sumter had fallen but had signed up for only one year.

He had fought at Bull Run, but when his year was up, he had left the army and determined never to fight in the Civil War again.

Waco's train of thought about the war was broken when a voice behind him said, "That's a right nice sign you got there, Waco."

Waco turned and smiled at the speaker, Micah Satterfield, and paused, studying the police chief.

Satterfield was a heavyset individual with a square face, a pair of sharp blue eyes, and a neatly trimmed mustache. He had served Little Rock as police chief for three terms and kept a tight lid on the city. "You're getting to be a respectable citizen."

Shaking his head, Waco gave Satterfield a brief grin. "Never thought I'd be one of your taxpayers, did you, Chief?" He was six feet two inches tall and had to look down on Satterfield, as he did on most men.

Satterfield glanced up at the large sign that announced SMITH & BARTON HARDWARE. "Hope to get rich, do you, son?"

"I doubt that. All I've ever done is raise horses." He shrugged his broad shoulders, adding, "Will—he's the smart one."

"So I understand. You two must have been friends for a long time."

"Nope." Waco studied the sign and murmured, "I worked on my grandparents' horse ranch most of my life. My grandfather died, so I ran the ranch for Grandma. Last December she died. Since I was the only kin, she left the ranch to me. I sold out and made straight for the big city. I was tired of cleaning up after horses and aimed to waste all that money I got on wild women and whiskey."

Sheriff Satterfield studied the tall man. "Well, you didn't do that as I thought you might. What stopped you, Waco?"

Smith took off his hat and ran his hand through his stiff black hair. "Well, I would have, but when I went into the bank to deposit the money I got from the sale of the horse farm, I met Will Barton. I guess I was boasting about what a fool I was going to make of myself, and he talked me into putting off such foolishness. We got to know each other, and somehow he convinced me to go into business with him." He stuck the hat on his head, pushed it back, and said, "I still don't know how it all happened, but the first thing I knew we took my money, Will quit his job at the bank, and for the next six months we just about killed ourselves working twenty hours a day getting that hardware business started."

"You put up all the money?" Satterfield had some doubt in his voice. "That's unusual."

"Oh, Will had a little money. Mostly he took care of the finances of the business. He knew how to keep books, and he knew hardware. I just turned out to be a strong back and a weak mind. You know, Sheriff, I thought breaking horses was hard, but running a business. . .that's worse. Sometimes I wish I was back there in the simple life."

Suddenly a voice called out, "Well, are you going to stand and stare at that sign all day, or are you going to come in and give me a hand?" Both men turned and saw that Will Barton, Waco's partner, had emerged from the store. He was wearing an apron and shook his head. "I can't pick up those kegs of nails. That's your job."

"My master's voice." Waco nodded toward Satterfield, bid him good-bye, and with a rolling gait moved to the front door. "When are we going to hire somebody to do all my work, Will?"

"Not anytime soon." Will Barton smiled then and added, "If you think handling stock is hard, you ought to try balancing a set of books for a new business that's out of money. Put those nail kegs over by the wall, will you?"

"Sure." Waco moved over where six nail kegs were stacked,

picked one of them up, and carried it easily with a strength that surprised most people. He moved the rest of the kegs then leaned against the counter and sighed. He opened one barrel and pulled out a cracker and then reached into another and pulled out a pickle. He took a bite of the pickle, made a face, and said, "These things are sure sour."

"Well, stop eating them. That's my profit."

"I wish I had never run into you, Will. If I had gone right down to having my fun, I could be living it up with the hostesses down at the Golden Nugget."

"Hostesses! That's a nice word for 'em."

"Well, it doesn't do any good to be nasty. That's what they call themselves."

"If you had done that, you'd be broke and probably in jail."

Suddenly Waco grinned, which he'd been told by several ladies made him look much younger, and reached out and put his hand on Will's shoulders.

The man was his opposite in almost every way. Barton was only five feet eight and was almost fragile. He had blond hair and hazel eyes, and his face was composed of delicate features. Waco's hair lay thick and black and ragged against his temple. He had high cheekbones, and minute weather lines slanted out from his eyes across smooth bronze skin. His mouth was broad below an aqualine nose, and his eyes were a shade of gray that was almost blue.

Will had been to college for a year when his father had died. There had been no inheritance. Will had found a job as a clerk at the bank and had done well enough.

"I was just kidding, Will," Waco said. The feelings of his partner were easily hurt, so he had to be careful.

Instantly Will gave Waco a smile. "Take the cash from the sales to the bank, will you? I don't like to keep it at the store."

"Sure."

"And take the pistol. You might get held up."

"I'll be right careful." Waco moved to the drawer behind one of the counters, pulled out a .44, checked the load, stuck it in his waistband, and sighed. "Do you reckon business will pick up after this war's over, Will?"

"Bound to, and it can't last much longer," Will declared. "Grant's got Lee penned up in Richmond."

"I wish it would end today. I lost some good friends in that fracas." Waco turned and called out as he left, "I shouldn't be long."

"Sounds good."

Waco left the building, but not before hearing Will turn back to the books with a sigh.

As Waco left the bank, he was greeted by a blond woman who grinned at him. "When you coming down to visit me, Waco?"

"Oh, I'll be there. You just hang on, Rosie."

Stepping outside, he looked up and studied the sky, then muttered, "There's some rain in those clouds." He walked down the street to the train station. When he got there, he stopped to talk to Oscar Riggs.

"You still aim to go hunting after a deer with me this weekend?" Oscar asked. He was a muscular man with a pair of sharp black eyes.

"Yep, we need some venison at our place."

"We'll go on Sunday morning."

Oscar shook his head violently. "I'm plum nervous about hunting on the Sabbath."

Waco was amused. "Well, you're a sinner just like I am, aren't you, Oscar?"

"Yes, but I don't want to make it any worse." He took a match out of his pocket, stuck it in his mouth, and began chewing on it. "Don't it scare you to think about what's gonna happen to us when we die?"

"Some. I try not to think about it much."

Oscar suddenly turned and said, "Well, there comes the 2:15. I hope there's no baggage for me to move."

The arrival of the train always drew visitors to the station. Men with nothing else to do, many of them veterans crippled up, gathered, and Waco idly watched as three men got off.

Then a woman stepped down, and the conductor reached up to take her hand.

"That's a right nice-looking woman," Oscar said.

"Sure is," Waco replied.

The two watched the woman as the conductor helped her locate her luggage, which she set down on the platform. She looked around as if confused.

Waco would have left, but he had gone only a few steps when Oscar said, "Uh-oh, that's trouble."

Waco turned and saw that two men had bracketed the young woman and were giving her a hard time.

"Those two ought to be run out of town."

Waco recognized Jasper Landon and Orville York. Both of them had served short terms in prison, and Waco had beaten Orville in an oozing fistfight in the Golden Nugget Saloon. The sight of the two giving the young woman a hard time brought the quick flare of temper that lurked somewhere below Waco's smooth surface. "Those fellows need a lesson in manners," he remarked.

"Better watch yourself, Waco," Oscar called out as his friend left. "They been spreading it around they're gonna wipe you out."

Moving to where the three stood, Waco paused.

Instantly the two men turned their attention on him. Both of them had anger in their expressions.

"You two be on your way. Leave the lady alone."

"What makes you think you can give me orders?" Jasper Landon said. He was a tall, lanky man with a lantern jaw.

Orville York was shorter but muscular. He spat out the words, "You might as well move on! We're doing right well without your help here."

Waco ignored them as he turned to the woman. "Young lady, you're probably going to the hotel. I'll be glad to escort you."

"Thank you very much." The woman was very attractive, with blond hair and blue eyes and dressed better than most.

"I'm going to wipe you out one of these days," Jasper said. "I hear you think you're a tough man."

Waco kept his eyes fixed on both and was not surprised when, without warning, Orville threw a swift punch. Waco had been expecting it. He blocked it with his left arm and struck the man a tremendous blow on the nose. Orville wheeled, cried out, and fell backward in the dust. Instantly Waco wheeled to see that Landon was reaching for a gun. With one quick move he pulled out his own gun before Landon could free his own weapon.

"I ain't drawin'!" Landon said quickly.

"Second thoughts are usually best. You two move on. I'm tired of the sight of you."

Orville scrambled to his feet. Blood was staining his shirt. "You won't always have that gun."

"I'll always have the gun, Orville. I'm not telling you again. Move on."

The two cursed but left.

Waco watched them to be sure they were out of the way.

The woman said, "I can't thank you enough."

Waco said, "Sorry you'd get such an introduction to our city. I'm Waco Smith. Could I help you with your luggage?"

"I—I don't know exactly where to go. I need a room for the night."

"Well, there's the Majestic Hotel. The name's more stuck up than the hotel, but it's clean."

"If you wouldn't mind, I'd appreciate it."

Waco picked up the two suitcases and then nodded. "Down this way, miss. I don't know your name."

"I'm Alice Malone. I'm very grateful to you for you help, but won't it make trouble for you?"

"Oh, those two will make trouble wherever they go, but they won't bother you."

They reached the Majestic Hotel, and Waco waited while the woman signed her name to the guest register.

The desk clerk instructed, "Room 206 up on the second floor. Got nobody to carry your bags."

"I'll take care of that," Waco said pleasantly. "Got a key, George?"

"Right here." George leaned over and pulled a key from a board and handed it over. "There you are, Miss Malone. Glad to have you in our city."

"Thank you."

Waco moved up the stairs with the young woman. When she got to the room, she unlocked the door, and he walked inside and put the suitcases down. He took off his hat and said, "Well, like the man said, welcome to Little Rock."

SABRINA'S MAN

She hesitated and bit her lower lip.

There was some sort of fear in her, at least Waco thought so. "Look, it's a little early, but those train rides can get you pretty hungry. Be proud to have you go down with me. We'll have an early supper or late lunch. Whichever."

"Oh, I am hungry, but it would be a bother."

"No bother at all. Come along."

The restaurant was only a quarter full. Waco pulled a chair out, and when she sat down, he moved across from her.

A woman came up and said, "Hello, Waco, what can I get you?"

"What's good today?"

"Got some good beef."

"Bring us some of that and any vegetables you can find. That suit you, Miss Malone?"

"It sounds wonderful."

The woman moved away, and Waco managed to make small talk as they were waiting. The meal came, and she ate hungrily. Waco, who was always hungry, downed his meal quickly.

Finally Alice seemed to be troubled about something and said, "I don't know exactly what to do, Mr. Smith."

"Waco's fine, ma'am. What do you mean you don't know what to do?"

"Well, I was living with my sister and her husband. They have a large family and a small house, so I felt like I needed to give them some freedom. I have another aunt that lives here. I need to find her. She invited me once to come and stay with her, but I haven't talked to her in some time. I'm just a little bit nervous."

"Well, be good to have you here. What's your aunt's name?"

"Bessell Gilbert."

"Don't know the lady, but we'll find her."

After they finished their meal, Bessell Gilbert turned out to be easy enough to find. At least her house was.

Sheriff Satterfield had been their source. When the two had found him in his office, he was slapping flies with the swatter, but he rose at once and nodded when Waco introduced Alice.

"My aunt's name is Bessell Gilbert. Do you know her, Sheriff?"

"Yes, I do, but I'm sorry to tell you she's not here."

Dismay swept across Alice's face. "I haven't heard from her. I wanted to come and stay with her. I really don't have any other place to go."

"Well, we'll find something. She got married and moved away out to Kansas somewhere. Perhaps we can find her."

"That won't do any good, I'm afraid," Alice said. "If she's not here, I'm sure she's sold her house."

"Yes, she did, and folks are living in it now."

"Come along. We'll figure out something," Waco said. "Let's go down and sit on the bench and watch the old Arkansas River flow by."

She did not answer, and he saw that she was upset. He himself had never had such a problem, and he felt an urge somehow to help her. "Here. Sit on one of those benches there, and we'll watch the steamboats."

Alice sat down, and he sat beside her. She was quiet for a long time.

Waco did not know how to handle the situation, but he felt that somehow she had to have help. "I'll tell you what. We'll find you a place to stay, and then you can decide what to do."

"I—I don't have very much money."

"We can probably find you a place with low rent. Don't let it worry you. Things like this always look bad when you're in the middle of them." The two sat there, and Waco spoke to her as cheerfully as he knew how.

Finally she rose and said, "I'm tired. I think I need to rest." Waco stood beside her, and she turned to look at the river. A steamboat was making its way up the stream, and she watched until it moved around the bend. "I'm really afraid. I've never had to really take care of myself in a situation like this."

"If you want to work, I'm sure we can find something for you to do."

She did not answer, but he saw that tears were in her eyes. She began to tremble.

Waco put his arms around her, drew her close, and said, "Don't worry about it. I'll see you're all right."

Alice did not move. She was looking at him with her face lifted, her lips motionless. The fragrance of her hair touched his senses. He saw the quick rise and fall of her bosom, and then an impulse took him. He drew her closer, bent his head, and kissed her.

He'd had little enough experience with a woman of this nature. Most of his women friends were rougher, but as she lay in his arms in an attitude of trust, he felt a sweetness and a richness that filled the empty places in him and allowed him for this short fragment of time to know what completeness could be. The best of life suddenly took him, but a sadness came, for he knew this would soon pass away.

She lay quietly in his arms, the rhythm of her breathing growing calmer. "I shouldn't have let you kiss me."

"Not your fault. Men are pretty selfish."

"You're not, Waco." She smiled suddenly, pulled out a handkerchief, and wiped away the tears. "Take me to my room, please."

He walked with her to the hotel and left her there, but she turned at the foot of the stairs and gave him a sweet smile. "Will I see you again?"

"Why don't we have breakfast? I'll come to call for you at the hotel."

"That would be nice. Good night, and thanks for helping me."

Waco nodded, put on his hat, and left the hotel. He went back to the hardware store where he and Will had made a temporary bedroom to serve until they could do better.

He found Will sitting at the table eating something from a bowl. "Have some of this stew. Not bad."

"I've already eaten."

Will looked up. "Why'd you do that?"

A sharp, uncomfortable feeling touched Waco as he told how he had met the young woman. "Will, you know all the businessmen in town. She's got to find something to do. We've got to help her."

Will held the spoon in his right hand, looked at it for a moment, and then said, "I don't know the lady, but I know you. Be careful, Waco."

Waco stared at him. "Be careful about what?"

"Well, you've had some experience with another kind of woman. This one is apparently different. You'd be right for the plucking."

"She's not that kind."

Will Barton smiled faintly. There was a doubt in his eyes, and he said, "They are all that kind sooner or later. Just be careful."

"Sure. But she's not that kind."

CHAPTER 2

William Barton walked to the sheriff's office.

Micah Satterfield sat in one of the rockers in front of his office reading a week-old paper. The news displeased him, evidenced by the creases along his forehead. With a twisted mouth he muttered, "The Yankees are going to get us. Ain't no doubt about that." He continued reading the paper, but a movement caught his eye and he looked up at the man who had approached. "Hello, Will. What brings you to my office today?"

Will Barton nodded to the sheriff. "I wanted to talk to you about something that's got me pretty worried. Are you gonna put a special guard on the bank, Chief?"

"Why would I want to do that?"

"Well, the First State Bank over at Jonesboro was robbed. That's not too far from here. We might be next. I don't want a bunch of outlaws to be getting the money I worked so hard for."

"Don't worry about it, Will. The thieves didn't get much over at Jonesboro if what I hear is true. Sheriff Conners has got a posse out running them down."

"Well, can't be too careful." Barton leaned up against the post and glanced at the paper in the sheriff's hand. "Not good news about the war, is it?"

"There ain't no war left, son. It's just a matter of survival, and the Confederacy won't do that very long."

"I'll be glad when it's all over. I wish we had never got into it."

"So do a bunch of grievin' widow women and men, too."

The two chatted about the war; both of them, like many Southerners, had practically given up on the Cause. Finally Satterfield folded his paper and tossed it into the chair next to his. "What's going on with Waco and that woman that come to town?"

"I never saw a man so dazzled by a woman," Will said sourly. "I thought Waco was a pretty steady man, but he's not. She's been here a month, and Waco just acts like a man bewitched. He'd run into a fence post if she was close."

"Well, you reckon he's going to marry her?"

"Might be, but I'd hate to see it."

"Don't you like the woman?"

"She's the wrong woman for him." Barton shrugged his shoulders. "They're different. She's a city woman. Waco doesn't know anything but horses."

"Well, he's learning the hardware business. That'll make him a city man."

"I don't think he'll ever become a city man. He does what I tell him, but he's not really got what it takes to make money."

"Well, you do, so I guess he'll be the strong back, and you can be the sharp mind."

"I don't think it's exactly like that. I'll see you later, Chief. You be sure you keep an eye on that bank."

"I'll take care of it, Will."

Stepping up out of the dust of the street onto the wooden plank sidewalk, Waco glanced up at the sign that said THOMAS'S JEWELRY STORE. He hesitated for a moment and shook his head. Then, taking a deep breath, he walked across the sidewalk and entered the store. It only took him ten minutes to make his purchase and exit the store. When he stepped onto the sidewalk again, he was still confused. He walked along until he approached the sheriff, who was, as usual, sitting in the rocker outside his office. "Hello, Micah."

"Hey, Waco. Say, I been meaning to talk to you. It might be a good time." Satterfield leaned forward, spat out an amber stream of tobacco juice on the floor, stared at it thoughtfully, then shrugged. "I've been needin' a new mount. You know horses, son. I want you to look at that stallion that Bill Green wants to sell."

"Already seen him. He's a fine horse. Can't go wrong with him." The two men talked about the virtues of the horse in question. Waco realized he knew more about horses than any other man in Little Rock, or in Arkansas for that matter. It was his strong point. Finally Waco glanced down at the newspaper. "What's the latest news?"

"Did you hear about Cold Harbor?"

"No. What's that?"

"Why, it's a place, son. Been a big battle there."

"I don't really keep up with the war. Just hopin' it'll be over soon," Waco remarked.

"Well, this was a bad one for the Yankees. Grant's followin' Lee's army all the way to Richmond, I reckon. He caught up with him at Cold Harbor."

"Is that pretty close to Richmond?"

"Not far. That's what Grant's aimin' for." A look of satisfaction swept across the sheriff's craggy face. "But Grant got more than he was askin' for this time."

"What do you mean?"

"Lee beat him to Cold Harbor and got his men in an entrenched position. They was just lyin' there waitin' behind them trees and rocks. Grant always thinks he can lick Lee anytime he can catch up with him. Well, he caught up with him, but he wished they hadn't! He sent his whole army in, but General Lee was in an impregnable defensive spot. Paper says seven thousand Union soldiers were killed in less than an hour. They're calling him 'Butcher' Grant now."

"I guess that's the kind of man the North needed."

"Guess he is. He can lose four men to our one, but if he loses a thousand men, he just sends word back to Lincoln and asks for a thousand more. Lincoln reaches out and makes a call to one of the states, and they send a thousand men without even thinking about it. Every time we lose a man it leaves a gap. No one to fill his place."

Sheriff Satterfield studied Waco's face and finally asked, "How's that Alice girl you been courtin'?"

Waco shot a quick glance at the sheriff. He had taken considerable ribbing about his courtship of Alice. "She's doing fine."

"How's it working out her working there in the hardware store with you and Will?"

"She's doing fine. She didn't know much about hardware, but then I don't either. She's smarter than I am though. She's learned all the prices, and Will's satisfied with her."

"I'm surprised that Will would let a woman work in the store."

"Well, I had to keep after him, but he finally caved in."

Waco shifted from one foot to another.

"What's the matter, son?"

"Well, I guess I've got a problem, Chief."

"You want some advice? I'm mighty free with that."

Waco grinned. "I guess I do." He reached into his pocket and pulled out a small box. He lifted the lid and said, "I just bought this ring."

"Why, that's a right fancy article," Micah said. "I'll take a wild guess and say it's for Miss Alice."

"Yes, but I'm not sure I ought to give it to her."

"Why not?" Micah asked with some surprise.

"Well, I bought it for an engagement but to tell the truth, I'm feeling pretty shaky."

"It don't take much advice here. You love that gal, don't ya?"

"Yes, but I'm not sure she cares for me."

Micah chuckled. "Take a run at it, son. Marry that girl. Get you a house full of kids and settle down."

Waco was not quite satisfied with Micah's advice. He looked at the ring for a long time, closed the lid, and then put it back in his pocket. "Doesn't seem right to get married with this war still going on."

"Well, it'll be over soon. Everybody knows that."

"Yes, but what'll happen to the South then?" Waco demanded. A stubborn look crossed his face, and he added, "The Yankees will come down here and tell us how to do everything. They're going to make life tough on us Rebels."

"There's always something to wait on, Waco. There ain't never a perfect time to get married or do anything else. If you love that gal, then grab her and tell her so and get hitched."

23

Waco suddenly smiled. His broad lips turned upward at the edges, and he said, "Well, that's just what I aim to do, Micah. Thanks for your advice."

Waco moved away, walking down the sidewalk rapidly, now sure of his decision.

Waco and Alice were walking along in front of the Olympic Theater. They stopped to look at a bill outside. A heavy rain had fallen earlier, and the smell of more rain was in the air, which carried the spongy odors of spring. The violent rain had stopped, but the stubborn clouds rolled overhead like huge waves from a rough sea breaker. It was late in the afternoon. There was little light in the day, and lights were shining up and down Front Street as the two paused and looked at the poster.

> MINSTRELSY, BURLESQUE, EXTRAVAGANZAS,
> ETHIOPIAN ECCENTRICITIES.
> *Nothing to offend ladies or children,*
> *for all are done in the most sensitive taste.*
> *Tickets fifty cents. Orchestra chairs one dollar.*
> *Boxes three dollars.*

Alice stared at the sign and then turned to face Waco asking, "What's an Ethiopian eccentricity?"

"I don't have no idea. You want to go in and find out?"

"It might be fun."

"It's early yet. Let's go. Maybe we can get something to eat later."

"All right."

Waco paid a little shriveled-up woman with bright black eyes the admission fee, and the two went inside. The room was filled with stale smoke from cigarettes, cigars, and pipes. Their seats were halfway to the stage. The show started almost at once, and they found it mildly amusing.

When it was over they left, and Waco said, "I reckon I could get along without seeing something like that every night."

"Oh, I think it was fun. I still don't know what an Ethiopian eccentricity is though."

The two walked down Front Street until they got to the Royal Café. They went inside.

A heavyset waitress with stains on her apron said, "What can I get you folks?"

"How about some roast beef?" Waco asked.

"Nope. Special is pork tonight. We got pork chops and pork ribs and pork roast."

"I'd like to try the ribs," Alice said. "I always like pork ribs."

"I'll have the same. Bring us some vegetables if you got any."

The two sat there talking about the show while the heavy waitress moved away.

Waco was nervous, which Alice noticed, and she asked, "Is something bothering you, Waco?"

"Why, no. Not really." He searched his mind for something to say. He finally said quickly, "I don't know much about you. Do you have much family?"

"No, I don't have any parents. My father was a gambler, but my mother didn't like that. My father left when I was only ten. Mother had to work hard to provide for the two of us."

"What did she work at?"

"Oh, whatever she could find. She was a good seamstress and

did that for a while. We moved around a lot."

Waco picked up one of the ribs. Chewing thoughtfully, he swallowed and said, "What about sweethearts? You have a lot of them?"

A smile came to Alice's lips. "I'm not supposed to tell about things like that, am I?"

"Oh, you can tell me." He studied her carefully.

She seemed to have a spirit glowing in her that showed self-sufficiency. But at the same time she always seemed on guard. She was a beautiful and robust woman with a woman's soft depth that could scarcely conceal a woman's fire. Alice's face in habitual response had an expression that stirred Waco. Finally he found himself trying to find a name for what it is. It was something like the gravity that comes when someone has seen too much, like the shadow of hidden sadness. There was also some sort of strength in her. She seemed to be the kind of woman who could, if necessary, draw a revolver and shoot a man down and not go to pieces afterward. She was past her first youth, but there was a beauty about her that drew him as no woman ever had.

"What about you?" she said.

"What about me?"

"What have you done all your life? How old are you, Waco?"

"Twenty-five."

"So am I. Did you go to school?"

"Oh, for a little while. Never got past the sixth grade. Most of what I know is horses."

"Yes, everybody says you know horses better than anyone. You ever have a sweetheart?"

Waco stirred and could not seem to find an easy answer. Trouble clouded him, and he cleared his throat then shook his head. "I've known a few women, but nothing serious. I guess I know more about horses than I do about women."

Alice obviously found this amusing. When she smiled, two dimples appeared at the corners of her mouth. "I'm glad to hear a man admit that he doesn't know everything there is to know about women."

A silence fell over the two. Finally the meal was finished, and he said, "I've been wanting to ask you something, Alice."

"Well, go ahead."

"Have you ever thought of me as a man you might marry?" The words were hard for Waco to get out.

Alice stared at Waco for a long moment. "I think a woman wonders that about every man she knows, Waco."

"I care for you more than I can say. I wish I had the words, but all I can say is I love you and you'll never know meanness from me. Would you think about marrying me, Alice?"

Alice reached over and covered his broad hands with hers. She rubbed the calluses that were on his palm and said nervously, "How strong these hands are." She grew silent and seemed to be thinking deeply. Finally she smiled. "I'll think about it, Waco. I will definitely think about it."

🝑

"Well, I wish I'd been the knight in shining armor to save you, Alice. Waco has all the luck." Will Barton spoke simply and with obvious sincerity. Alice had just told him that Waco had asked her to marry him.

"Why did you never come courting me?"

"Because I saw Waco was in love with you." He moved forward then and put his arm around her in a protective fashion. "If he doesn't treat you right, I'll shoot him, and we'll run off to the South Seas and eat coconuts."

Alice laughed.

She had once told Will that she liked his light sense of humor. He smiled, lost in thought. He suddenly came to himself and said, "But Waco would never mistreat a woman."

"No, he wouldn't."

An hour later, Will encountered Waco. He immediately said, "Alice has told me that you want to marry her."

"Yes, that's right."

"Well, congratulations."

Waco ran his hand through his hair with a troubled expression. "It's not exactly settled yet. She's got to think about it."

"I don't understand having to think about things like that," Will said, shrugging his shoulders in a gesture of disgust. "If you love someone, that's all there is to it."

"No, I don't think so, Will. A man and a woman have got to have something different, almost like magic. Or else why would they stick together no matter what?" Waco suddenly saw something in Will Barton and asked quickly, "Did you ever feel like marrying a woman, Will?"

Finally Will dropped his head and turned away muttering, "Just once."

"Why didn't you do it, then?"

Will's voice was no more than a whisper. "She favored another man."

"Come along, Alice. I've got something to show you."

"What is it?" Alice had been standing outside the hardware

store when Waco had walked up with a smile on his face. "Come along. I'll show you."

Alice looked puzzled but walked along. They cleared Front Street and turned and walked to where a few houses had been built on large lots.

"Come on and look at this." Waco led the way up on the porch of a painted frame house with gables and two windows covered by curtains.

When Waco reached for the door, Alice exclaimed, "You can't just walk in there, Waco!"

"Why can't I?"

"Because we'd be trespassing."

Waco laughed. "No, we wouldn't. This is our house."

Alice stared at him in disbelief. "What do you mean *our* house?"

"I took what was left of the money from the sale of the horse ranch and put it on this house. It'll take awhile to pay for it, but it's for us, Alice. Come on in and let's see if you like it."

Alice followed Waco inside. They went through the house room by room, and finally when they got to the spacious living room with the large fireplace, he walked over and put his elbow on the mantel and stared around the room. "I wonder if there was ever a murder in this room."

"A murder?" Alice stared at him in disbelief. "What are you talking about?"

"Well, lots of things happen in houses, Alice."

"But not murders."

"Maybe so. No telling what the history of this place is. Might have been a fellow standing right here where I am. A woman came in the door. He took one look at her and fell in love. They married and had children and grandchildren."

"That's much nicer than a murder."

"I just imagine things like that sometimes. Maybe there was a couple that lived here, and one of them was unfaithful and ran off with the hardware salesman or an insurance salesman."

"You know, Waco, you're a much deeper thinker than most people take you for."

He came to her and brought her to him with a quick sweep of his arm. He'd kissed her before, but lightly. This time he felt not only the desperate hunger of her lips, but running through him was an emotion almost like wildfire. She had this power over him, lifting him to a wild height so that he could know the vague hints of glory a woman and a man might know. When he lifted his lips, he said, "Marry me, Alice. I'll make you happy."

Alice put her hands behind his neck, drew him down, and kissed him again. "All right," she whispered. "I'll marry you."

⌘

"Alice has agreed to marry me, Will."

Will was adding up figures in a book. He looked up and said, "Well, that's fine. Of course that's no surprise to me. My congratulations. You're getting a fine girl."

"You mentioned you loved a woman once, but you didn't explain what happened."

Will shook his head, his lips clamped together. "No sense talking about things like that. When is the date of the wedding?"

"As soon as we get the house ready."

Will closed the book. "All right," he said. "Are you sure you love her?"

"I am."

"And are you sure she loves you?"

Waco did not speak for a moment, and Will saw uncertainty in his face. Finally Waco said, "She doesn't care for me like I do for her, but I can make her love me, Will. You just wait and see!"

CHAPTER 3

A violent rain had swept through Little Rock earlier, leaving the pungent odors of spring that followed a downpour. It was late in the afternoon, and there was a small light in the sky. Already some businesses were lighting lamps, but Front Street had become a muddy yellow street through which wagons, weary riders, and small groups made a river of mud illuminated by the street's gas lamps.

Alice had left the house and held an umbrella over her head to catch the few remaining remnants of the rainstorm. She moved along past Jackson's Confectionaries and next door smelled the dry, faint fragrance of cotton goods at John Maddox's shop. There was a jam of wagons locked hub to hub, and she heard the curses of the teamsters. She made her way to the shop that had become very familiar to her and arrived at the hardware store barely touched by the earlier rain.

As she collapsed the umbrella and shook it dry, a group of young men passed by and called out to her. Their raw comments brought only a look of disdain from her, and she did not bother to answer them.

Folding the umbrella, she entered the store and was greeted by Will, who put down a box that he was lifting up on the counter. He turned to face her. "Surprised you come out in all this rain," he said, smiling at her.

"Oh, the worst of it was over. Is Waco here?"

"No. I sent him out with a load of equipment to Walnut City. Should be back fairly soon. What are you doing out in this weather?"

"I was going to get him to go with me and pick out a wedding dress."

Will came over and leaned against the counter and studied her thoughtfully, a slight smile on his face. "You excited about getting married, Alice?"

"Why, of course." Her remark was perfunctory, and she had a calm look about her.

"You don't look excited."

"Well, do you want me to jump up on the counter and do a dance?"

Will laughed. "That would liven things up. Customers would like it, I'm sure."

Alice turned to smile, then said, "Well, I guess I'll have to go alone."

"James is here. He can handle the place for a while. I'd like to go with you."

"Shopping?" Alice looked surprised. "Not many men would want to help a woman go look for a dress. Most men, I understand, hate shopping."

"Oh, not me," Will said cheerfully. "I like shopping with pretty women. Why, I shopped with my mother all the time."

"Will, why is it I have trouble believing you when you make statements like that?"

"Because I'm such a nice fellow. Let me get my coat, and we'll go find you the prettiest wedding dress in Little Rock. Money is no object."

"Oh, it is, too."

"Nope. This will be on the store." He slipped into a lightweight coat, picked up her umbrella, and said, "We might need this before we get back."

They left the store and walked down the rain-soaked street.

"I love the smell that comes after a rain," Will said. "It's even better when you're out in the country somewhere."

"You aren't a country boy, Will."

"No, I wasn't. I have at least been there after a rain. Which store we going to?"

"We'll go to Maddox's. He has some nice things."

The two made their way down the main street of Little Rock, which was less crowded than usual, for the rain had kept people in.

When they passed by one of the saloons, Alice glanced in and saw the men playing poker around a table. "You never seem to have any fun," Alice said. "Don't you ever go out and play cards or something?"

"I'm a terrible poker player. Terrible gambler for that matter. I always lose more than I win. Cheaper to stay out of it."

"I'm a pretty good poker player."

Will glanced at her with surprise. He turned his head to one side and asked, "Where in the world did you learn to play poker?"

"I had an uncle who was an inveterate gambler. I must not have been over twelve years old, and he taught me how to play." She laughed. "He was surprised when I beat him. We were just playing for matches, and he told me I was a bad girl to beat her old uncle."

"He sounds like a pretty nice uncle."

"He was the only one I had. He used to take me places. His name was Luke Carmody." She did not speak for a while, and then she said, "When he died, I cried for a week it seemed like. I was closer to him than anybody."

"What about your folks?"

"Oh, I had my mother. My father left sometime when I was very young, so it was just Mother and me and Uncle Luke. He was her only brother, or at least the only one she knew about."

They reached Maddox's store, turned, and went inside.

Alice at once went to the section set apart for women's dresses and began pulling them off of a table and holding them up. She held one up that was obviously too large. It had large figures on it and was fairly hideous.

"Oh, that'll be the one." Will grinned. "You'll get fat enough to fit into it one of these days. You won't have to buy any more dresses."

"It's awful!" Alice put it back and began going through other dresses. She was amused by Will, who did not seem at all embarrassed by the looks he got.

The owner, Mr. Maddox, came over and said, "Well, good afternoon, folks. Some storm we had."

"We needed the rain. We got plenty of it," Will said.

"What do you need today, Miss Alice?"

"Going to buy a new dress. A wedding dress."

"Oh, that'll be back here if we have any that'll fit you. If we don't, Minnie Stover could make you one. She's right good with a needle."

They moved back to where Maddox had indicated the dresses might be, and for the next half hour they looked at different dresses. Finally they got one that Alice remarked about slowly, "I rather like this one."

"Well, go try it on. Let's see what it looks like."

"You don't have to wait around, Will."

"I wouldn't miss it. Go on now. Let's see what you're going to look like on your wedding day."

Alice moved into the room that was set apart for women to try on clothes and wondered where the men tried theirs on. For the most part, the men of Little Rock wore rough clothes. It was still a frontier town, more or less. She slipped out of her dress, into the new one, fastened it, and then stepped outside. There was a full-length mirror. She came in front of it and examined herself critically. "What do you think?"

"It doesn't do you justice. It's not gaudy enough. You need to get something that will knock everybody's eyes out when you walk down the aisle of that church. I wonder if they have any bright red dresses."

Alice laughed. "You fool! Brides don't wear red dresses."

"Well, you can set it in motion."

He kept teasing her, and finally she gave up and said, "I guess it will have to be Minnie Stover."

"Well, let's go down and tell her we've got to have it in a hurry."

They left Maddox's and walked down Third Street, where they turned left and found Minnie Stover's shop.

There was a dress in the window that caught Alice's eye. "Now that's the dress I like."

"Not bad. About your size, too."

"I wonder how much it is."

"Don't worry about it. You only get married once. The store

36

has made a better profit than usual this month. We'll get the dress if it fits."

The dress did fit except for a few minor alterations. Minnie Stover, a short, round woman with bright, merry blue eyes said cheerfully, "Might have been made for you, Miss Alice. I'll have it ready for you tomorrow."

"Oh, the wedding won't be for a week."

"Well, you can pick it up tomorrow anyway."

The two left the store, and Alice noticed that Will had fallen silent. "What's the matter? Cat got your tongue?"

"No, I was just thinking. You ever heard that old saying about brides? You need something old, something new, something borrowed, something blue?"

"Yes, I've heard that."

"Well, I want you to have this to wear." He reached into his pocket and pulled out a box. "I've been carrying it with me since yesterday. I found it in my things."

She opened the box and saw a beautiful pearl necklace. "Why, this is wonderful, Will!"

"It belongs to my grandmother. Very old."

Alice looked up and saw that there was a sadness in his face that he could not hide. "You should keep this for the woman you marry."

Will Barton seldom showed his emotions, but there was some sort of grief in him. "I doubt if that will ever happen."

They continued on their way, and Alice glanced at Will several times. When they reached the store and went inside, she said, "Tell me what's the matter."

"I can't hide my feelings very well. I guess that's the reason I'm not a good poker player."

"What's wrong, Will?"

"I guess I feel left out somehow."

"Left out of what?"

"I don't know. I had a partner. Now I don't."

"Why, you'll still have Waco."

"No, I won't. You'll have him, Alice." Will turned, picked up her hand, held it, and looked at it for a moment. "You have beautiful hands." Then he said with a note of gloom, "The way marriage is, at least as I understand it, one man, one woman. They make some sort of group."

"Don't feel that way." Her hand tightened on his. When he looked at her, she reached up and put her hand on his cheek. "Don't be sad, Will. You know we both love you."

Will Barton stiffened and seemed to find something in her words that he needed to hear. "That's good to know," he said softly. "Now we'll have to find you something blue and something new."

❧

Waco sat in the parlor of Reverend James Stoneman's house next door to the framed Methodist church. Stoneman was a middle-aged man with iron-gray hair and smooth cheeks. He wore a black suit, the typical uniform for a Methodist pastor of the day, and he had been speaking for some time about the general arrangements for the wedding. Finally he said, "I wish Alice were here."

"Why is that, Pastor?"

"Well, I like to have meetings with the bride and groom together before the wedding."

"Meeting for what?"

Stoneman leaned back and ran his hand over his gray hair. "I want to warn 'em that things won't be easy. Usually when a couple come in and want to get married, they have stars in their eyes. They see nothing but a long road filled with only good things and joyous days passing as they grow older."

His words troubled Waco, who leaned forward in his chair and asked, "Isn't it like that?"

"Well, no. There are difficulties."

"I don't think Alice and I will ever have any."

Stoneman suddenly laughed. He had perfect teeth, and they showed against his tanned complexion. "Even Adam and Eve had problems. Every couple I know has some."

"You and your wife, you have problems?"

The question seemed to disturb James Stoneman. He half turned away and looked out the window. "The birds have been building a nest out there," he commented. "You see it? I've told my wife to leave it there. The mother bird comes every day and sits on those eggs. I'm looking forward to the time when she brings their supper to them."

Waco did not speak for a while. Finally he said, "You're not telling me about the trouble you had."

"All right," Reverend Stoneman said heavily, and a sober look chased away the good cheer that seemed to be habitual with him. "Well, my wife and I were deeply in love when we married, but we separated."

"I never knew that, Reverend."

"Not many people do. It was a long time ago in another town."

"What happened? I don't mean to be nosy, but—"

"It's all right, Waco. Maybe you need to hear this. My wife left me."

"Well, why did she leave you?"

"My fault. I became infatuated with another woman. Ran off with her."

The news was somehow shocking. He had never thought of a preacher having that kind of a problem. "I can't believe it. You're still a minister."

"It wasn't easy. I soon found out I had made a terrible, terrible mistake. I had to go back and beg my wife's forgiveness, and she forgave me, and I had to go before the church to confess what I had done. I was out of the ministry for five years. I was too ashamed to even speak to God. My wife helped me though. I got her forgiveness, she stayed with me, and the church members were kind. None of that was easy." He turned and said, "There are a great many ways for a marriage to go wrong, and only one for it to go right."

"What's that one way?"

"When you both love each other so much that nothing else matters."

As Waco entered the store, he found Will and Alice putting up stock. Will said, "Well, about time you got back. You deliver the goods?"

"Sure. What have you two been doing?"

"Oh, Waco," Alice said, her eyes shining. "I found a wedding dress." She began to describe it.

Will shushed her, saying, "Don't tell him a thing. When you walk down that aisle, let it be the first glimpse of it." Will had been sitting on the counter chewing on crackers. He was a cracker addict and kept the barrel pretty well filled, but now he slid off and shook his head. "You know you have everything, Waco. You got a good business, and now a fine wife."

Waco did not know exactly how to answer that and was troubled by it.

Will said, "I've got to go to the bank. You two watch the store."

After his friend left, Waco turned to Alice and said, "You know, I feel bad about Will."

"I know. He was telling me how he would be all alone."

"Well, he'll have us."

"He said a marriage was sort of a closed corporation, a man and a woman, and nobody could really get inside."

"Why, that's foolish! They could have friends. They should have. I'll tell you what. Maybe we could find a young woman for Will to court and marry."

Alice suddenly laughed. "It's not like buying groceries, Waco, or a loaf of bread."

"No, I guess not. You know I've never been a Christian man, Alice, but I can't help but believe that God put us together, you and me."

Alice smiled and put her hand on his chest. "You are a romantic, Waco. I never knew that before. I'll bet you like stories with happy endings."

Waco reached out and drew her to him, holding her tightly. "Don't you?"

Alice suddenly grew serious. She bit her lower lip and then said quietly, "I don't think that happens very often."

"Look, Alice, horses could be your friends."

"I've always been afraid of them, Waco."

The two had come out to the livery stable. Waco had determined to teach Alice to ride. He had been shocked when he discovered she had never ridden, and now as they stood before the chestnut he had saddled for her, he said, "You shouldn't be afraid of horses. They're really nice." He patted the horse and said, "Aren't you nice?"

The horse threw its head up and drew its lips back.

"Haven't you ever been hurt by a horse?" Alice asked.

"Well, a few times, but I always thought it was my fault. Horses are good until somebody hurts them."

"Well, I'm sorry to give you your first disappointment in marriage. I know you love horses, but I'm going to be too busy being a wife. You'll have to get a buggy for the honeymoon."

Waco grinned, shoved his hat back, and said, "I'll make you a fine rider, Alice."

Alice shook her head. "You know, I noticed something about you. You think you can change people, but I don't think so."

"Why, sure you can. Haven't you ever changed?"

An odd look crossed Alice's face. "I don't think so. I always knew I needed to change, but I never could." She turned abruptly, saying, "Let's go back to the store."

They made their way back to the store, and when they walked in, Will showed them a new line of boots that he had managed to get. "Our men are walking around in worn-out boots falling to pieces. Some of them they had in the army."

"Well, what's happening to General Lee?" Alice asked.

Will shook his head. "The Confederate Army is whittling down. I'm afraid it's only a matter of time until the South is forced to give up."

They discussed the war until Alice insisted they turn the conversation to lighter topics. The talk turned again to the wedding and who they were going to invite.

Waco finally said, "Invite whoever you want. I will just be happy when we are married."

Alice replied, "Don't let yourself get too happy, Waco. Nobody should. Usually when a person does, something bad happens."

"Never happen to us." Waco grinned.

He had no sooner spoken than a man entered. He was a sullen-looking man with one pant leg pinned up and a crutch. He hobbled in.

Waco said, "Hello, Jake."

Waco knew Jake Callahan resented the fact that Waco and Will did not serve in the Confederate Army. He knew that Waco had served as a soldier for a year at the very beginning, but to Callahan that did not count. Confederate men served until they died or were injured so badly they could no longer fight, and he always let his feelings be known. Callahan had a thin face with a pair of muddy brown eyes. "Gettin' hitched, I hear, Smith."

"That's right."

"This your little woman here?"

"Yes, it is."

"I guess you ain't been by the post office today, have you?"

"No, I haven't."

Callahan grinned. "You won't like it."

"What is it, Jake?" Will asked.

"You don't know either? Well, the notice just went up, and I talked to Colonel Johnson in charge of the troops here in Little Rock. It's a new law."

"What kind of new law?" Waco asked cautiously. "What's it all about?"

"It's called the Conscription Law."

"Conscription? What does that mean?"

"It means that the Confederate Army's got to have men, and at least one of you is headed that way. Conscription Law says every able-bodied man's got to serve in the army. I guess that means you."

Waco could not answer for a moment. There was a triumphant look in Jake's eyes as he said, "You will be gone pretty soon. You'll catch up with General Lee somewhere in Virginia. Let me know how you make out."

As he turned and left, the three were quiet for a time.

"Look, there's Micah. He'll know about this," Will finally said. He went to the door and hollered, "Sheriff, come over here, will you?"

Micah Satterfield came in and looked at the three. "How're the bride and groom?"

"Never mind that," Waco said. "What's this about a Conscription Law?"

"Well, that just came out. The notice is on the post office wall."

"Is there any way to get out of it?" Will asked.

"Sure. Run. I guess if you make it to the North, you won't have to serve."

"It won't be too bad," Waco said.

"I knew something like this would happen," Alice said, her voice tight and a tense look in her eyes.

"It ain't as bad as it sounds," Micah said. "This war can't last too much longer. You fellas just go on and stay out of the way of any bullets."

Alice turned and ran out of the store even before Micah.

"She's plumb disturbed," Satterfield said. "Women are crying all over the Confederacy, I guess. She'll feel better, Waco."

"I don't know. I don't think I will."

"Well, one of you might be able to stay to run the store. It's a pretty lame excuse, but it might work."

Waco quickly replied, "I'll be going back for sure."

"You didn't believe much in the Confederacy, did you, son?"

"No, I didn't, Sheriff. Oh, I did at first when the bugles were blowing and the flags were flying and we were winning, but it became pretty obvious that we couldn't win this war. I knew that a long time ago."

"Well, you better go talk to Alice," Will said. "Women are weak, but she'll stay with you."

Waco's world had been shaken. He had talked to Satterfield several times and to the commanding officer of one of the Confederate groups and got the same story.

The major was a tall man with a fierce mustache. "Lee's penned up, and Grant will get Richmond surrounded. That'll be the end of it. Your woman will wait for you."

He did not go back to the store for some time but just walked around town.

Finally when he returned, Will said, "Where have you been, Waco?"

"Thinking." He stopped and gave Will a sober look. "I can't marry Alice, Will."

"Why, of course you can."

"What if she got pregnant? Who would take care of her and the baby? When I come home, I may be blind or crippled. She needs a whole man."

"You've got to do it, Waco. I wish you didn't have to go. Just trust the Lord. He'll bring you through."

"You don't believe that any more than I do. I don't know about you, but I've ignored God so long He's forgot about me."

45

Later in the afternoon, Waco and Alice were in the store.

Will had gone on one of his errands, and he came back with his face alight. "I've been talking to the major. He says a man can pay a substitute to go into the army in his place."

Waco stared at him. "That's a pretty sorry kind of man to hire somebody to do his fighting for him."

"No, listen. Here's what we'll do. I'll be your substitute. Then you can stay here, get married, and take care of the store."

Waco shook his head firmly. "You know I couldn't take care of this store. We'd be broke in a week. But you're right. One of us has to stay."

They argued about the situation most of the day, and after closing time, Will said, "You may not like it, but one of us has to stay here and take care of the store and Alice."

"You're the only one to take care of the store, Will."

"And you're the only one who can take care of Alice. Here's what we'll do. We'll cut cards for it. The high card goes to the army. The low card stays here and takes care of things until this war is over."

"I don't like it," Alice said. "It doesn't seem right."

"I don't like it either," Waco added.

In the end, though, Will had his way. He walked over and took a deck of cards out of the drawer and said, "Here. Alice, you hold the cards out, and I'll pick one and Waco will pick one."

Waco watched as Will picked a card out and showed it to them. "The nine of spades."

Waco reached out and said, "It'll take a high card to beat that." He picked a card out and stared for a moment. When he turned it over, he said, "Queen of hearts. I guess I'm going after all."

"I still think it should have been me," Will said.

"We did this your way, which was fair. As I said earlier, the store needs you anyway."

"Well, it shouldn't be for long. You'll go off to the army and get the fighting done. When you get back, the store ought to be doing well, and you and Alice can get married then."

Seeing the stricken look on Alice's face, Waco smiled and said, "Well, that's the way it's got to be. I'll be back before you've even missed me. Now I'd better be getting you home."

Alice and Waco left the store and walked together. She said, "I knew something would go wrong."

"Wars break up things, Alice. I'll be careful. I'm no hero."

"You can't promise that."

"Well, there are ways to keep from being shot. Take one of the wounded men out of the battle back to the hospital. It won't be for long. You can fix the house up. Will will help you."

Alice said sadly, "I thought my life was planned. Now it's a wreck."

"Your life is all right, sweetheart." He stopped, turned her around, and held her tightly. "I'll be back, we'll be married, have a house full of kids, and grow old together."

"If you say so, Waco."

CHAPTER 4

The law office of L. G. Simms was cluttered to such an extent that Waco wondered how any work ever got done there. All the walls had shelves going up to the board ceiling, which were packed with books, magazines, newspapers, and souvenirs. The big desk, with its back to the single window, was illuminated by sunlight, and the surface was filled with artifacts, books—some of them open, some of them closed—and old newspapers.

Simms himself was a large man bursting out of his clothes almost. He had a large stomach decorated by a gold chain that led, no doubt, to a gold watch in his pocket. His white shirt had the sleeves rolled up, and the buttons seemed ready to burst off. All in all, L. G. Simms was a disappointment.

Waco had not known the man, but he and Will had come in to have him do some work.

"So, you're going off to war. Is that right, Mr. Smith?"

"That's right," Waco said sparingly. "We have a little legal matter we want to take care of before I go."

"Very well. That's my specialty, little legal matters." Simms grinned, pulled a half-smoked cigar from a desk drawer, stuck it in his mouth, then struck a match on his thumbnail and sucked the blue flame in. As soon as the purple smoke was rising as if from a miniature engine, he said, "What can I do for you, gentlemen?"

Will spoke up at once. "Mr. Simms, we went into business, a hardware store, as partners. We're doing real well, but then this conscription thing comes up and throws us into a bind."

"I should imagine it does." Simms had small eyes and glasses that were propped up over his head.

"Yes sir, it really does." Will nodded. "But only one of us has to go."

"So I hear. So what's your decision?"

"We cut cards for it, and I won, I guess you might say." Will made a face. "I didn't like it. I still don't like it. It's not right. It's not fair, and I hate the whole idea."

"Will, we already thrashed this out." Waco shrugged. He turned to look at Lawyer Simms and said, "What we want to do is put everything in Will's name, the business and a house we recently bought."

"Well, that should be simple enough. You have the papers here?"

"Here are the Articles of Partnership," Will said, opening up a folder. "And here's the papers for the mortgage on the house. Still a little bit owing on it."

"Well, this will be fairly simple. You gentlemen just wait one minute. I'll get this matter out of the way."

Waco watched as the lawyer worked on the papers. He appeared to be rather messy and almost turned the ink bottle over once, but he got through the business without total disaster. "Here, you two gentlemen sign right where I have marked. That's all that will be necessary. You'll need to go to the court with this at the capitol building."

Will shook his head but leaned over and signed his name carefully. He handed the pen to Waco, saying, "I still don't like it, Waco."

Waco shook his head. He signed his name and said, "How much do we owe you?"

"Ten dollars ought to cover it, I reckon."

Waco fished in his pocket, but Will beat him to it. He came up with cash and said, "Thank you, Mr. Simms."

"Well, good luck to you both." He turned to Waco. "And you dodge them bullets now."

"I'll do my best."

As soon as they were outside, Waco said, "I guess we might as well head for the train station. From what I hear, the train will be pulling in sometime this afternoon. Trains don't run on schedule with this war going on."

The two walked along the boardwalk, and finally Will said, "Waco, can I ask you something?"

"Sure."

"Are you scared? I mean scared of getting shot?"

"Not right now, but they're not shooting at me." Waco managed a grin. "I will be when about five hundred Yankees are trying to kill me." He glanced over and saw a flight of blackbirds circle the town, making their harsh, guttural cries, then disappear behind the taller buildings. "I remember when I served the last time. I didn't like it a bit."

Will was quiet for a while and said, "We've never talked about this, but do you believe in God?"

"Of course I believe in God. What do you take me for? Just

look around you. With a world like this, there's got to be a world maker."

The two trudged silently on, threading their way between the people going to work and soldiers wandering the town, and finally Waco said, "You know I'm not afraid of dying."

"I would be."

"Well, it's what comes after that bothers me."

Will shot a quick glance at his partner. "Maybe you'd better go talk to the minister."

"No, I reckon not."

"I expect he can tell you how to get right with God."

Waco turned and shot a hard glance at Will, saying, "Will, I've been ignoring God all my life. Now you think if I run to Him and tell Him I've been a bad boy, He's going to let me into heaven? That would be like trying to buy insurance on a house when a house was on fire. I may be a sinner, but I'm no hypocrite."

They continued their walk, and when they approached the train depot, Waco said, "Look at that crowd."

Will shook his head. "They don't look like much, do they?"

"No, the Confederacy is skimming the bottom of the bucket."

The two of them moved back and leaned against the station house, and Waco's attention was drawn to an older man.

A woman was hanging to him and weeping, and a young woman with a small boy was standing by, watching with a worried look in her eyes. "You'll be all right, Carl," the young woman said.

"Sure I will."

The boy perked up and said, "Are you going to kill the Yankees, Grandpa?"

"I reckon as how I'll do my best."

The woman was weeping violently. "Why'd they have to take

51

you, Les? You're fifty-five years old. You're too old to be a soldier."

"Well, I got to go, Liz. That's all there is to it."

The scene disturbed Waco, and he shook his head in despair. "That old man doesn't need to leave his grandson and his wife."

"No, it's not right, but it's the way it is."

Ten minutes later, a very young lieutenant with rosy cheeks and bright blue eyes and dressed in a new Confederate uniform appeared. He shouted out as if everyone were deaf, "I'm Lieutenant Burl Gibson. When I call your name, sing out." He began calling out names.

When he called out Waco Smith, Waco raised his voice: "Here, Lieutenant."

The officer called out several more names, and then he called, "Charles Abbott." The lieutenant waited. "Charles Abbott, are you here?"

There was no answer, and one of the men said with a wry smile, "He lit out last night, Lieutenant, headed for the West Coast, I guess."

Lieutenant Gibson turned rosy, blushing furiously. "He'll be sorry when we catch up with him."

An older man, obviously seeing a younger son off, said, "You ain't gonna catch Charlie, Lieutenant. He's going all the way to the West Coast, sign on a clipper ship, and get down to the South Sea Islands. I wish I was going with him."

Gibson stared furiously at the older man, completed the roll call, and said, "You men stay where you are. The train will be here any minute."

He had no sooner spoken than Alice came, almost out of breath. She was holding a fairly large box. "I fixed you something to eat on the train, Waco."

Waco took the box and said, "Feels heavy. What you got in here?"

"Cake and sandwiches and pickles. Everything I could get in there."

"Thanks, Alice. That'll come in handy, I'm sure."

Alice looked around, her eyes falling on the older couple, and then she burst out, "I hate this war! I hate everything about it!"

"I reckon we all do, Alice."

"Grant wouldn't let this bunch in his army," she said.

"No," Waco said, "but Lee has to use what the South has got. This is it."

"You know the best of the men went off in the first excitement," Will said thoughtfully.

"That's right. Most of them got killed. I was in that bunch. We were all excited. Thought we'd be home before Christmas. Pretty soon it'll be the fifth Christmas."

They stood there talking awkwardly as none of them knew exactly what to say. Finally Waco lifted his head. "There it comes. I heard the whistle."

They stood waiting, and everybody watched as the old wood burner pulled onto the narrow-gauge rails. It huffed and puffed and let loose a tremendous blast of steam and the wheels made a grating noise as it came to a stop.

Lieutenant Gibson shouted, "You men get on those flat cars!"

Alice threw her arms around Waco and pulled his head down. Her lips were desperate, it seemed to him, and he held her close, aware of the soft contours of her figure.

When he lifted his head, he whispered, "I've got to go."

She said, "Be careful! Oh, be careful, Waco!"

"Sure." He turned around and put his hand out, but Will

ignored it and put his arms around him and hugged Waco. He had to reach up, of course, as Waco was so tall. "Take care of yourself, partner," he said huskily. "Don't worry about this. I'll take care of everything. You get home. You'll be a rich man. You'll have your wedding, and things will be good."

"Thanks, Will. I know I can count on you."

Waco moved to one of the flat cars, noting that the riding stock was filled already. He clambered on board and sat down and heard his name called. He turned around and saw a young man with bright blue eyes and a cowlick in his red hair. "Howdy, Mr. Smith."

"Why, it's Chad Royal, isn't it?"

"Yes, sir. My dad worked for you on your horse ranch. Ain't this great?"

Waco stared at the young boy. It was as if he went back in time and saw himself in this sort of attitude back when he had first signed up just before Bull Run. He had been excited, and the train had stopped at stations. Young women had come out with lemonade and cake, cheering them on. Suddenly he felt a pang to think that most of the young men who had been with him on that train were now in shallow graves. "It's good to see you," he said.

"I'm glad we're going together. I'm a little bit scared to tell the truth."

The two sat there talking, and a man named Roger Sanders was sitting by listening. When he heard Waco mention that he was engaged and had to put his wedding off, he said, "Well, I hope she's faithful to you."

Waco turned quickly, anger in his eyes. "She will be."

"Sorry. I've already served three years. Got invalided out, and now here I am going back. I tell you this. . .I'll run the first chance I get."

"You can't do that," Chad said.

"You hide and watch me, sonny."

The train gave a lurch forward and then began to move slowly out of the station. The last sight that Waco Smith saw as it pulled out was Alice and Will standing together. Will had his arms around her, and she seemed almost ready to faint. He watched until they faded from view then turned grimly and glanced into the direction of Richmond, where he knew he would be likely to be buried in a narrow grave.

❦

"Well, here it is April," Les Dickson said. The old man had stayed up with the younger men even more than others had thought. Waco had become fond of Dickson. He was a good man; he didn't complain, did his job. He and Dickson, along with Chad Royal and even Roger Sanders, who complained constantly but had never run as he had threatened, had stuck together through all the months of warfare.

It had been a dance of sorts. Grant would bring his army down, attack Lee, and there would be a battle. The first one was The Wilderness, which was a horror. It was a thicket of trees, grass, and vines, and somehow it caught fire. Men burned to death, screaming as they were consumed by the flames. Then came Spotsylvania and Cold Harbor, all butcheries. Grant lost five thousand men in Cold Harbor in less than an hour, but he was grinding Lee down.

"What do you hear from that gal of yours, Waco?" Sanders asked.

"Haven't heard lately. The mail service is not too good in the army, if you noticed."

"Nothing else is."

"Where we going?"

"I heard Lieutenant Gibson say we was going to some place called Appomattox."

"What for?" Chad Royal asked. "Are we going to fight the Yankees there?"

"I don't think so," Les Dickson said. "We don't have enough to fight a battle."

"We'll fight 'em until we can't fight no more," Chad said.

"I think that time's gone," Waco said. Indeed, the talk was that the war was over. Lee had evacuated his army from Richmond, and it was now in the hands of the Union. They were headed along a dusty road toward some little place called Appomattox.

Finally they reached it and found there a courthouse, but there were more people gathered around a white house with a front porch that ran the length of the house. There were all kinds of officers there.

"Looky there. Some of them men are Union," Chad said. "I could hit one from right here."

"Better not," Waco said. "You could hit him, but they got plenty to take care of that. No, this is the end."

They were halted and told to be at ease. Time passed slowly, and finally Roger Sanders said, "Look, there's General Lee."

Indeed, as Waco looked, he saw Robert E. Lee riding Traveler, his favorite war horse. He rode up to the house and dismounted, and one of the soldiers took his horse. Lee turned to look at the ragged scarecrows left of the Confederate Army and said nothing, but his eyes were sorrowful. Turning, he walked into the house.

"We lost even with Robert E. Lee," Waco said.

"Well, we were outnumbered in every engagement," Roger said.

The two waited, time passed, and finally Chad said, "Look, who's that?"

Everyone turned to look at a short man in a Union uniform but with no insignia except four stars on the shoulder. It was dusty and grimy, and Chad said, "That's General Grant, I bet. He's come to take Lee's surrender."

Grant hurried into the house, and there was a long time of waiting. There was nobody to tell them what was going on, but finally Robert E. Lee stepped in the door, looked out, and said, "Men, the war is over. I've done my best for you. Those of you who want horses are permitted to take them home." He turned, mounted Traveler, and rode slowly away without looking back.

Captain Dorsey Hill came over quickly and said, "Hey, Waco."

"Yes, Captain?"

"Pick you out a good horse."

"Why, I'm no horse thief."

"No, the Yankees gave us our horses from what I hear. Pick you a good one and get home to that girl of yours. Marry her. Just remember to name your first child Dorsey after me."

"I'll do it, Captain. I'm going home, getting married, and selling hardware." He quickly turned and went to the horse herd, where he picked a tall, rangy gray stallion, slapped a saddle on it, and rode out, headed toward Little Rock as straight as an arrow.

CHAPTER 5

Waco had made the trip back from Appomattox to Little Rock in company with his two fellow soldiers. The young man, Chad Royal, had stuck close to Waco from the first day in the army, as had Les Dickson, the grandfather whom all called "Gramps."

Dickson glanced across at his two fellow travelers and said, "Well, I'm going to leave you fellows here. That road leads to my place. That wife of mine will be mighty glad to see me."

"You go on and have some more grandchildren, Les," Waco said.

"I ain't ever going to forget you fellows."

"I guess I'll take off, too," Chad said. "I'll ride a ways with you, Gramps. My folks got that place over in Windy Hollow. They'll be right surprised to see me."

Waco moved his horse around closer to Chad and stuck his hand out. "Chad, I haven't forgot how you saved my bacon when the Yanks had me pinned down."

Waco noticed how the young boy's face had become mature. In a year's time, solid battles all the way from The Wilderness to the last fight at Fort Steadman added more than just time, and he knew that Chad and Gramps, like he, would never forget their time together.

"You fellows get on. We'll all be in the same area. Come into my store, and we'll go out and have a meal."

"We'll do that." Les kicked his horse into a run.

Chad followed, waving and shouting, "I'll see you later, Waco."

Waco had gotten a good mount, a tall, rangy roan that he called Sarge for no reason except his face kind of resembled his first sergeant, long and sober. "Come on, Sarge, let's get home."

As he rode, the skyline of Little Rock showed itself over the horizon. He kicked Sarge into a lope, but all the time he was thinking about the last time he had said good-bye to Alice. He had never forgotten how she whispered, "Waco, I can't bear it! How can I wait? I love you so much." He remembered the firm pressure of her lips on his, the urgency in her voice, and her arms around his neck. It was a memory that he had lived on for the last year. Suddenly he kicked Sarge into a dead run.

He approached Little Rock and rode down the main street, noting that the war that had wrecked so many Southern towns had not hit Little Rock so hard. There were many soldiers wearing Confederate uniforms, or part of them. He remembered a line of poetry he had heard somewhere: *All things are passing.* He muttered, "They sure are, and I'm glad the war has passed!"

He rode down Main Street eagerly and pulled up in front of the hardware store, but when he looked up, he got a shock. Instead of the old sign SMITH & BARTON HARDWARE, the new sign, still white with paint, said SAUTELLE HARDWARE. As he stood under the sign, he had an odd feeling. *Something's wrong about this.* He had not heard from Will or Alice for months now, but there could be letters he had missed. Mail service wasn't too regular in the Confederacy.

He dismounted, tied up his horse, and opened the door leading to the office. He noticed that it had been enlarged and redecorated. It had been a combination office for him and Will where they did their book work and kept supplies. Now there were three large rolltop desks along the center of the room. Filing cabinets were neatly ranked along the back wall with a series of charts and maps on each wall.

As Waco entered, a man looked up. He was tall and expensively attired. Turning to a younger man, obviously a clerk, he said, "We'll finish this later, Ray." Then he turned and said, "May I help you, sir?"

"Well, I'm looking for Will Barton."

A flicker touched the man's gray eyes. "Well, I can give you his mailing address."

"Mailing address?" Waco frowned. "Isn't he here?"

"No, I'm Ralph Sautelle, the owner."

The alarm that had been very faint suddenly grew very evident in Waco's head. He settled back on his heels, studying Sautelle's face. Finally he said carefully, "I'm Waco Smith. That name mean anything to you?"

Sautelle shook his head. "No, I'm afraid not. Have you done business with me?"

"I own this place. My partner is Will Barton."

Suddenly the man nodded to his clerk and said quickly, "Leave us alone, Ray." After the door closed, Sautelle said carefully, "You're out of the army, I see."

"Just out." Impatience stirred Waco, and he said, "What's going on here?"

Sautelle nervously pulled a cigar out of his pocket, his hands unsteady as he lit it. After taking a few puffs, he jerked it out and said, "I bought this place from Barton two months ago. He never said anything about a partner."

Waco froze. Finally he took a deep breath then expelled it, holding on to his temper. "He didn't say anything to me about selling the place."

"I think we'd better check into this, soldier," Sautelle suggested. "Do you have a lawyer?"

"Yes, I do."

"Go see him—and then, unless I'm mistaken, you'd better go to the police."

"The police?"

"Yes, that's right. I went over this business very carefully before I bought it. There's always a chance that a lot of debts aren't listed in the books. For example, I made sure the title was clear. According to my lawyer, Will Barton was the legal owner."

"We put the place in his name when I went into the army to make it easier for him to handle the business."

Sautelle's eyes flickered, and he shook his head slowly. "Mr. Smith, go see your lawyer and then come back. It looks like you've been taken."

"I don't think so," Waco replied.

"He's not living at his old address," Sautelle said. "I know that much. A month ago I needed to talk to him about something that had come up. Sent a man around, but he returned saying that Barton had moved, apparently right after he sold the store. I have the address he left with his landlady." He turned, walked over to a file, opened it, and pulled out a slip of paper. "Not much help, I'm afraid."

Waco stared at the note. *General Delivery, New York City.*

"Soldier, take the advice of an older man. Go to the police at once. Your friend has sold you out."

"I'll be back." Waco whirled and walked out, mounted Sarge, and headed down toward the house he had bought. He felt like when he had almost taken a bullet in battle. It had left him empty in the stomach and his pulse beating rapidly. He pulled up in front of Will's house and saw that it looked basically the same. He dismounted, walked up to the door, and knocked.

When the door opened, a woman greeted him. She was in her midthirties, he thought, with a wealth of brown hair and brown eyes. "Can I help you?"

"I'm not sure," Waco said slowly. "Is the man of the house here?"

"No, my husband, Samuel Trent, works for the railroad. He won't be back for two more days. I'm Hattie Trent. Is there something I can help you with, Mr. . . ."

"I'm Waco Smith. May I ask when you bought this house?"

"Well, we moved here only three months ago. The house was such a bargain. Mr. Barton said they were leaving to go east, but he didn't say where."

"He didn't leave an address of any kind?"

"No, I'm afraid not. Is something wrong?"

"Did you meet his wife?"

"Yes, I did. They hadn't been married too long. I did find that much out."

Waco knew that further questioning of this woman was useless. The truth was sinking in on him, and he had a hollow feeling in his chest. Slowly Waco said, "Thank you," turned, and walked away. He mounted his horse, moving slowly. He did not urge Sarge but let him walk slowly down the street. When he came to the sheriff's office, he was relieved to see that Micah Satterfield still held the position. Waco dismounted, tied Sarge to the rail, and then walked inside.

Micah was sitting at a desk. When he looked up and his eyes lit on Waco, he jumped to his feet and cried out, "Waco!"

"Hello, Micah."

"It sure is great to see you back from the war safe and sound."

"I'm afraid I've got some trouble here, Micah."

"What's the matter? You got wounded?"

"Not by a bullet, but I found out Will sold the store and house and ran off with Alice."

"Well, I knew they left together." Micah looked down at the floor as if he hated to look into Waco's eyes. "I sure did hate to have to face you with it. I guess they got married just before they left town. I heard about them selling the house and the business. Have you been down to talk to the new owner?"

"Yes, I have."

Micah said, "Well, I don't know what charges we can bring. The lawyer who handled the sale said that Will was the only name on the property."

"That's right, Micah. I signed it all over to him so it would be easier." He grinned wryly and said, "Of course I didn't realize he'd be taking it all anyway."

"We'll see if we can run him down."

"I don't guess it would do any good." He hesitated as if he wanted to say something else, then turned and said, "If you hear anything of them, let me know."

"Where'll you be staying?"

"I'll get a room at the hotel." Waco left, but instead of going to the hotel, he rode down Main Street. His mind seemed to be closing. He couldn't think clearly. "I can't believe I was so wrong about a man—and a woman."

He glanced down the street and saw the sign THE GOLDEN NUGGET. It was an old saloon that had been there for years, and although Waco was not a drinking man in any sense of the word, he turned Sarge toward the saloon. He tied the horse up at a rail and went inside. He was struck by the acrid smell of alcohol, stale tobacco smoke, and unwashed male bodies. Walking over to the bar, he hesitated.

A heavyset barkeeper nodded and said, "What can I serve you?"

"Whiskey."

"Sure." The bartender put a shot glass on the surface of the bar, poured it full from a bottle, then started to take the bottle away.

"Leave the bottle here."

"Right."

Picking up the bottle, Waco went over to a corner of the room where there was a table with two chairs. He sat down in one, put the bottle down, then held up the shot glass. He studied it for a moment, and bitterness seemed to flood him. He was not by nature a bitter man, but he had been dealt a harsh blow. This was worse than being called back to the army! Worse than anything he'd ever had happen.

For a time he drank the whiskey off, bracing himself as the fiery liquor bit at his throat then warmed his stomach. He filled the glass again and downed it quickly. He sat there alone until one of the women who frequented the bar came over. But when he shook his head, she sneered and walked away from him.

An hour later, Waco knew he was drunk. He dropped some coins on the bar and was aware that there was a dullness of sound and knew that he had lost it. He got up, walked over to the barkeep, paid for the drinks, then left.

He knew he had very little money left, but he went to the hotel and got a room. Going inside, he lay down on the bed and closed his eyes, making the room seem to swim. The bitterness had turned into hatred, and he lay there thinking of his "friend" Will Barton and his new bride, Alice Malone. He could not turn his mind away from the two of them, and he finally passed out, still thinking of how he would get his revenge if he ever saw them again.

❧

"That young man sure got a rotten deal," Micah Satterfield said. He was talking to his deputy, Zeb Willis. They were both seated in the sheriff's office.

"He sure did." The deputy was a tall, lean man with a ferocious mustache and a pair of mild blue eyes. "As I see it, he let himself in for it. Must be a trusting sort of fellow, signing his business and house over to Barton like he did."

"Yes, I guess he was trusting. He always was an easygoing man. Don't know if he'll ever trust anybody again."

"Well, trusting someone to keep something for you is dangerous business. I think he'll have trouble getting his money back."

"He thought Barton was his friend," the sheriff said. He remembered now how Waco had unloaded to him, and the sheriff knew there was really no recourse for Waco Smith to regain his business or his woman. But he had to check out every opportunity.

A silence fell between the two men. Then Willis said, "I hear he's staying drunk most of the time."

"Yes, he is, and that's different, too."

"Well, I don't know where he's getting the money, but he's sure trying to drink the Golden Nugget dry."

"Waco never was a real drinking man. Never any trouble in that way."

"I reckon he thinks he's got a good excuse. Bad enough to have to go to that war, but to come home and find your best friend skipped out with your cash and your woman. That's tough." Zeb leaned back and said thoughtfully, "You know he's got a pretty hard look in his eyes. I don't blame him a bit."

"Well, he's been hurt pretty bad. Last night I went by to try to talk him out of drinking, and he said, 'They done me in, Sheriff, but they won't do it again.' You know, I don't think he was talking just about Barton and that woman. He's not going to trust anybody for a long time."

The deputy got up and left, leaving Satterfield to his thoughts. He sat for a long time, trying to think of a way to trace Barton, but knew there was little he could do.

Finally he looked up to see Waco and called out, "Come and sit."

Waco stopped, hesitated, then came and lowered himself into a chair. He said nothing.

Finally Satterfield said, "Well, you got to put this behind you, Waco."

"How do you do that?" Waco's voice was harsh and had an edge to it.

His eyes, as the sheriff had noticed, were hard and sharp, something unusual for him. "You need some money?"

"No. I got a little grubstake. My grandmother left me a little plot of land. I sold it. My partner didn't know about it, or he'd have that money, too."

"Well, why don't you go back into business, Waco. The town is booming and—"

"Nope, I'm pulling out."

"But you've got friends here."

"It's not the same anymore. I need to get away."

"I sort of figured you might. Where will you head for?"

"Someplace far out in the woods where the only company will be squirrels and timber wolves."

Micah Satterfield was a student of men, and he studied the stubborn cast to Waco's face. The two had been close, and with a heavy heart he realized this was not the same happy young fellow he had known before the war. The easy ways and the careless manners were gone. What he saw now was a man filled with cynicism that obviously was turning into something much worse.

Finally Waco shook his head and said, "I've had enough of people to do me for a lifetime. This is probably good-bye. I'm leaving early in the morning."

"Keep in touch. Drop me a line when you can."

"I won't promise that. I never was much for writing."

Something much like grief touched Micah Satterfield. He hated to see a man go wrong, and if he ever saw a man on the way down, it was Waco Smith. "Look, boy, it's not the end of the world. Not everybody's a crook like your partner was. Not everybody's a hussy like that woman was."

Waco shook his head and said, "No, I'm going to get out of here. Far away from everything I know. I don't know where I'll go. Maybe get on a ship and go to England or somewhere."

"You won't like it there."

"Probably not." Waco put out his hand and gripped the sheriff's hand hard. "You've been good to me, Micah. I know it won't please you, but I think I found a place where I can just live and won't have to fool with any man or woman."

"Where's that?"

"Indian territory. Out in Oklahoma at the edge of Arkansas. Judge Parker is out there now, but he's got some marshals. It's a huge territory. A man can do anything he pleases."

Satterfield shook his head. "No. No man can do that. There's still laws and rules."

"I'm through with all that," Waco said. "So long, Sheriff." He turned abruptly and walked outside.

Satterfield stared at the door, shook his head, then murmured, "He's headed the wrong way, and there's not anything I can do to stop him."

❧

Waco had pushed his way slowly westward, and as long as he had money, he stopped at small towns and drank himself insensible at bars. He would then carry a bottle with him and get drunk on the way.

The whiskey destroyed something in him. He had not known alcohol could have this much effect. All he knew was that he had lost his good opinion of men, and at some point on his journey he reached a conclusion that he never would have thought of back in earlier days. "I'll take what I want as long as I live." That was the sum of his philosophy. It gave him a grim satisfaction to realize that he was headed for the one place in the United States where that would be totally possible—the Indian Nations where the only law were a few scattered marshals who could not possibly keep up with all the wrongdoers.

He was almost to Oklahoma when he drew up and saw that a wagon was pulling up close behind him. He pulled Sarge over and hid behind a bush. He saw that it was a Union Army wagon.

They're bound to have some money on there. At least those soldier boys will have, he thought. *I'll get what they've got in their pockets.* Pulling his pistol, he waited until they were close enough then stepped out and called loudly, "Pull up there, or I'll shoot!"

One man was driving the wagon; two more were on horseback. One of them immediately reached for his gun.

Waco fired, not to kill but just close enough where the man might have heard the bullet whizzing by his ear. "If you want to die, go ahead and pull for that gun," Waco called out and was gratified to see that the man stopped. "No shooting," he said. "Now, you two drop your weapons and get off your horses. You get out of that wagon, sonny." He waited until all three men were down and were disarmed. "Okay, you head back down the road. If I still see you in five minutes, I'll shoot you."

The three stared at him and saw something in his face that kept them silent. "Come on," the oldest of them said. "Let's get out of here. We're not going to die for this."

Waco watched until they were mere blue dots down the road, and then he climbed into the wagon. He found more than he bargained for. There was a strongbox there. It was locked, but he shot the lock off and opened it up. "Look at that," he said. It was filled with papers, but there was also a pile of gold coins. He looked at the papers and discovered that this was the payroll for a small fort almost in Oklahoma. He found a sack, put the gold coins in it, cut the horses loose, and then mounted Sarge after tying the gold to his saddlebag. "Come on, Sarge, we got financing."

The horse leaped ahead, and Waco Smith, for one moment, had some sort of guilt. He had never stolen anything before except for some livestock, mostly chickens, when he was in the army. But this was a different Waco Smith. He reached into his saddlebag, got out the whiskey bottle, drained it, and threw it away. "Well, here's my new rule," he announced to the air. "I'm going to do what I please and take what I want!"

CHAPTER 6

Indian Territory, April 1870

Trey LeBeau leaned back and threw his cards on the table. There were several men there, including the James brothers, Frank and Jesse. His band included five other men, but only Al Munro and Zeno Shaw were at the card table.

Trey let his eyes go over to the woman who sat at the table, not playing cards but just simply sitting and watching. Calandra Montevado, whom everyone called Callie, was the most beautiful woman he had ever seen. She had a pure olive complexion and large almond-shaped eyes with long lashes. The color was blue, a particular shade of blue. He had seen a stone that was called lapis lazuli. Her eyes were that particular shade of blue. She had hair as black as the darkest thing in nature and sensuous lips.

He let his eyes rest on her, admiring her figure as usual. She lifted her glance and met his gaze coolly. They had been together now for nearly a year, and he had never gotten the best of her in any way. In any case, she added something to his life that was missing.

"We got to pick up somebody to take Butch's place," Al Munro said. He was a small man with pale blue eyes and hair that was prematurely white. A deadly man with a gun, a knife, or any other weapon.

"I don't know where we'd get one," LeBeau said.

Zeno Shaw was the biggest man at the table. He was six feet two and weighed well over two hundred pounds. He had brown hair and brown eyes and was a ferocious saloon fighter. He was not particularly accurate with a gun, but in any activity requiring brute strength he was a good man to have. He glanced over at LeBeau and said, "You might think about that fellow Waco Smith. I've heard lots of talk about him."

"He wouldn't be interested," Callie said. "He's a loner. He takes what he wants, but he's not a killer. Not like you fellas."

The insult, if that was what it was, did not move the other men from the table. Frank James said, "Why don't you look into it." He glanced over and said, "Jesse and me are going to be leaving pretty soon. We're going back to civilization."

Jesse James smiled slightly. "Yeah, this is hard living here, Trey."

"Pretty safe though. You go back to Missouri or somewhere, you'll have sheriffs and deputies and all kinds of lawdogs on your trail all the time. Here all we got is a few marshals."

"I don't like it here," Jesse James said. "You better look into this fellow Smith. What's he like?"

"Well, he's evidently pretty tough. I've never met him. I don't think many have. He stays in the territory mostly with Indians. I hear Judge Parker has put a special price on his head."

"If he ain't a killer, I don't know how we can use him," Al Munro said.

"The man will do what he needs to do if there's enough money involved." LeBeau nodded. "But anyway it's a good idea. I wonder where he is?"

Frank James said, "I heard some talk about him when I was over at Travis's store. He's around there somewhere. He comes in for supplies."

"That's not far from here," Trey said. "What do you say we go look him over, Callie?"

"That sounds good to me. I'm bored with watching you men lose at cards."

LeBeau laughed and said, "Come on. We can be there in two hours."

As they were on their way, LeBeau said, "You watch out for Waco Smith. Stay away from him."

Callie laughed. "You don't own me, Trey. Don't tell me what to do."

🙶

They reached Travis's store and were surprised at how easy it was to find the man called Waco Smith.

"He comes in here pretty often, but he's got a camp over by Red Canyon." Travis, the barkeep, explained how to get there. "I wouldn't try to sneak up on him though. He's as quick as a snake with that .44 of his."

"Oh, it's just a friendly visit."

The two mounted again, and two hours later, as Travis had said, they came upon a camp, but they did not get far before a voice said, "Hold it right where you are."

Immediately Trey LeBeau held up his hands. "No trouble. We come friendly."

Callie glanced around and saw a man emerge from behind some bushes. He was very tall with black hair and a tapered face. He had a coppery tan, and he held a .44 loose in his hand. Not pointing it at them, just saying that it was there.

"I'm Trey LeBeau."

"I'm Waco Smith."

"Sure," Trey said. "We come looking for you. This is Callie Montevado."

"I'm glad to know you, Miss Callie. Why are you looking for me?"

"Is it all right if we get down and talk?"

"Sure. Just be careful that you don't make any moves that would set me off. I'm a nervous type."

"I doubt that." Trey smiled, and his eyes crinkled when he did. He stepped off his horse, as did Callie, and kept his hands carefully away from the gun. "The thing is, I've got a pretty good bunch of boys. We've taken in quite a bit of coin. Somebody said you might be interested in joining up with us."

"I don't think so. I'm doing all right on my own."

"Well, we can talk about it, can't we?"

"Sure. Come on and sit on the front porch."

The three sat down in front of a shack that at least had a porch with a roof on it.

Waco brought out a bottle and three glasses. "If you're dry, this is pretty good whiskey."

"Any whiskey is good whiskey," Trey said. When he swallowed it, his eyes flew open, and he gasped. "That's like liquid fire."

"Yeah, the Indians like it."

"What are you doing out here all by yourself?" Callie asked.

"That's what I am. All by myself. I got tired of people back East. Here I do as I please."

"You couldn't be making much coin selling whiskey to the Indians."

"I don't need much."

"Of course you do. Every man needs a lot. Look, you go in with us, and in six months you'd have enough cash you wouldn't have to sell whiskey to the Indians."

"Well, tell me about it."

Trey was a good talker, and for a while he outlined the plan for making money. "Robbing trains, that's where it's at. My boys are good at that, but like I say, we lost a man."

"You don't know me."

"Well, you don't know me either. You watch me and I'll watch you."

"I wouldn't do it if I were you, Smith," Callie said.

Her remark obviously interested Waco. "Why not, Miss Callie?"

"You just look like a loner."

"That's what I intend to be."

"Callie, you keep out of this," LeBeau protested. "We need some help."

The conversation went on for an hour, and Trey was pleased to see that Waco was interested.

Waco said finally, "Well, I'll come along with you, and we'll see if I fit. If I don't, I can always come back."

"Sure. We're not too far away from here. You can come back anytime." As they shook hands, Trey was mentally counting all the money Waco Smith was going to help them take from all those unsuspecting trains.

Waco had been welcomed by LeBeau's band. Frank and Jesse James were gone, but the rest of them seemed to find him acceptable. It was not that he did anything, but they were careful in their movements around him for they had heard he was deadly with a gun. He did not have the reputation of a killer, but he had pulled and drawn on several men before they could even move.

One interesting thing was that Callie seemed to be fascinated by him. They went on several brief hunting trips together, and on one of them she said, "You have many sweethearts, Waco?"

"I almost had one once, but she didn't love me."

"Did she say that? Tell you she didn't love you?"

"No, she waited until I was gone to war, and then she ran off with my best friend. He was my partner in business." A wry expression touched his face. "He took all I had."

She was quiet for a while before she said, "Trey is jealous of me. Haven't you noticed how he looks at you when we go out together?"

"I've noticed."

"Are you afraid of him?"

He grinned. "All LeBeau can do is kill me, and he couldn't kill me but once."

"Doesn't that bother you?"

"No."

She suddenly said, "What do you feel for me?"

"You're the most beautiful woman I've ever known."

They were sitting under a tree, and he read an invitation in her eyes. He reached forward, pulled her close, and kissed her. She lay soft in his arms. Then she put her arms around him and drew him closer. Her warmth became a part of him, and her nearness brought up a constant, never-lessening want. He was conscious of her in a way he had never been conscious of any woman, not even Alice.

The effect of the kiss worked at him. They were along the edge of the same mystery every other man and woman face, neither of them knowing what good would come of it, nor what tragedy. As she pulled him closer, she knew what they shared was physical and not a thing of the spirit.

⁂

LeBeau was being taunted by Al Munro about losing his woman. "You shouldn't have let that good-looking guy come in. Callie is crazy about him."

"Shut up, Al!"

Munro knew better than to go too far, but humor was in his eyes, a sly humor that LeBeau did not miss. Thirty minutes later, Waco and Callie came in, returning from one of their trips. As soon as they were inside, Trey said, "Everybody sit down. We're going to make a big haul. We're wasting time robbing trains for watches and rings. This one is going to have a good gold shipment."

"How do you know that?" Rufo Aznar said. He was Mexican, trim with an olive complexion and dark eyes. He had a knife scar on the right side of his face. "They didn't send you an invitation, did they?"

"No, I paid a lot of money to find out."

"Money to who?" Waco asked instantly.

"A man who works for the railroad. He knows if he lied I'd kill him. Anyway, we'll do some planning here."

⁂

The plans were all made, and Callie warned Waco as the men left. "Don't turn your back on him."

"I won't."

They rode out, and as always Waco kept to one side where

he could watch all the men. Trey had made a good plan pointing out that there was one spot where the train had to slow down practically to a stop in order to make a sharp curve.

"You and me will get on that train, Waco," Trey said. "We'll go up and force the engineer to shut down. The rest of you go through and find that gold."

Waco did not particularly like it. He didn't like working with other thieves. He made up his mind he would leave after this particular robbery.

The heist went as planned. The train had to slow down, and it was no trouble for Trey LeBeau and Waco to get on board. They made their way along the top to the engine, jumped down and put their guns on the engineer and the fireman, who was holding a shovel and staring at them with wide-open eyes.

"You fellows be still, and nobody'll get hurt," Waco said. But no sooner had he spoken than he heard a shot.

Trey had shot the fireman, then turned and shot the engineer. Even as they were falling, he had raised his gun and brought it down on Waco's head.

As everything began to fade to black, Waco realized he had been betrayed yet again.

Out of the darkness Waco came, and he heard voices. He felt something tying his arms, and when he opened his eyes, he saw that he was a captive. A man with a star on his vest said, "Well, I hope you enjoyed your robbery. You're going to hang for it."

"I didn't shoot anybody."

"I'll bet," the lawman said. "We'll let the judge decide about that."

Things moved much more quickly than Waco had ever known legal matters to. He spent two weeks in a vile jail, then was brought up before Judge Parker. During the trial, the fireman, who had survived his injuries, testified that it was another man who had shot both him and the engineer, who had died. "He hit this fellow in the head, but this man didn't shoot anybody."

"Well, the longest sentence I can give you for holding up a train is ten years," Judge Isaac Parker said. "I wish it were for life. If you give me the names of the rest of the robbers, I'll make it five."

For a moment he was tempted to do it, but then he said, "No, I won't squeal."

"Honor among thieves," Judge Parker said cynically. "All right. Go on to jail then."

The days passed in his cell, then the weeks, the months, and finally the years. Time had crawled by more slowly than Waco could have imagined. He had put in days on a road gang chained to other prisoners. Sometimes he had been locked up in the cell for months without getting out to the sunshine.

Finally one day Mel Batson watched him scratch on the wall and said, "What's that for, Waco?"

"My anniversary. I've been here five years today."

"Well, you only got five more to go," Batson said. "You won't get no parole. You've been a bad prisoner. Me, I'm trying to be a good boy."

"I'm not licking anybody's boots. I'll do my ten." Waco lay

down and thought of the five years that lay ahead of him. He had been beaten and mistreated, but his spirit had never been broken. *I'll do five more,* he thought bitterly, *and then I'll go looking for Mr. Trey LeBeau. . . .*

PART TWO

PART TWO

CHAPTER 7

Memphis, Tennessee, 1870

"Dulcie—you've got this water too hot!"

Sabrina Warren had stuck her toe in the zinc bathtub and jerked it out immediately. Glaring at her maid, her voice filled with irritation as she went on. "Can't you even draw a bath right?"

Dulcie, at age twenty, was as black as nature would allow. She was an attractive young woman, but now her lips drew tightly together as she glared at her mistress. "I doin' the best I kin. If I don't get it hot enough, you raise a ruckus! I get it too hot, you do the same thing. How I'm supposed to know what you want?"

Sabrina glared at Dulcie. "You're supposed to have a little sense! Test it yourself before I boil my feet off!" Sabrina Warren knew she was tall for a woman at five ten. She also knew she was quite beautiful with her auburn hair, green eyes, and peaches-and-cream complexion. To top this off, she had a splendid figure. No one had ever questioned her good looks, but she readily admitted, to herself anyway, that her temper was more volatile than one would expect of a young woman in her position. "Well, pour some cold water in there and cool it off!"

"Then it'll be too cold. You watch what I says." Nevertheless, Dulcie picked up a bucket and dumped half of it into the tub. "All right. See if that suits you. Nothin' else does."

"You're getting too uppity." Slowly Sabrina stepped over the edge of the tub, and when she stuck her toe in she found it suitable. She stepped over with the other foot and, holding on to the edges of the tub, lowered herself down into it. A look of relaxation came to her eyes then, and she forgot about Dulcie, her fit of temper quickly over. She slid down into the tub, luxuriating in the warm water, and as she did, she looked around the room that had been converted from a large bedroom into a spacious bathroom.

Many houses had taken this method of adding a bathroom, for most of the mansions in Memphis had not made provision for bathing back when they were built in an earlier day. She glanced around and saw that the ornate gas chandelier had been left in place so that it shed its luminescent beams over the marble floor. She knew it had come from Italy for she had ordered it herself. Her father had almost fainted when he saw the bill, but she had patted him on the cheek and said, "Now, Daddy, you know we've got to have a good bathroom."

She eased down more into the tub and thought, *I'm going to get rid of this zinc tub. It's ugly.* As a matter of fact, it was rather ugly. It had a flat bottom and a raised back, but it did not suit her sense of decorum. The walls had once been papered, but the steam from the hot water had caused the paper to begin to peel. So she'd had to work to take it all off and put instead wooden panels that she had had painted a beautiful shade of orchid. There was an ornate dressing table over to one side and two chairs in front of a full-length mirror. As she closed her eyes, she thought, *Must have been awful not to be able to take a bath back in the old days.*

She lay in the bath until it grew tepid then said, "Get some of that rainwater, Dulcie. I want you to wash my hair."

"You done washed it yesterday."

"Well, wash it again!" Sabrina snapped.

Grumbling under her breath, Dulcie found the bucket of pure rainwater, and selecting a soft soap, she wet Sabrina's hair down and worked up an ocean of suds. "Don't see no need in all this washin' anyhow," Dulcie grumbled. Actually she did not mind helping Sabrina. She knew she had an easy place and was not at all unhappy in her situation.

Sabrina sat up in the tub, and as Dulcie washed her hair with the soft water, she began thinking about Lane and the ball she was going to attend. *I wish Lane were more dashing.* The thought came to her mind, and it was not the first time. Indeed, Lane Williams was not a dashing man at all. He was, as a matter of fact, two inches shorter than Sabrina. He had brown hair that he kept carefully trimmed, along with a brown mustache and mild brown eyes. He was neat in all of his ways but had never taken a risk in his life.

Sabrina sighed and relaxed while Dulcie finished her hair. Finally Dulcie rinsed the soap out with several buckets full of soft water then began to dry it. "There. Get out of there, and I'll dry you off."

It was difficult to get out, for she had relaxed almost to the point of going to sleep, but finally Sabrina stood.

With a huge, fluffy white towel, Dulcie dried her off carefully.

"Don't dry me off so hard," Sabrina complained.

Dulcie ignored her curt words. "You sit down there, and I'll fix your hair."

"All right." Fixing hair right was the one thing Dulcie

could do excellently. Sabrina knew that many society belles of her station had to put up with much worse, and she sat quietly, thinking about the ball, smiling slightly. As a matter of fact, her life was made up of parties, balls, teas, an occasional trip to the Memphis symphony, and a traveling opera on occasion. Her family was not in the upper regions of society but just in what was not far from it. Sabrina had grown up with never wanting for anything, and now at the age of twenty-four she was one of the belles of Memphis society. "Don't pull my hair out by the roots!"

"I ain't pullin' nothin' by no roots. You just set still."

Finally, when her hair was fairly well fixed, Sabrina sent Dulcie off to get some perfume, and while she was gone, she slipped into her underwear that Dulcie had laid out. The garments were all made of silk or fine linen.

When Dulcie came back, she stopped dead still and stared at Sabrina. "You ain't got yo' corset on."

"No, I don't, and I'm not going to wear that old thing," Sabrina said. "I don't need it." Indeed she did not, for her waist was small. She smiled at Dulcie and said, "You don't have to wear one. You don't know how uncomfortable those things are, and the bustles are just as bad."

"All the respectable women wear corsets to them balls."

"I don't need one. It rubs me wrong."

"You know your momma ain't gonna let you go to no ball without a corset."

Sabrina laughed. It made a pleasant sound. She knew well how to work her parents. "We just won't tell her, Dulcie."

Dulcie was shocked. "Maybe you won't—but I will."

"No, you can't tell her."

"Why not?"

"Why should I wear an old corset? I look well enough without it." Indeed she did, but corsets were standard equipment for young ladies of her station. An idea came to Sabrina, and she said, "I'll tell you what, Dulcie, if you don't tell Momma that I'm not wearing a corset, you can have that red dress of mine that you covet."

"It's a sin to covet," Dulcie said righteously. "I ain't studyin' no red dresses."

Sabrina drew closer to the young woman and said, "And you can have the petticoat and the shoes that go with it."

Sabrina was amused as she watched the struggle going on within Dulcie's soul. She knew that the girl had longed for that particular dress, but this came in conflict with her idea that her mistress needed to wear a corset. She said nothing, and finally Dulcie threw her hands up in a gesture of despair. "Well, if you's bound to dress like a hussy, I guess I can't help it."

Sabrina laughed and said, "You can take it today. Maybe there'll be a party you can wear it to. You'll have to take it up a little bit."

"I ain't studyin' no parties." Dulcie pouted. "I'm thinkin' 'bout how you treat your poor momma and daddy. You ain't never minded them a day in your life."

"Of course I do—when I want to."

"Well, I'll tell you one thing," Dulcie said, "you better start being nicer to Mr. Lane or that Aldrich girl is gonna take him away from you."

"Melissa Aldrich couldn't take anything away from me." She was confident and knew that none of her friends could take her gentleman friend away from her. "Well, finish my hair."

"All right. I'll finish it, but you better ask forgiveness for foolin' your poor old momma. If she knew the stuff that goes on in your mind, she'd be shocked, and your daddy, too."

"Oh, I never tell them things like that, and you don't either, Dulcie."

"I don't reckon I can, but you're gonna get caught one of these days."

As Dulcie finished her hair, Sabrina was thinking of the ball, though not with any particular excitement. It was just another ball, and she had been to a thousand of those it seemed like.

Mick Sullivan pulled the buggy up in front of the Warren mansion and clambered down to the ground. He was a ruddy-faced Irishman, sturdy, with huge hands, and was known to be the best horse trader in Memphis. He walked up to the front steps and knocked on the door.

A butler came to the door and said, "May I help you, sir?"

"I've got a horse here for Miss Sabrina Warren."

"Well, you can't bring the horse in here," the butler said.

"All right, but I've got to have her sign for it."

"You take the horse around to the stable. I'll tell her you're here. You wait until she comes."

"I ain't waitin' forever," Mick growled. He went back, unhitched the beautiful bay mare, and led her around the house. This was what was once the center of Memphis and now was merely a neighborhood. There was plenty of room, and the grass was green. Mick shook his head. "These folks got too much. Spoiled rotten is what they are, especially that girl." He had sold horses to Sabrina before and knew there would be no question about money. He found Morris Tatum, the groom, sitting on a barrel whittling.

"Got a horse here for Miss Sabrina."

Morris jumped down and said, "Well, she's a beauty, ain't she? How much did you gig her for?"

"I give her a fair price. Don't you worry about that."

Morris was a small man. He had spent some time working as a jockey. Now his blue eyes sparkled. "The last time you gave anybody a fair price, Adam and Eve was in the Garden of Eden."

"You got anything to drink here?"

"Soft or hard?"

"Just whiskey."

"When's the last time you had water?" Morris made a face. Nevertheless, he disappeared inside the stable and came back with a bottle. "Here. Don't drink it all."

Mick took a long drink, then another, and handed it back to Morris. "That girl. She's spoiled to the bone."

"Well, I can't help that. You're right though. I don't think she's ever wanted anything in her life her momma and daddy didn't get for her."

"One of these days," Mick said, "she's gonna want something she can't get. We'll see what she does then."

Five minutes later Sabrina came out and said, "Hello, Mick."

"Hello, Miss Sabrina. Here she is. Prettiest mare in Memphis."

"Oh, she is a beauty," Sabrina crooned. She stroked the smooth hide of the mare and said, "I'll take her."

"We ain't settled on a price yet."

"Well, I know you'll name a price, and I'll tell you it's too high, and you'll come down. Why don't we just skip all that."

"All right. Price is eight hundred dollars."

"I'll give you seven hundred."

"Seven-fifty."

"Oh, that's all right. I hate these things."

"Okay. Here, sign this. These are the papers on the mare." Sabrina signed the papers, and then Mick nodded, saying, "Thank you, Miss Sabrina. I'll let you know when I get some more good-looking stock."

"Thank you, Mick." Sabrina stood there stroking the silken nose of the mare then said, "Morris, rub her down and be sure to watch her diet. I think I'll take her out for a ride tomorrow."

"What about today?"

"Oh, I've got to go to a stupid ball. I'd much rather go with you, sweetheart."

"Is that what you named her? Sweetheart?"

"No, I haven't given her a name yet. I think I'll call her Cleo for Cleopatra."

"Well, she's a beauty, Miss Sabrina. I'll take care of it."

Charles and Caroline Warren were entertaining Sabrina's escort, Lane Williams. They were in the larger of the two parlors. There was a large fireplace of polished marble at one end, and the pictures on the walls were either seascapes or Dutch pastoral scenes with cows.

The long green velvet curtains splayed out on the floor and sagged with braided sashes. There was a large cut-glass bowl of roses on a low mahogany table between two chairs, and all in all the room had all the Victorian clutter that had been so popular and still was.

"I expect there'll be a crowd at that ball, Lane," Charles said.

"Everybody I know is going except us."

Lane Williams was a small young man, shorter than Sabrina. "There probably will be, but I'm not going to stay for the entire ball."

"Well, you'll have a lovely time," Caroline Warren said. At the age of forty-seven she was an attractive woman with the same auburn hair and green eyes that she had passed along to her daughter.

"I hate balls," Charles Warren said. He had a square face, was six feet tall, and weighed over two hundred pounds. He was forceful and stubborn. Founder and owner of Warren Steel Mills in Memphis, he loved his family, his church, and his business, in that order. He had planned on having sons to help him with the business, but that had not happened, so he always thought what sort of partner one of the girls' suitors would make.

They were interrupted when Marianne Warren came into the room. She was nineteen, with beautiful smooth blond hair and blue eyes. Her parents had long ago learned that she was very romantic. She read romances by the ton it seemed, and once her mother had said, "Marianne, you're waiting for a knight in bright shining armor to come and sweep you off, but there aren't any white knights in armor these days." She had realized, of course, that that would mean nothing to Marianne.

She was wearing a beautiful bright green satin dress trimmed with glittering black lace and black velvet ribbons. Three black feathers were arranged in her blond hair, held on by an impossibly large emerald and a diamond stick pin.

"You look beautiful tonight, Marianne. You'll be the belle of the ball." Caroline Warren smiled at her daughter.

"Oh no. Sabrina will be the belle of the ball."

Charles grinned, and then a thought came to him. He turned to Sabrina's suitor. "I can't keep up with you two. Are you engaged or not?"

"We were yesterday, but this is another day." Lane smiled wryly. "I ought to keep a record or a journal or something. You can ask her, and then we'll both know."

Even as he said this, Sabrina came in. She was wearing a beautiful dress of her favorite Nile green color, and it was as elegant as the water in the sun. It was stitched with silver beading and seed pearls. The waist was tiny, and the bodice crossed over in front with the bosom cut low.

"You look beautiful, Sabrina." Lane smiled. "You'll be the belle of the ball."

"She always is," Marianne said. "I wish I could be just once."

"Well, when we're married, your competition will be gone," Lane said. "By the way, your father wants to know if we're engaged. What's the score on that?"

It was a question that came up often, and Sabrina stared thoughtfully at Lane. "I'll let you know before the evening's out. If you step on my toes, the engagement's off."

"Well, let's go," Lane said.

They left the house, and as soon as they were gone, Charles said, "I don't know about that young man. He doesn't have much strength it seems."

"You think everybody who's not as driving and forceful as you are doesn't have enough strength, Charles. He's a fine young man. He'll be good to Sabrina."

"She'll wear him out just like you wore me out."

Caroline came over and put her arm around his waist. "No, I didn't. You always get anything you want from me."

Charles laughed and said, "That's the way it's supposed to be in a marriage."

☙

The ball at the Steens' mansion was held for the betrothal of their daughter. It was glittering, glamorous, and grandiose. At the entrance to the ballroom was a long table covered with a snowy white tablecloth, and gentlemen's silk top hats, canes, and gloves were arranged in militarily precise rows. The strains of a slow waltz filtered through the twelve-foot-high double doors, which were open but still guarded jealously by two gigantic footmen.

Inside the great ballroom the scents and sounds and sights were overwhelming. Women glowed in hundreds of butterfly colors. All of the men were striking in full evening dress of white ties and tails. The flowers smelled luscious, the chandeliers glittered like diamonds, and the music of the twelve-piece orchestra resounded magnificently.

Almost as soon as they were inside, a tall, handsome man with a beautiful beard came and said, "I'm going to have to ask for a dance from your fiancée, Lane."

"All right. You try to steal her at every ball. Go ahead, Harold."

As the two whirled off to the music of a waltz, Lane said, "It seems a shame to spend all this money on something as frivolous as a dance."

Marianne looked around. Thousands of flowers lined the walls in great stone urns. There were old ivies, deep green, long, trailing, curling up the walls. "It is rather frivolous, I suppose, but it is exciting."

"May I introduce myself?"

Neither Lane nor Marianne had heard anyone because of the music, but when she turned quickly, she saw a man six feet tall, very trim, and very handsome.

"My name is Gerald Robbins. I'm here on business. I hardly know anyone at this ball, so I thought I'd ask the most beautiful woman here for a dance."

"There you are, Marianne," Lane said, smiling. "You're already attracting the men." He said, "I'm Lane Williams, and this is Miss Marianne Warren, daughter of Charles and Caroline Warren."

"And may I have this dance, Miss Marianne?"

Marianne was flustered. He was the best-looking man in the hall as far as she was concerned, and there was something dashing about him, always an extra for a man.

He led her to the dance floor, and soon they were moving around smoothly. "You dance beautifully, Miss Warren."

"Why, thank you, Mr. Robbins. You say you're new in town?"

"Yes, just here on some business."

"Well, where is your home?"

"Oh, out West. I deal in cattle quite a bit. Have a large ranch."

"Oh, how exciting!"

Robbins laughed. "Well, that's one way of looking at it, but taking care of a thousand cows is not very exciting. That's why I come East every once in a while just to have some real culture."

Marianne was fascinated and peppered him with questions about his ranch and his life. He had a smooth voice and had all the wit that one would expect in a man. "You don't look like a cowboy."

"Well, I don't wear spurs and chaps and a ten-gallon hat to a ball like this." Robbins smiled. "What does your father do?"

"He owns an ironworks here in Memphis. Actually, it's called Warren Steel Mill."

"And you have brothers and sisters?"

"Only one sister. She's around here somewhere."

For the rest of the ball, Marianne either danced with Gerald Robbins or else waited for another chance.

When Lane prepared to see her and Sabrina home by going outside and sending for the carriage, Robbins said, "I'm a lonesome bachelor and usually wouldn't be this forward, but there's a concert tomorrow in the park. I just wonder if you would accompany me."

"Oh, I'll have to ask my father. But I'm sure he'll say yes," Marianne said.

Robbins bowed slightly. "I'll pick you up, if you'll give me your address, tomorrow. I think the concert begins at two o'clock."

Marianne watched as he walked away.

After he had returned to the party, Sabrina joined Marianne with their coats.

"Oh, I wanted you and Mr. Robbins to meet before we leave. He is so wonderful, Sabrina. I know you will just love him. He is taking me to a concert tomorrow. That is, if Father agrees to his taking me."

"You know how to work Father. Just give him that pitiful look you do when you want something, and he will give in as usual. Now let's go. Lane is waiting for us."

"But Mr. Robbins. . ."

"I'll meet him some other time, Marianne, all right? Come along now. My feet hurt. Let's go home and relax."

Marianne relented. "Well, I think you will have many other opportunities to meet him as I plan on seeing Mr. Robbins many more times after tonight." She sighed contentedly as she left with her sister. She knew she would in fact see him in her dreams that very night.

CHAPTER 8

July had brought a heat wave into Memphis. Dulcie had washed some of Sabrina's finer clothes and was now hanging them out on the line. She mumbled to herself as she often did. "There comes that no 'count Caesar. He's gonna try to get next to me just like he always does, but he ain't gonna have no luck."

"Well, hello. How's my favorite young woman?" Caesar, the carriage driver, was a tall, well-built, handsome black man. He had a beautiful smile and graceful moves that had made him a favorite with the ladies. Now he came and stood next to Dulcie and said, "What you been up to today, Miss Dulcie?"

"I've been eavesdropping."

Caesar blinked his eyes. "Well, that ain't nice. Who was you eavesdropping on?"

"I was listening to Miss Sabrina and Miss Marianne. Then I listened to what Mr. Charles and Miss Caroline had to say about them daughters of theirs."

Caesar reached over and put his hand on Dulcie's shoulder. "That's always nice to be able to listen in on the rich folk." This was his term for the Warren family. "I don't get to eavesdrop on nobody except you and some of the other ladies around this neighborhood."

His grasp tightened, and Dulcie suddenly looked up with her eyes flashing. "You get your paws off of me, Caesar!"

"Why, honey, I'm just being affectionate."

"I know what you're being. You're trying to get next to me like you always do."

"Why, you can't blame me for that," Caesar protested. "After all, you're the prettiest lady in this whole town of Memphis. As a matter of fact, I came over to give you an invite."

"Humph! I know your invites. What is it this time?"

"Well, it's so hot I thought later in the afternoon when it cools off, we go down to the river. You know where the big trees overhang and there's a nice grassy bank there. We could take something to eat and have a little picnic."

Dulcie glared at Caesar. She knew his reputation, and although she was tempted to give in to his invitation, she knew better. "I remember," she said loudly, "how Clara went to the river with you, and she got a baby out of it."

"Well, that's so, but ain't that boy baby handsome? Just like me."

"You think mighty well of yourself, Caesar, but I'm a Christian woman, and I'm not about to put myself in any kind of a way with you."

"Well, I goes to church every Sunday."

Dulcie bent over the basket, picked up one of Sabrina's gowns, and clipped it onto the clothesline. The breeze stirred it slightly, and it smelled of lavender, for Sabrina liked her clothes to have this scent. "Bein' inside a church don't make you no Christian—no more than bein' inside a stable makes you a horse."

Caesar grinned and shook his head. "You is a mighty clever woman, Dulcie. Just think what it'd be like if you and me had some children. They'd be handsome like me and pretty like you. They'd be smart like you. They'd be nice and easy to get along with like me. Now, tell me what you heard them women and Mr. and Mrs. Warren talkin' about."

"Mostly they was talkin' about that new man that Marianne has got on her mind."

"What did they say?"

"Well, Miss Sabrina tried to tell Marianne how foolish she was to make that much of some man that ain't goin' to be here. Mr. Charles and Miss Caroline said about the same thing. They's worried about her."

"Well, what do you think, Dulcie?"

"That girl Marianne, she's a sweet child, but she ain't had no experience with men to speak of, and right now she got some romantic notions. Them things is bad for a person. They can get her into bad trouble, and Miss Marianne don't need no trouble with a stranger, which is what that man is."

Caesar listened carefully as Dulcie talked on. When she finished, he pushed his case for a picnic again. He looked surprised to hear her say, "All right. I'll go to the riverbank with you, but I'm takin' one of our knives from the kitchen. You try to put your hands on me in a way that ain't proper, and I'll cut your fingers off."

"I'll be just as good as the driven snow. We'll have us a time, Dulcie."

⁂

Sabrina was sleeping peaceably, but the door opened and then closed, waking her up. She sat up in bed and looked startled, then said, "What are you doing interrupting my nap, Dulcie?"

"You done had enough nap. You won't sleep tonight."

"You want to run my life. You're my maid and sometimes you act like I'm the maid and you're the mistress."

"You need to get up. Miss Marianne done had a long talk with your momma and your daddy."

"You always listen to people."

"Well, why shouldn't I? White folk treat house servants like they was furniture. What do you think, we don't hear nothin' or see nothin'? You just plumb forget about us. You better get dressed. You need to talk to Miss Marianne about that man she's been seein'."

Sabrina took a deep breath and nodded. "I guess you're right about that, Dulcie. Help me get dressed."

Sabrina had almost finished dressing when Marianne burst in. "I'm going out with Gerald late this afternoon. We may go out to Rudolph's Restaurant. That's the nicest place in Memphis."

Sabrina turned so that Dulcie could fasten the buttons on the back of her dress. Her mind worked rapidly. She had thought a great deal about this man whom Marianne was seeing, and when she turned around, she said, "That's fine, Dulcie. Why don't you go take some of those clothes that you washed this morning and iron them."

Dulcie gave Sabrina an insulted look. She well knew that this was her signal to leave.

Marianne waited until Dulcie had left the room then said, "I'm so excited. You're going to have to help me pick out a new dress. I don't have a thing to wear."

"You've got plenty of dresses, but let me tell you, Marianne, you don't need to be thinking about Gerald as a man you could marry."

"Why not?" Marianne demanded instantly. She was not a quarrelsome girl. As a matter of fact, she was far more docile than either their mother or Sabrina, but she was sensitive about Gerald and defensive.

"Well, in the first place you don't need a man who is not a Southerner."

"Well, he is a Southerner."

"Where is his home? I don't know anything about him. Neither do Father or Mother."

"He grew up in Mississippi. As a matter of fact, he served as a cavalry officer in the war. Fought under Robert E. Lee." She shook her head and said defiantly, "He and Lee were close friends."

"That's what he told you?"

"Yes, and the man couldn't be a close friend of General Lee unless he was a good Southerner."

"Where is he from? What does he do?" Sabrina said. Now as she looked at her sister whom she loved dearly, she saw a vulnerability there that, for some reason, frightened her. Sabrina herself had always been forthright, saying pretty much what she thought without apology, but Marianne had a far gentler attitude. She could not bear to hurt anybody or anything.

As Sabrina stood before her sister, she studied her face and saw there a quiet calmness that she herself did not possess. Sabrina had always been outspoken, forthright, and willing to argue with anyone, even her parents. But Marianne had a gentleness that she envied. Marianne's face was a mirror, which changed as her feelings changed, and she had never showed herself capable of robust emotion. But now that seemed to be what Sabrina was seeing in her.

Marianne's hair had a rich yellow gleam, and she was wearing a gray dress that deepened the color of her eyes and turned her hair into a more shining color. She had a pleasantly expressive mouth, one that, Sabrina had learned, showed her emotions very easily. She was growing up now, and Sabrina saw that her hips, which had been straight as a boy's only a short time ago, were rounded, and the light from the windows ran over the curves of her shoulders, and the light was kind to her, showing the full, soft lines of her body, the womanliness in breast and shoulder.

Suddenly Sabrina said, "Marianne, I think you're paying far too much attention to this man. He's not going to be here long, is he? Didn't you tell me he'd be leaving for the West?"

"Not for two weeks, and he asked me to go with him tonight to see *Hamlet*." Marianne's face was as clearly expressive at that moment as Sabrina had ever seen it, graphically registering the light and shadow of her feelings. Pleasure and wonder and the fullness of her youthful heart seemed to flow, and a strange small stirring of hope followed. She wasn't smiling, but the hint of a smile was at the corners of her mouth and in the tilt of her head.

Sabrina sought vainly for something to say that might change Marianne's mind. She was a little bit surprised, for she had always been able to guide Marianne's thinking, for the younger woman was easily led, but now there was a strength in her and a manner of decision. Sabrina saw there a new strong and self-assertive pride.

"I'm sorry you don't like him, but I don't care why. I'm going to keep seeing him. Besides, you've never met him."

"Well, I'll meet him soon enough, I guess. I do hope you have a good time tonight."

"Thank you, Sabrina. I'm sure you'll change your mind about Gerald once you do meet him." Marianne left the room.

Sabrina suddenly sat down. She was discouraged and not at all happy with the way she had handled the situation. She took a deep breath, released it, and sighed. "Somebody needs to be able to talk to that girl. She doesn't know what in the world she's getting into."

"I don't think this man playing Hamlet is much of an actor."

Marianne looked up at her father, surprised. "Why, you don't ever go to the theater, Father."

"No, but I listen to people. They say his father was a great actor, but the rest of his family are second rate."

"But he's so handsome. I saw him in *Julius Caesar*."

"Yes," Caroline said, "but that's not everything."

"I wish you'd go with us to the theater."

"I'm not going to see any play. I don't want to," Charles said. "And I wish you wouldn't go. I'm disturbed about this man you're seeing. We don't know anything about him."

"But I do," Marianne said. "He's a fine man. He's got a big ranch out in the west part of the country. He's built it up to where it's hundreds, maybe even thousands, of acres."

"Well, why don't you invite him to dinner one night so we can get to meet him?" Caroline said.

"He's been very busy, but I'll ask him."

After Sabrina came home that evening, Dulcie told her about Marianne's going to the theater.

"I heard you went down to the river with Caesar. You need to be more careful, Dulcie. You know what a bad man he is."

"He ain't bad. He's just a man."

"Well, you don't let him take any liberties."

"I reckon I know how to take care of myself. You don't need to give me no sermons."

꩜

Frank Morgan, at the age of twenty-eight, was a trim young man almost six feet tall and athletic. He had fair hair and dark blue eyes and had worked for Charles Warren for a long time. He had become an indispensable man at the factory.

Charles sat back and listened as Frank went over a new method he had discovered that would make them money. "You could sell this for a lot of money to U.S. Steel, Frank."

Frank shook his head. "I don't work for U.S. Steel, sir. I work for you."

"Well, you deserve something for your work. I'd like to make it right with you."

"No need of that, Mr. Warren."

"It's a business, and I insist on paying you outright or making you a stockholder."

Instantly young Morgan's eyes lit up. "I'd like that very much, sir, to be a stockholder."

"Fine." The office was quiet now for it was after office hours and all the help had gone. Charles Warren studied the young man and thought, *I've done at least one thing right.* "You know, Frank, I started this company with a son in mind to take over when I'm gone, but I have no son and never will now. As a matter of fact, Frank, you're closer to being my son than I had ever thought anyone could be."

"Well, I'm glad you feel that way, sir." Frank nodded. "I've never been able to thank you for all you've done for me."

As a matter of fact, Charles had practically raised young

GILBERT MORRIS

Morgan. He was the son of Charles's second cousin, and when both of his parents died of cholera, Charles took him into his own family. He sent him to college, and now one of the chief prides of his life was the way Frank Morgan had turned out. He looked out the window at the buildings of the factory, took a pride in it, then said, turning back to face the young man, "I worry about my family, Frank. If I were killed, nobody would know about the business. That's why I decided to make you executor of my estate."

"Why sir, I never thought of such a thing." Frank was genuinely surprised.

"Well, one of my friends died. His money was all used poorly. I know you've got a solid head for business and you'll take care of my wife and my daughters. You know, my wife and I had always hoped you and Marianne would make a match of it."

Suddenly Frank flushed. He had a fair complexion and hated it when a flush revealed his true deeper feelings. "Well, that's what I'd like, but I'm not the kind of man she wants."

"Why not? You're not bad looking. You're smart. You know the business. You've got a good future. Why don't you just go ask her, Frank?"

"I wish I could, but Marianne is interested in a more romantic fellow than I could ever be."

Warren got up, walked around, and put his hand on Frank's shoulder. He said quietly, "I'm sorry, son, but she may change her mind."

"I don't think so." Morgan smiled at Charles, turned, and left the office.

After he left, Warren stood there thinking of how a man's plans for his life seldom worked out.

104

Dulcie knew Sabrina was leaving early but was pleased she came in to see how Dulcie and Marianne were getting along with the new dress. It was a beautiful satin gown of a china blue color that matched Marianne's eyes.

"I look awful," Marianne said.

"No, you don't," Dulcie insisted. "You looks fine. Just fine."

Sabrina agreed. "Yes, it's a beautiful dress. I picked it out myself. Now, you sit down and let Dulcie fix your hair. I have to leave, but before I go, I thought you'd like to wear some of my jewelry. Here's this sapphire necklace and earrings that match." She put the earrings in then put the necklace around her sister's neck and said, "Now you truly look wonderful."

Marianne touched them and smiled gratefully. "Can I have some of the perfume that Lane gave you that he bought in Paris?"

"Of course you can. You know where it is."

As Marianne left the room, Dulcie said, "I wish you wouldn't run off. That girl needs somebody to look after her."

"Well, she's got you. You try to boss everybody on the place."

"He may be fine-looking, but he's a man."

Sabrina left, headed for the horse race in which she had a mount that she thought would win.

Dulcie went back and watched as Marianne eagerly applied the perfume behind her ears and in other strategic locations. "Don't you let that man take no liberty with you, Miss Marianne."

"He wouldn't."

"Yes, he would. He's a man, ain't he? I'm going to pray that you come home as sweet and innocent as you leave here."

"Oh, you worry too much." At that moment Clara, another

servant, came and said, "Your gentleman friend is here, Miss Marianne."

Marianne got up and left the room, excitement aglow in her face.

Dulcie shook her head. "I just hope that man is decent."

Clara stared at her. "Seems to be. Just for the night, ain't it?"

"That's all it takes—one night."

Marianne had enjoyed the drama tremendously. Her father would not let her go to many plays, and she had been conscious of Gerald's arm pressing against her. They left the theater, and he took her to have a light meal then drove her home.

He got out of the carriage, and she waited, knowing that he would come around and help her down. *He has such fine manners,* she thought.

When he took her hand as she stepped down, he didn't release it but held it for a moment. "You've given me great pleasure tonight, Marianne."

"It's been wonderful."

Suddenly something changed in Gerald's face, and Marianne, though inexperienced, knew that he was going to kiss her. She had thought long and hard about how she would handle such a situation, but she had no choice. She had nothing to do but surrender. Whatever plan she had left her, for she felt the lean strength of his body, and he was smiling in a way she had never seen in a man's eyes. She breathed more quickly, and as the moonlight highlighted his face, he pulled her closer and then lowered his head and kissed her.

Marianne knew nothing of actual passion, but she learned it

at just that moment. The full growth of woman came into being at that time, and she knew that she cared for this man in a way she had never felt for any other man. She felt fragile in his embrace, but he was not rough.

When he lifted his head, he said huskily, "You're sweet, Marianne. I've never known a sweeter young woman in all my life."

The kiss had been an experiment. She discovered she had the power to stir this man and found herself feeling a wave of emotion she had not anticipated. She put her hand on his chest and stepped back.

He smiled at her. "I shouldn't have done that," he whispered.

"It's all right."

"I ask your pardon, yet the fault was not entirely mine."

She knew that this was absolutely true, and when she turned to go into the house, she knew she would not forget that kiss for a long time.

CHAPTER 9

"I really don't think you should be running off on a shopping trip, Sabrina." Caroline Warren had come up to Sabrina's room and had at once begun speaking about her proposed trip to New Orleans. "It's just not a good time for you to go."

Sabrina, as usual, was headstrong and merely smiled, then came over and patted her mother on the shoulder. "Mother, I've planned this trip for weeks now, and I have friends who will be expecting me there. I really have to go."

"But at such a hard time. Neither your father nor I know what to do about this man that Marianne's been seeing."

Frank Morgan had come in to stand beside Caroline, and he added his plea to hers. "I really don't think you should go, Sabrina. Ordinarily it would be all right, but this is different."

"Oh, Frank, you and Mother, and Father, too, are just worried too much. Marianne will be all right. I'll only be gone for a few days. Maybe two weeks. And then when I come home, I'll meet that man and decide what he's like."

"Every day your sister falls more in love with him," Frank said quietly. "You really ought to show more consideration."

The remark touched off Sabrina's temper. "I think I am better aware than you of what my sister is, Frank. I know you mean well, but this is just not possible. I'll come back, and it'll take me a few days, but I'll get Marianne to see her foolishness."

"She's never been this serious about a man," Caroline said. Her hands were unsteady as she reached up and pushed her hair away from her forehead. "I've never seen her like this."

"He's romantic from what I hear. That's what she's always been looking for. She reads too many of those romance novels," Sabrina said then added, "She just needs to wake up."

Frank shook his head and for once dared to cross Sabrina. "She's not like you, Sabrina," he said quietly, but there was a steadiness in his voice that was unusual.

The argument went on for some time, but in the end Frank and Caroline left, and Dulcie entered. "You ought to listen to your momma. She knows what she's talkin' about, and Mr. Frank, he knows, too."

"Dulcie, I'm not going to argue with you. I'm going on this trip, and you're going with me."

Dulcie was sullen for a while; then as she continued to help Sabrina pack, she said, "You always think you can fix things."

"Well, it's true. I can fix things. All it takes is a lot of determination. Nobody's really showed any of that with Marianne."

"I don't know how you think you'd do anything about it. You ain't been listenin' to her. She's really gone on this man. We don't know nothin' about him. None of the family does."

"Well, when I get back I'll handle it."

"How you gonna do that?"

Sabrina threw a petticoat into the trunk that was already

packed then turned to say, "I'll meet this man and decide about him. If I don't like him, I'll hire a private detective to find out what kind of a man he is. Now help me get the rest of this stuff packed. We've got to be on that steamboat by two o'clock today."

⬬

Marianne had met Gerald for lunch, and after he watched her carefully, he said, "You've got something on your mind, Marianne. What is it?"

"I was wondering if you would come and have dinner with us tonight."

Gerald smiled. He had a good smile, broad, and humor sparkled in his eyes. "I guess your parents want to see what kind of a man you've been running around with. I've been wondering when this would come up."

"I wish you wouldn't tease me, Gerald. I've never been as serious about a man as I've come to feel about you."

"I didn't think your family would let you."

Marianne's eyes blinked; then she nodded slowly, realizing the remark was true. "They've always been very protective of me. Very careful about what I do and who I see."

Gerald leaned back in his chair, sipping his tea. "Not like that sister of yours, are you?"

"No, she's very strong."

Gerald set the cup down and stared at the young woman. He was quiet for one moment; then he turned his head to one side and said, "What if you had to choose between the man you loved and your family? Would you go against their will?"

Marianne was troubled by the question. She looked down for a time and said, "I just don't know, Gerald."

Leaning forward, he took her hand and held it. "If you love a man, Marianne, you give him everything. Just as he'd give you everything he had in him."

"That's sweet, Gerald. That's what I've always thought."

"One thing you have to understand, Marianne. I'm not a rich man. Not like your father. You'd have a comfortable life here if you choose to stay. You'll find some man, and your father will give you more than I ever could."

Marianne suddenly smiled. "I don't care about that."

"It's hard living out West. Not like living in a big city. You can't run down to the store every morning to get a pound of butter."

"It'd be like at pioneer times. I've read so many stories by James Fenimore Cooper about how difficult the pioneer life was. It would be like that, I think."

"Well, it's pretty rough all right. As for tonight, I'll be glad to come to dinner. This may be the last time we meet together. I fully expect your father to see me as a greedy man after his money through his daughter."

"They'll love you after they get to know you, Gerald."

❧

Gerald Robbins had come to dinner dressed in the latest of fashion. Caroline Warren saw there was a roughness about him, but he was also able to put on a fine manner and was pleasant. Her husband had probed carefully around, trying to find what kind of man he was, but had not been very successful.

Charles now asked their guest, "I understand you are in the cattle business."

"Yes, Mr. Warren, that's about all I know. I've done well at it." He took a bite of the steak on his fork, chewed it, then said,

"Of course I haven't done as well as you have. It's hard to make a fortune in the cattle business unless you're someone like the King Ranch with unlimited space and money to go into it."

"Where do you sell your cattle?"

"Well, now that the railroad is in, we just take them down to the stockyard. Some of them get shipped to Chicago. I would imagine some even come here. We try to grow the finest cattle in the world."

"I imagine that's a lot of hard work, isn't it, Mr. Robbins?" Caroline said. She had been impressed by Gerald Robbins's manners, and for some reason had been expecting less.

"Yes ma'am, it is a lot of hard work, but I've got a good crew. They've been with me a long time, so we make out very well."

"Is your ranch very far from town?"

"It's not around the corner, but of course we have plenty of good horses and carriages. No trouble to go once we make up our mind."

"I imagine it's pretty lonely out there, isn't it?" Mr. Warren said.

"Well, you know, you get used to that and you get to where you even like it. As a matter of fact, I get to feeling all crowded in when I'm in a big city like this one. From the ranch you can look over to the west and see the peaks of the mountains. Beautiful mountains. I go there for a hunting expedition once in a while. Plenty of deer and any other kind of game you like to shoot, but then out on the flatlands that's right pretty, too. In the springtime the wildflowers make a riot of color. Very beautiful. The country gets to you."

Marianne had said little. "Oh, that sounds so beautiful. Just like I read about in the books."

The dinner went on for some time, and then they adjourned to the drawing room for coffee and more talk. Finally Robbins took his leave.

After he left, Marianne came to them at once, her eyes sparkling. "Isn't he a handsome man, Mother?"

"Very attractive."

"But he's talking about a hard life that you've never had." Marianne's father sought for the words. Caroline knew he felt deep in his soul that something was wrong here, and finally he said, "I don't believe you ought to see him, Marianne. You're infatuated with him."

"I am not. I actually care for him."

That was the beginning of the closest thing to a quarrel that Marianne Warren had ever had with her father. Caroline and Charles were determined that she should stop seeing Robbins, and she was equally set on seeing him even more. Marianne finally left the room in tears.

Charles shook his head. "This is a real problem. I wish Sabrina hadn't gone off."

Caroline shook her head. "I don't think it would make any difference. I've never seen Marianne this stubborn before. It's just not like her."

"You got two letters?" Dulcie asked.

"Yes. One from momma and one from Marianne." She opened the first letter and began reading.

Dulcie asked, "What does she say?"

"She's worried about Marianne, of course, but we went over that before I left. She'll be all right." Sabrina opened the second letter and was quiet as she read it.

"What did Miss Marianne say?"

"She is besotted with that man Robbins."

"I told you! Didn't I tell you? We ought to go home."

"No, I've got more shopping to do, Dulcie. I may not get back here for a year. We'll leave Wednesday. Now don't argue with me anymore about it. Things will be all right. When I get there, I'll see to it that Marianne settles down."

CHAPTER 10

Waco lifted the eight-pound sledgehammer over his shoulder and was about to swing it down and break a large rock into fragments when the shrill whistle of one of the guards stopped him. He could have gone ahead and smashed the rock, but he was determined not to do one thing that he was told to do if he could get out of it. Carefully he lowered the sledge and looked over at Cecil Petit, his cell mate. "There's the whistle, Cecil. Let's go wash this dust off and maybe get something to eat."

"Sure, Waco." Petit was a small man no more than five-seven and thin. He had been unable to handle an eight-pound sledge so the guard had furnished him with a five-pounder. Even this was too much for the young man. He was barely past twenty years old and was the typical Southerner with light greenish eyes and tow hair and a Southern accent.

The guard rode by, his shotgun in the crook of his arm, his eyes darting here and there. "Okay. Get on in and wash that dirt off."

Waco turned wearily and slapped Cecil on the shoulder. "That's about enough for one day." Indeed, it had been a terrible day. The blistering sun had burned those who had light-colored skin. Fortunately for Waco, he had his tan from his work on the horse ranch and his years in prison out under the sun.

The prisoners all formed a single line and went by an outdoor shower of sorts. It was simply a hose that was attached to a well that ran on a windmill sort of pump. Waco pulled his shirt off, and when his turn came the tepid water seemed almost cold it was in such contrast with the blazing sunlight. He would have liked to take off all his clothes, but he knew that the guard wouldn't let him.

"Okay, Smith, move on. You're clean enough."

Waco stepped outside, pressed the water from his hair, and waited until Cecil had gotten his shower. The two of them made their way to the long building that contained, among other things, the mess hall.

"Sure wish they'd have something good to eat tonight," Cecil said. He was almost gasping for breath, for the hard manual labor was almost more than he could take. "You know," he said, "I was down in New Orleans one time. We had shrimp, fish, and gumbo. Sure wish I had a mess of that. Or even some catfish out of the Mississippi River."

"Shut up or I'll break your head, Petit."

Quickly Waco turned to see that Ring Gatlin, a hulking brute of a man, was glaring at Cecil. "Take it easy, Ring," he said.

Gatlin was the bully of the prison. He had whipped everybody except Waco Smith. The two had fought it out under the hot sun, and the guards had merely laughed and watched. Waco had walked away, but Gatlin lay unconscious, his face cut and slashed.

"You makin' this your fight, Waco?"

Waco didn't answer. He just simply stared at Ring to see if he would make a move. Then he shrugged and said, "Come on, Cecil. Let's see what we've got to eat."

The two men filed into the mess hall, which contained six-foot-long tables with benches. At one end there was a mess line, and the prisoners were lining up in front of it. When Waco looked down at the food that was in metal pans, he said, "Well, Cecil, no good old fish or gumbo tonight."

"No, I didn't reckon there would be."

The two men filled their plates, walked back, and sat down at a table. Waco stared down at the food, which amounted to a tough piece of pork, beans not fully cooked, and rough bread. There was also a small amount of cold rice. Cecil went at his food like a starved wolf, for as skinny as he was he ate ferociously. As the two men ate, there was little talking.

After all the men had been fed, the guard blew a whistle. "All right. Get into lockup."

Cecil and Waco made their way out of the mess hall and under the watchful eye of one of the guards went with other inmates down through a long corridor. On each side were steel bars fencing in a small cell no more than ten by ten. They stepped inside, and Waco sat down on the lower bunk. He was so much larger, and Cecil found it easier to scamper up into the top bunk.

For a while the two men rested up. Waco felt even the bad food allowing strength to flow through his body. He said, "You ought to sleep good tonight, Cecil, after a day's work like that."

"I reckon I will."

The two lay still for a time, exhausted by the hard labor. Finally Waco heard a scratching sound, and a bluish light illuminated the cell.

Cecil had the stub of a candle that he had obtained somehow, and now he came down from the top bunk and set it down on the edge of Waco's bunk. "I've been readin' here in the Bible somethin' that you ought to know about."

"I don't guess I'm interested."

"You ought to be. It's about a guy like us."

Waco looked at Cecil with what little fondness was left in him. The two had grown close, especially after Waco had saved Cecil from a beating by Ring Gatlin. "Why don't you give up on me? You've been preachin' at me for three years now."

Indeed, Cecil had been converted when a visiting minister had spoken. He had become a fervent Christian and had obtained a Bible, which he read in all of his free time.

"God ain't never give up on nobody, Waco. Now you just listen to this." He began to read. "This is when they crucified Jesus. Nailed Him up on a cross, and it says here in Luke 23, verse 32, 'And there were also two other, malefactors. . .' That means criminals, Waco. They were 'led with him to be put to death. And when they were come to the place which is called Calvary, there they crucified him, and the malefactors, one on the right hand, and the other on the left.' Then, Waco, the Bible says people made fun of Him, the rulers mocked Him, and the soldiers made fun of Him, too. They called out, 'If thou be the king of the Jews, save thyself.' And here's the part I want you to hear. Starts on verse 39.

" 'And one of the malefactors which were hanged railed on him, saying, If thou be Christ, save thyself and us. But the other answering rebuked him, saying, Dost not thou fear God, seeing thou art in the same condemnation? And we indeed justly; for we receive the due reward of our deeds: but this man hath done nothing amiss.'

"Now listen to this, Waco. Are you listenin'?"

"Yes, I'm listening, Cecil."

" 'And he said unto Jesus, Lord, remember me when thou comest into thy kingdom.' Waco, you've got to remember this guy lived like us. He was a criminal, and Jesus was the Son of God, but he asked Him to help him. 'And Jesus said unto him, Verily I say unto thee, Today shalt thou be with me in paradise.' " Cecil chortled, shook his head, then slapped Waco's broad shoulders. "Ain't that somethin' now. There's a guy no better than us. He was in jail just like we are, and he was gonna die that day, but Jesus said he would be with Him in heaven. Ain't that a great story, Waco?"

Waco closed his eyes. He had grown accustomed to Cecil preaching to him, and actually he did not mind. He had developed a fondness for the young man and was determined to see that he was not bullied. "I've heard that before. An evangelist came to town, and my grandpa and grandma took me to hear him. He preached the same text."

Cecil considered this, and then he said, "Well, why didn't you get saved, Waco?"

"Don't ask me, Cecil. I don't know. Maybe I'm just too lost to be saved."

"No, that ain't right. Jesus said, 'Whosoever will may come.' "

The two men sat there by the feeble, flickering light of the candle until there was a sound of a whistle, which meant everybody had to be quiet. The guards had ways of enforcing this, so Waco said, "Better put that candle out. We don't want to burn the place down."

Cecil laughed. "Couldn't burn down this place. It's made out of stone." Cecil put the candle out and said, "You think about that criminal, Waco."

119

"Sure," Waco agreed. He waited until Cecil had scampered to the top bunk then stretched full-length on his cot. It had nothing but a straw ticking, and for a long time he lay there.

It had become his habit to go to sleep as quickly as he could and to avoid thoughts of what life was like before he had been thrown into prison. But tonight sleep eluded him and he thought back on the time when his grandfather taught him how to break horses. Then he thought of the meals his grandmother cooked. Every morning biscuits six inches in diameter and fluffy.

He finally began to doze off, but suddenly he came wide awake. He shifted in his bed and sat up, looking around, but he could see nothing in the darkness.

"What's the matter, Waco?" Cecil whispered.

"I don't know. Something's wrong."

"What's wrong?"

"Can't say, but if anything happens, you stick close to me, Cecil."

"Ah, nothin's gonna happen."

"Probably not."

Waco lay back, but five minutes later he heard the sound of a voice, and then the steel door at the end of the corridor that led to the cells opened. He sat up at once, for he knew that this was not something that happened every night. Suddenly a voice broke the silence, and a man shouted, "Wake up! We're getting out of this place!"

Waco stood up then.

Cecil joined him as they looked out. "That's Ring Gatlin," Cecil said.

"Yeah, and his two buddies, Tad Mason and Shortie Tyler. They're all three troublemakers."

"How'd they get out of their cells, Waco?"

"I don't know."

Ring had keys in his hands and started unlocking the doors. "Come out of them cells."

When Waco's cell door opened, he stepped out to face Ring. "What's up, Ring?"

"We're gettin' out of this place." Gatlin had a wolfish-looking expression. "I done killed one guard, so I'll kill whoever I have to. They can't hang me but once."

"You can't get out of here. There are guards everywhere," Waco protested. He saw the wild light in Gatlin's eyes and knew that the man would stop at nothing.

"We're going to shake the warden down and get the key to the weapons room. We're gonna get a gun in the hand of every prisoner here, and we're gonna shoot our way out. Anybody gets in our way, that's their tough luck."

Waco shook his head. "You'll never make it. Count me out."

Suddenly Ring snarled, "Get out of that cell, Smith. You're either with me or against me." He held the revolver up, pointed directly at Waco's face. "You either help us do this or I'll kill you now. And I'll kill that cellmate of yours, too."

Waco knew Ring, and he was not entirely sane. He had no idea how the big man had worked this, but he knew that he was telling the truth about shooting him. He took a deep breath and said, "Well, you've got the best of the argument, Ring."

"All right. We'll get you a gun, and then we're leaving this place." All the cell doors were open, and there were at least twenty inmates in that cell block. Ring hissed, "Everybody be quiet. We're going to the warden's office."

Waco kept his eyes open. The three men were all carrying lanterns throwing a feeble yellow light over the scene. They passed the body of the guard whom Ring had killed, turned down a corridor, and stood before a door that said WARDEN CRAWFORD.

Ring lifted the gun and said, "All right. Get ready." Ring opened the door and stepped inside, and his two friends shoved Waco through the door along with Cecil. Waco saw that Warden Morgan Crawford was shocked. He stood up immediately, a small man with dark hair and dark eyes. "What's going on?"

"We're bustin' out of this place, Warden. Give us the key to that weapons room where you keep the guns."

"I won't do that, Gatlin."

"Then I'll shoot you and take it off your body."

Waco was shocked to see one of the guards go for his gun in spite of being under the guns of the three inmates.

Ring shot him down, and he lay kicking for a moment then grew still. "You're next, Warden."

"Wait a minute, Ring. I'll get the key," Waco said. He walked over to the warden, who was standing with the remaining guard. He had his eyes on the gun that was at the guard's belt.

Ring laughed. "Give him that key, Crawford, or you'll be dead. Get that guy's gun. Find the key to the weapons room."

Waco's mind was working rapidly. He knew he had no choice, but he also knew he couldn't go along with Ring. This could never work. He walked across the room. His eyes met Warden Crawford's. He took the gun from the guard then stepped in front of the warden. "Drop your gun, Ring. You're not going to do this."

Ring lifted his pistol and fired two shots as Waco knew he would. The first shot grazed him, but Waco felt the other bullet strike him. He then shot off three rounds, one at Gatlin and the other two at his companions, before he felt the world turning black. He then fell, conscious only of the smell of gun smoke then of nothing at all.

Dr. Simmons was talking to Warden Crawford. "He's going to be all right, but those two slugs hit him. I guess if you have to be shot twice it was pretty good. One missed the lung and lodged in the shoulder. The other creased his head. If it had been an inch to the right, he'd be dead."

Warden Crawford had come to the prison hospital and watched as Simmons had patched Waco up. Waco's shots, to the warden, had been miraculous. He had put all three men down, Ring dead and the other two so badly wounded that the guards were able to come and overpower them. "He saved my life, Dr. Simmons. Do your best for him."

Waco came out of a deep darkness. He was conscious of pain, and when he opened his eyes he saw a face peering down at him. "Well, Warden, he's going to live."

The face disappeared, and Warden Crawford's face appeared. Waco could not put it all together. "How'd I get here?"

"Well, you got here by saving my life and maybe the lives of half a dozen others. You got Ring dead center. And the other two, after they shot you, you kept firing until they both went down. Waco, I want to thank you for saving my life. I owe you for that, and I always pay my debts."

Waco was weak and felt himself drifting off. He tried to put it all together but could not think. He knew somehow that Warden Crawford was saying something very important. He tried desperately to remember it as he drifted off into sleep.

CHAPTER 11

Sabrina looked around the room as Dulcie shook her head. The room was piled high with packages of all shapes, and dresses and other garments were hanging from anywhere the two could find a place to put them.

Finally Dulcie said, "You don't need no more new clothes. You couldn't wear all you got now in a year."

"Hush, Dulcie," Sabrina said. She held up a dress that she had not been sure of, and now she shook her head. "This is just a little bit too daring. Look at that neckline. I would never wear it."

"Then what you buy it for?" Dulcie shot the question. "I told you when you tried it on it showed too much of you, but would you listen to me? No, you never listens to me."

Sabrina suddenly laughed. "I don't know why you're fussing so much," she said, staring at the dress. "You get all my old clothes."

"You ain't got no old clothes."

"What are you talking about? I always have clothes that I give you when I buy new things."

"You give 'em to me, but they ain't old. You ain't never wore out

124

a dress or a petticoat or a pair of pantaloons in your whole life."

"Well, you probably have the best wardrobe of any servant in the United States."

Indeed, this was true. Sabrina knew Dulcie did not keep all the clothes, for she had friends who needed them, and there were certainly not enough places for her to go where she might wear the fancy dresses. But still she grumbled. "You got enough stuff here to start a store."

"Well, come on. We're going to go out to one more place."

"One more place for what?"

"There's one more place that makes stylish dresses. Just one of a kind. Come on. I want something absolutely different."

The two left the hotel and walked down the streets of New Orleans. It was the city that Sabrina loved, for it was so different from any other town or city that she had ever seen. They passed down a street where there were organ grinders and a fair where they were selling all kinds of things that nobody in the world had a need for but bought anyway. They went by the square where Sabrina glanced at a cathedral. It seemed to be doing not nearly so much business as the shops.

Dulcie followed her as Sabrina went into one of the stores, looking around. "They ought to have something here for me."

"I reckon they do," Dulcie grumbled, "and it's gonna cost you an arm and a leg."

Sabrina had long ago given up looking for bargains. Now she simply bought what she wanted. She noticed that there were, strangely enough, couples there, men with women. The women were Creoles, beautiful women, and she suspected they were the mistresses rather than the wives of the men they accompanied.

She was interrupted when a man who had come up to stand

beside her said, "Well, I don't believe we've met."

Sabrina turned and studied the man quickly. She had become quite a student of males for she had been pursued since she was in her midteens. She was wise enough to know that some of the pursuers were simply after her father's money, and she had quickly learned to identify that species instantly. "No, we haven't met, and I don't think we will."

She was studying the man, who was tall and darkly handsome with black hair and eyes a deep brown. He had a trim mustache and a clean-cut jaw, and his clothes were absolutely everything except cheap. The quality and cut of his suit, the perfect-fitting shoulders, the smooth, flat lapels—all were impeccable. He was dressed in a pure white soft silk shirt and a wide, flowering cravat tied meticulously, and his jacket was a fine wool. The price of his boots would have fed a poor family for a month.

He was a handsome man with a face full of humor and undisciplined imagination. "I take it you are a visitor in New Orleans."

"Yes sir, I am."

"Well, we are happy to welcome you. My name is William Blakely." He hesitated for a moment then said, "At this point it's customary for a lady to give her name."

Sabrina ordinarily would do no such thing, but she knew she would not be seeing this man again, so she said, "I am Sabrina Warren from Memphis."

"Fine. Now we are acquainted, and I think we should have lunch."

"Don't you have work to do?"

"No, not a bit."

"Well, what do you do for a living?"

"Nothing."

His honesty and mischievous look attracted Sabrina.

"My father made a pile of money, so all I do is flit around going to social events."

He was a charming, witty man, obviously with plenty of money. Most women would have been flattered with his attention, but Sabrina was merely amused. "Doesn't it embarrass you to come right out and tell people you're a parasite?"

"Not a bit," Blakely said. "Dad knows when he goes up the flue I'll have to take over the business. Then I'll become a boring businessman like all the rest."

"Are you married?"

"No. And I hope you're not either. . ."

"I'm also unmarried."

His smile widened. "Great. I'll tell you what. I think it would be suitable if you and I would go to lunch as a welcome to our fair city."

Men did not often amuse Sabrina. He was obviously a scoundrel and a wastrel but a wealthy one and a witty one. She turned and said, "Dulcie, you go back to the hotel. Can you find it?"

Dulcie gave her a disgusted look. "You think I get lost in this place? Of course I can find it."

"Well, you go on back and wait for me there."

After Dulcie left, Blakely said, "Come on. I'm going to take you to the finest restaurant in New Orleans, and I'm an honored guest. They'll give us the best they've got."

They moved outside, and several minutes later he led her into the Boudreaux Café. The tables were covered with snowy white tablecloths, the silver glowed with a richness and a warmth almost alive, and the lights illuminated the richness of the décor.

A man dressed in a fine black suit came forward. "Well, Mr. Blakely, we haven't seen you lately."

"Hello, Franklin. This is Miss Sabrina Warren. She's a visitor in our city, and I brought her to the best restaurant in New Orleans."

"Kind of you to say so." Franklin beamed. "Come. I'll give you your usual table."

A few minutes after they were seated, Franklin extended a menu, but Blakely said, "Just bring us the best you have. It'll be good." He leaned forward and said, "I've never gotten a bad meal yet."

"Thank you," Franklin said. "Your food will be out very quickly." He turned and left their table.

"Well, now. Tell me about yourself, Mr. Blakely," Sabrina said. "If you don't work, what do you do?"

Blakely turned his head to one side and seemed to think. "Well, I suppose my chief occupation at the present time is looking for a bride. As a matter of fact, I've got a list of prospects for the job. My mother and father made it out. The usual things for a rich wastrel like myself. She must be not hideous, have lots of money, come from a good family, and be respectable. As I say, my parents made it out. I'd like to add you to the list."

"It would never work, Mr. Blakely."

"Just call me William. Now, why wouldn't it work?"

"Because we're both used to getting everything we want."

"Well, that doesn't matter. We've got money enough between us to take care of that."

"We'd fight constantly."

"I'd rather like that. Every couple needs a good fiery argument at least once a week. Then they can have fun making up. What about you, Sabrina? Has your family tried to marry you off to a suitable candidate?"

Ordinarily Sabrina would not have spoken to a stranger about her life, but something about William Blakely made her open up. She said honestly, "My family feels like yours, except they're looking for a suitable husband."

"Well, this is going to work out fine." Blakely smiled. He leaned forward and whispered, "After we eat we'll go to my house. You can apply to my parents for the position of my wife. I think they'll give you a high rating. I'm afraid," he said sadly, "they're trying to marry me off to Emma Gibbons."

"What's the matter with her?"

"Well, she's rather homely, to be truthful. Stacks of money. Comes from an old-money family, and lots of poor men without money are after her. Oh, I think you can beat Emma out."

Sabrina laughed and said, "That's very tempting, but we're too much alike. Both spoiled to the bone."

"Well, I like being spoiled, and I expect you do, too, right?"

"Pretty much."

"Any brothers or sisters to inherit the money?"

"I have one sister, but she's younger than I am. As a matter of fact, she's very romantic, which I am not."

"Oh, I think you might be if you had the proper...encouragement."

"No, I've had the proper encouragement. I'm very practical. My sister is expecting a white knight to come riding in and carry her off. She's being courted by a handsome one right now. My parents are afraid of him." She went ahead to explain the situation, and finally she shrugged. "My parents are worried sick, but I can handle it."

"What will you do, shoot the poor man?"

"Oh, there are ways of getting rid of fellows like that. I've had quite a bit of experience."

Blakely smiled and stroked his mustache. "Well, it occurs to me maybe I could go back with you for a double purpose. I could shoot the fellow, maybe not kill him, just wound him and persuade him to leave. Then I can persuade your parents that I'm just the sort of son-in-law they need."

"I don't think that would work out. My mother's not very astute, but my father's sharp. He got rich by knowing men. He'd see you, William, in a minute as a poor choice for a son-in-law."

"That breaks my heart, Sabrina, but let's at least enjoy the lunch. Then tonight we'll go out together, and I'll have another chance with you."

Sabrina enjoyed the lunch and enjoyed the chatter, but immediately following the meal she said, "Good-bye. It's been nice talking to you. You're a charming fellow, but I'm looking for a man with a little bit more backbone."

"I don't have much of that, I'm afraid." Blakely shrugged. "If you change your mind"—he reached into his pocket and gave her a card—"here's my name and address. Just write me, and I'll come on that white horse to carry you off."

Sabrina took his hand. He offered to accompany her, but she said, "No. This is good-bye forever, William."

When she got back to the hotel, Dulcie was waiting for her. "Well, did you get rid of that triflin' man?"

"Why, he's rich, handsome, and charming."

Dulcie said sourly, "He's a trashy man. You don't need no trashy man, Miss Sabrina. You needs a good man."

"Well, I'm trying hard. I seem to have run through the available list in Memphis."

"But there's plenty of good men out there, and one of them would be a good man for you, but you is too picky."

"Well, let's look at these dresses now." She threw herself into the task of trying on dresses again, knowing full well she would send some of them back.

The following day, Sabrina was awakened early by Dulcie, who said, "There's done been a telegram come for you."

"A telegram?" Sabrina sat up in bed and blinked her eyes, trying to come awake. "Where is it?"

"It's right here." Dulcie handed her a single slip of paper.

She peered at the signature. "It's from Father."

"What does he say?"

Sabrina scanned the telegram. "It says: 'Sabrina, Marianne insists on marrying Gerald Robbins. It's a tragedy. Please come home at once and help us change her mind.'"

Sabrina threw off the bedcovers and got up. "Help me get dressed, Dulcie," she said. "We've got to leave today."

"I told you so! Didn't I tell you? You didn't have no business leavin'. Now you got to go home, and I don't think you can do nothin' about Miss Marianne."

"Yes, I can. Now help me get packed."

"Gonna take an extra railroad car to get all this junk back," Dulcie muttered, but she began stuffing dresses into suitcases and trunks.

As the carriage drew up to the front door of her home, Sabrina got out. The footman was there to help her. She turned and said, "Dulcie, you take my things. See that it's all hung up."

"Yes, ma'am," Dulcie said.

Sabrina was met by her mother, who threw herself at her daughter. Sabrina held on to her, patting her back and saying, "Now don't cry, Mother. It's going to be all right."

"No, it's not going to be all right. It's going to be awful. She won't even listen to her father and certainly not me. You've got to change her mind and tell her about this man."

"Well, I haven't even met him."

"He's not a man for her. You'll find that out."

"Where is she?"

"She's up in her room. We had an awful fight. She went off and told me she didn't want to see anybody."

"Well, she'll see me," Sabrina said grimly. She released herself from her mother's embrace and headed up the stairs. As she did, she tried to make up a speech. *I've got to be firm. She's too young to get married. She's not mature enough to marry anybody. Not this knight in white armor she's been looking for.* She had already formed a poor opinion of Gerald Robbins without having met him. She had heard him described well by her parents and ecstatically by Marianne, and none of it pleased her. She reached the top of the stairs, went to the door of Marianne's room, and knocked. "Marianne, I need to see you."

"Go away!"

"I'm not going away." She opened the door and saw Marianne lying across the bed.

Her younger sister raised her head. Her eyes were red with weeping. "Leave me alone, Sabrina."

"I'm not leaving you alone. I'm going to talk sense to you."

For the next ten minutes Sabrina did her best to "talk sense" to Marianne, but it was like talking to a dead stump.

Marianne would do nothing but shake her head and say, "I

love him, and I'm going to marry him."

"You're not going to marry him. Why, I haven't even met him."

"Your mind is made up against him. So is Mother's and Father's, but I don't care. I love him, and I'm going to have him."

Sabrina was set back somewhat. Marianne had always been the gentle, easily led one of the two. Sabrina had been the bossy, demanding type, but now she had run up against a problem she had never encountered before. Marianne was obstinate; her mouth was set in a stubborn fashion, and she was glaring at Sabrina with resentment and anger. "We don't really know this man," Sabrina said. "We don't know anything about his family."

"I know one thing. I know I love him."

"You're just in love with romance."

"Don't start on me, Sabrina. I'm not going to listen."

That, in essence, was Sabrina's effort to cause Marianne to listen. But after ten minutes of total silence from her sister, Sabrina gave up. "We'll talk about this some more when you feel better." She waited for Marianne to answer, but when she still refused to speak, Sabrina got up and left the room. She went downstairs and found her father and mother waiting for her.

"What did she say?" her father demanded. His face was lined with care. He obviously expected her to have a good word.

"She won't listen to me now, but I'm not through yet. We can't give up."

"She's like a different young woman," Caroline Warren said. Her face was swollen from weeping, and she said, "Can't we just bundle her into a carriage and take her away?"

"She's not a child," Charles Warren said.

"She is behaving like a twelve-year-old," Sabrina said angrily. She was disturbed at having failed in her first attempt. Always before, whatever she pleased, she could get Marianne to agree to it, but this was a different young girl, and Sabrina's mouth set in a stubborn line. "I'm going to stay here and not let her out of my sight. And I'm going to meet this Gerald Robbins. I've got a word or two to say to him."

"We've said everything we can think of to him and to her," her father said. "It's a hopeless case."

"No, it's not hopeless. I can fix it," Sabrina said stubbornly. She turned and walked out of the drawing room and up the stairs.

She found Dulcie sitting in the midst of a pile of her clothes, waiting. "Did you talk her out of marrying that scoundrel?"

"You don't know he's a scoundrel."

"I bet he is. He ain't no good man."

"You wouldn't think any man was good enough."

"That doesn't change that he's a scoundrel. You mark my words on that."

"I'll make up my own mind on that," Sabrina said. "I'm going to see him tomorrow."

"You might have met your match this time. I don't think the Good Lord Himself could change Miss Marianne's mind."

Sabrina could not sleep well that night. She woke up late. Dulcie was not there, so she put on a simple dress, brushed her hair, and started down the stairs.

She was met halfway down by her father, who had a sheet of paper in his hands. His face was pale.

"What is it, Father?"

"Read this."

Sabrina took the paper and read it in one glance. It was in Marianne's handwriting, but where her handwriting was usually neat, this was obviously scratched at a moment's notice.

I know you're all going to hate me, but I can't help it. I love Gerald, and I'm leaving with him. I would like to be married here, but he says we can be married after we get to his home, that he knows a good parson there. Please don't try to find me. Gerald is my life. I love you all, but I must do this.

Marianne

"When did she leave, Father?"

"Nobody knows. She went to bed early, and she was gone this morning. She must have made arrangements for Robbins to take her in the middle of the night." He slumped over against the rail and looked as if he were about to fall.

"Don't worry, Father. We'll find them."

"How? We don't know where she's going. We know very little about the man."

"We'll find him. Don't worry. This isn't the end of this thing yet." But even as Sabrina spoke, she knew that somehow something had ended in the life of their family. It was almost like a death, and Sabrina, for the first time in her life, felt helpless.

She had tried her best to change Marianne and failed. Now the thought that if she had stayed it might have been different came to her. She slowly descended the stairs, determined to give her mother all the comfort she could—which wasn't a great deal.

CHAPTER 12

Caesar was sitting in the kitchen eating a huge piece of cake, stuffing his mouth full.

Dulcie glared at him. "You eat like a hungry dog. Take little bites."

"It's so good I can't hep it. You the best cook there is in addition to being the best-lookin' one around."

"Don't you come at me with none of your ways. I ain't gonna stand for it, Caesar."

Caesar's eyes opened wide. "Why, I was just being appreciative. You is good-lookin', and you is a fine cook."

Dulcie did not object to these two descriptions of herself, but she plopped herself down, and her head drooped. "This place is a madhouse."

"Sho' enough is. They all act like Miss Marianne died. She didn't die."

"About the same to them. She says she's going to marry that man, but he ain't said one word to Mr. Charles 'bout marryin' her. I don't think he's got marriage on his mind. He didn't look like a marryin' man to me."

"Well, he was a fine dresser and good-lookin' gentleman."

"Gentleman? He ain't no gentleman."

"How can you tell?"

"I've been around enough gentlemen to know one when I sees one. Mr. Frank Morgan, now he's a gentleman. Mr. Charles, he's a gentleman. Even that Mr. Lane Williams that been courtin' Miss Sabrina is a gentleman. But that fellow Robbins, he wasn't no gentleman. He's gonna ruin Miss Marianne, that's what."

Caesar took a small portion of the cake and put it in his mouth. At once it was gone, and he took a larger portion. He washed it down with a glass of milk and said, "Miss Sabrina, she's plumb upset. I took her downtown today, and she snapped at me like I wuz a snake."

"She's worried. First time she's ever been worried about anything."

"She knows it's her fault."

"How could it be her fault? It was her sister who run off."

"If she had stayed here and helped, she could have done somethin'. No, she had to go to New Orleans and spend a lot of money on clothes that she didn't need nohow."

"She surely was upset. She didn't even look like herself."

"Her father is going to have to have a doctor for his wife. She about to lose her mind."

The two sat in the kitchen, continuing to discuss the plight of Marianne.

❧

Downstairs in the larger of the two parlors, Charles was trying to comfort Caroline, who was weeping. "Dear, you simply must get ahold of yourself. I think we'd better have the doctor."

"What could he do?" Caroline wailed. "He couldn't bring Marianne back."

"No, but he could give you something for your nerves."

"What are we going to do? What can we do?"

"I tell you what I'm going to do right now. I'll leave Sabrina here to care for you. I'm going down to the police."

Caroline's eyes widened. "Do you think he kidnapped her?"

"I'm sure we couldn't charge him with that since she went willingly enough, but at least the police will know how to find her. . . I hope. I'll go get Sabrina. You try to lie down and get some rest."

Charles Warren left the drawing room and went at once to Sabrina's room. When he knocked on the door, she opened it up. "Sabrina, I'm going to town. You stay with your mother. Try to keep her calm as you can."

"Why are you going to town, Father?"

"I have no idea how to find my daughter. I'm going to the police."

Sabrina at once said, "That's a good idea. Let me go with you."

"No, you stay here with your mother. I don't know how long I'll be. If your mother gets worse, call Dr. Simpson. Have him come. Have him give her something that'll make her sleep. And make her stop worrying so much."

"I'm not sure there is anything like that." Then she said bitterly, "I need some myself."

Warren looked at his daughter and saw with surprise that her face showed signs of tears. "I haven't seen you cry since you were seven."

"It's all my fault! I should have stayed here."

"I don't think it would have made any difference, but you do what you can now by taking care of your mother."

"Come back home as soon as you find out something."

"I'll do it, daughter. Try not to worry."

"I won't do that. I should be worrying. I should have been more careful." It was an admission that his strong-willed daughter did not often make.

As Charles left the house he thought, *This thing has broken Sabrina. That shows how bad it is.*

"I'm sorry that we're not able to do more, Mr. Warren."

The chief of police was a personal friend of Charles Warren. His name was Louis Stone, and he was a good policeman.

It was the day after Warren had come and laid his problem before the chief. Now Stone shook his head. "I've had my best detectives out, and they can't find a trace of the man. Nothing solid. I don't think Robbins is his real name."

"Any leads at all?"

"Well, they found the hotel where he lived. Several people knew him, but he didn't talk about himself. We did find out one thing. . . ."

"What's that?" Warren asked eagerly.

"Strangely enough it was from a boot black. He was polishing Robbins's shoes, and Robbins started talking to a man sitting next to him. The boy's name is Jason. Seems like a reliable witness. He told my men one thing that might give you a lead."

"What's that?"

"He mentioned Robbins going to Oklahoma."

"Well, that's a big place. It would take forever," Warren said sadly.

"Well, he went a little bit more into detail," Chief Stone said.

"Said Robbins mentioned Judge Parker's territory. You know what that is?"

"I don't believe I do."

"Judge Parker is the judge over the whole Indian Territory. It's supposed to be just for the Indians, but every hard case, gunman, and crook running from the law in the country goes to Oklahoma Territory. Jason said this fellow laughed and said he could hide out there for a hundred years and nobody would ever find him."

"It sounds like he thinks somebody might be coming for him."

"That's what I thought, so I tried to find a confirmation on trains leaving, but no luck so far. I think this fellow is a criminal of some kind, and he's run off to Oklahoma Territory."

"Thanks, Chief."

"You might go see Donald French. He's the best private detective I know. If anybody can find out anything, he will do it."

"I'll go right there. Where's his office?"

"In the Hall Building."

"Well," French said, "I've done my best, Mr. Warren. I did find someone, after interviewing a hundred people, who saw a couple get on a train headed for Oklahoma. Couldn't be sure, but he gave a brief description of the man. Said he had blond hair and was well dressed."

"What about the woman?"

"She was small with blond hair and blue eyes. And the witness said she was hanging on to this man. It's not much, but I did find out from the conductor that one of them asked him how long it would take to get to Oklahoma."

"Well, that's what Chief Stone said."

"I think that's where you'll find them."

"Thanks, Mr. French."

"Well, I didn't earn the money, but I'll take it. And I'll tell you this. If he's taken that girl of yours to Oklahoma Territory, he's no good."

The chief's words discouraged Charles Warren, but he went home and repeated them to his wife. He softened the blow as much as he could, but it sent her into another torrent of grieving. He told Sabrina to put her to bed, and when Sabrina finally came back down, she saw an odd look on his face. "So the police and the private detective think this man's taken her to Indian Territory?"

"That's what they both said."

"What are you going to do?"

"Hire more detectives."

"What can they do?"

"Well, not much. Even if they found he had taken her there, they couldn't go in after her. It's against the law."

"But they do have some law, don't they?"

"Judge Isaac Parker is judge over the whole territory. He has about two hundred marshals. They go in and hunt the criminals down, but they're badly outnumbered, and he's lost about fifty of them."

"What do you mean, lost?"

"They were killed. It's a dangerous place." He hesitated. Then when he looked up, he saw an odd look on Sabrina's face. "What is it, Sabrina?"

"I'm going to find Marianne."

Warren's eyes flew open with surprise. "Why, you can't go into Indian Territory. In the first place, it's against the law. In the second place, you're not a marshal."

"I'll hire one of the marshals. I'm going to find her, Father."

That was not the end of Sabrina's announcement. The next day she left the house. Dulcie was crying and begging to go. Sabrina hugged her and said, "It won't be any place for you."

"Who's going to take care of you?"

"I'm going to find me a man," Sabrina said. "And we're going to go get my sister and bring her home."

There was more talk and more weeping on the part of Caroline Warren.

Her father pleaded with her not to go, but Sabrina Warren was cursed with a stubbornness that was almost endemic in her spirit. At two o'clock that afternoon she was on a railroad car. As it pulled out of the station headed West, she said under her breath, "I'll find me a man, and we'll find that scoundrel and bring my sister home!"

PART THREE

PART THREE

CHAPTER 13

The narrow-gauge coal-burning engine that touched into Fort Smith emitted a scream that sounded to Sabrina like a banshee. She was weary of her trip and had scarcely ever been more uncomfortable. The hard seats in the carriage car that she sat upon forced her into either an upright position or slumping down with a curve in her backbone. The windows were open most of the time, for it was hot. They admitted mostly hot desert air and cinders from the locomotive that chugged along toward its destination.

She had brought few clothes with her, and the garments that she wore were rather prim and severe, at least for Sabrina's taste. Her dress was a chocolate brown velvet, and she wore only a pair of earrings for decoration. Three black feathers were arranged in her hair, but they were now drooping and looking as if they were ready for the garbage heap.

Relief came when the conductor, a small, scrawny, ill-looking man in a crumpled black suit and a stiff-billed cap, came through shouting, "All out for Fort Smith! Everyone out for Fort Smith!"

Quickly Sabrina rose and straightened her back with a grunt.

She had expected a rough ride, but nothing as uncomfortable as this relic from the Civil War days that made the daily run from Fort Smith.

Passengers began filing off, and when Sabrina stepped down, the scrawny conductor was there. He reached up his hand, and she looked at it then shrugged and took it. When she stepped down to the brick surface, she said, "I need to find the courthouse."

"Oh, anybody can tell you about that. Just start walkin'."

"I have luggage."

"Yeah, I seen that. Well, let me get it for you."

He waited until the car was empty; then she guided him by saying, "That gray one is mine and that dark brown one—and the large one."

"You must be coming to stay for a spell, miss." The conductor waited to be enlightened about Sabrina's intention.

She merely nodded, murmuring, "Thank you, sir." She looked around and saw the ticket office, and leaving the luggage, she went inside.

She walked up to the window where a very fat man with a pair of startling green eyes peered at her and grinned. "Howdy, miss. Just get in I see."

"Yes, I need some directions."

"Where you be going, ma'am?"

"I need to see Judge Parker."

"Oh, well, the courthouse is right down that street to your right. You follow it, and you see the biggest building there three stories high. You'll find the judge somewhere around in there, I reckon. What do you need to see the judge for?"

"Private business!" Sabrina snapped. "Can you have someone put my luggage in a safe place?"

"Well, I don't know as there is a safe place around here."

Sabrina took a deep breath and withheld her comment on that. She saw a man sitting with a small wagon and said, "Does that man carry passengers?"

"Yes, ma'am, he does. His name is Zeke Cousins. He fit in the big war, he did. He'll take you anywhere you want to go."

"Thank you."

Zeke Cousins turned out to be a tall, lanky man dressed in a pair of bib overalls with a worn straw hat pushed down over his eyes. He moved slowly as if he were crippled getting out of the wagon but had no sign of a wound. Sabrina said, "I need to go to a hotel, and then I need to go to the courthouse."

"Yes'um. It'll cost you two dollars though."

"That'll be fine. My luggage is over there."

"I'll jist get it fer you."

She watched as Cousins moved slowly, carefully, as if he were about to step on dynamite, and wondered how a human being could move that slowly. The heat from the July sun was pouring down, and she was wet with perspiration, her clothes droopy.

Finally Cousins brought all three pieces of her luggage and said, "Just hop right in there, ma'am."

Sabrina was accustomed to being helped into carriages and vehicles. She saw that Cousins was not about to offer that service so, gritting her teeth, she stepped on one of the spokes, clambered onto the hard seat, and sat down. She found she was sore from sitting for many hours on the hard railroad seat, but there was no point complaining to her driver. "Take me to the best hotel."

"Sure, I'll do that, ma'am. That'll be the Starlight Hotel. It's run by Mr. and Mrs. Jamieson. They get along purty good 'cept they had a fight some time ago, and he lit out. But he come back, and they made it all up. Never did know what it was all about. Sure was sad for a while."

Such talk continued about people Sabrina had never heard of, and Cousins attempted, from time to time, to pry her name and purpose in coming to Fort Smith from her. Finally he pulled up in front of a two-story building. "That there's the Starlight Hotel, ma'am. You tell 'em Zeke Cousins brought you. They'll give you a good deal."

"Well, could you carry my luggage in?"

"Oh, that'll be an extra quarter."

"Fine." She handed him three dollars and said, "Keep the change."

"Why, that's right thoughtful of you, ma'am. I do appreciate it." He hopped down, but as soon as he touched the ground, his feet grew slower as if they were magnetized to the earth.

Finally the luggage was inside, Cousins left, and Sabrina walked up to the desk.

A young man, no more than eighteen it seemed, with his hair parted in the middle and wearing a string tie and a white shirt said, "Yes, ma'am, can I help you?"

"I need a room."

"Just for one night or for several days?"

"I'm not sure."

"Well, you better hold on to it for two or three days. Rooms are kind of scarce right now."

"Yes, that'll be fine. Three days."

She waited while the young man pulled out a leather-bound register, opened it, and said, "If you'd just sign your name right there, please."

Sabrina signed her name.

He turned it around and stared at it. "Miss Sabrina Warren—or is it Mrs?"

"It's Miss. Now, is there any chance at all of getting a bath in this hotel?"

"Yes ma'am, but that's extra. I'll have to have some boys bring up some hot water."

"That'll be fine. What's the room? Give me a key, please."

The young man turned and said, "My name's Joel Barnaby. Anything you need you just let me know. Here's your key. Room 206. Boys will be up with the hot water as soon as they can get it het up."

"Thank you."

"We ain't got nobody handy now. Let me help you with your luggage, Miss Warren."

Sabrina picked up the smaller suitcase, and the clerk carried the other two. When they got to the room in the middle of the hall, he put them down, opened her door, and then carried the suitcases in.

She entered behind him, said, "Thank you very much," and handed him fifty cents.

"You don't have to do that, ma'am."

"I appreciate it."

"Well, I'll have the fellers bring the water up as soon as they can get it."

"Thank you."

Sabrina waited until the door was closed and then took off the lightweight jacket. Her hair seemed to be drooping, and she knew the heat had done that. She looked around the room and saw it contained the bare necessities: a double bed with a corduroy-looking spread and a small table with a pitcher of water and a basin, the basin being cracked and the pitcher being broken at the lip. There were no closets, but there were nails driven into the wall. "I suppose that's where my clothes will go."

There were two chairs in the room, both with hard seats, and the wallpaper was sort of a leprous gray so ancient it was impossible to tell what it really was. She walked over to the window, which was open, and even as she did, two flies came zipping in. She shooed them away and looked down on the street. "Well, Fort Smith, there you are, and you're not much," she said grimly.

She watched as people moved below, noting that it seemed to be a typical Western outpost. The men wore pants tucked into high-heeled boots. Many of them carried guns and holsters, and all of them wore big hats. The women were dressed mostly in plain calico or printed cotton. They wore bonnets, and some of them carried umbrellas. "Well, here I am."

For a moment she felt a sense of despair. She knew her errand would not be easy, but she was a determined young lady. When she made up her mind, she ran at the job as if her life depended on it. She sat down on the bed instead of on one of the hard chairs and waited impatiently.

Finally there was a knock on the door, and three men came in. One of them was carrying what appeared to be a brass bathtub, an elongated affair. The other two both had two buckets of water. "Got your bathwater here, ma'am," the leader with the tub said. "You want it right here?"

"Yes, that's fine."

"Fill her up, boys."

Sabrina watched as the two men emptied the water out of the buckets into the tub and noted with satisfaction that at least the water was steaming. She thanked them all.

The tall man carrying the tub said, "If you need any help, just holler." He leered at her.

She stared at him disdainfully. "Good day, sir."

"Well, good day, ma'am. Enjoy your bath."

Sabrina recognized the look in his eye and knew that she was in rough territory.

After the men left, she opened one of the suitcases, took out a fresh outfit, then stripped down. The door did not seem to be locked, so she put one of the chairs under the knob and hoped for the best. She touched the water cautiously, and sure enough it was far too hot. She also realized she didn't have a washcloth or a towel, and none were furnished. "How am I going to wash?" Fortunately she had brought some soap with her.

She waited until the water had grown almost tepid. She stepped inside and sat down slowly, sighing with pleasure as the water lapped over her. She let her body slip down under the water. As she lay there soaking, she grew sleepy but knew she had to hurry. She stayed as long as she could, then got up and dried off as best she could with the dress she had worn. It was dusty, and she hated having to use it this way. She made a note to buy some washcloths and towels. As she dressed, she thought, *I've got to see Judge Parker, and he's got to help me!*

She went downstairs and said, "I need to see Judge Parker."

The clerk shook his head and said apologetically, "Well, ma'am, that ain't going to be possible until after the hanging."

"The hanging?"

"Yes ma'am, there's a hanging. Takes place in about thirty minutes. They're going to hang five men."

"At the same time?"

"Yes, ma'am. Go on down the street, and you'll see the

courthouse, and right across from it you'll see the gallows. The town's fillin' up. They always come for a big hanging. There ain't been five men hanged here in a spell."

Sabrina left and moved down the street, aware that indeed a crowd had come. The street was packed with wagons and mounts with saddles, and there was a babble of voices in the air. She finally saw the courthouse and had to endure the pressure from the crowd. She thought, *Do I want to see a hanging? It must be horrible.*

She almost left, but she said to a woman who had come to stand next to her, "Does Judge Parker come to the hangings?"

"Oh, he does. Look up there."

Sabrina looked up where the woman's gesture indicated, and the woman added, "That's him right there in the window. He comes to every hangin' right there at that window. I don't know how he stands it, all these men dying and all on his conscience."

"Well, he's a judge. That's what his job is."

"I reckon so, but I'd hate to be meetin' my Maker with Isaac Parker's record." It was only a few minutes later before a group of men came out of the courthouse. "The jailhouse is down underneath the courthouse," the woman said. She was a middle-aged woman with a wealth of freckles and reddish-blond hair. She was well padded and nodded, saying confidentially, "Looky there. They're all going to meet God. Ain't that a shame."

Sabrina watched the men. Indeed they were a mixed crew. One of them, the first one out, was a hulking giant who glowered at the crowd. *He has some Indian blood in him,* she thought, for his skin was dark and bronze. The man next to him was small and neatly dressed. Beside him were two men of medium height. Both of them were terrified. It showed in their eyes. The fourth man was tall and spindly, and the fifth man was a Mexican apparently, who looked down at the crowd as if they had come to be his entertainment.

"That's him right there! That's George Maledon. He's the hangman for the judge." She was a talkative woman, and she began to say, "My husband owns the store, and Maledon came in to buy some rope to hang men with. Nothin' suited him. He ordered it all the way from El Paso. He found the thickest hemp he could, and he buys linseed oil, and he spends hours working it by hand into the fibers until those ropes are plied just as well as your hair is. It will just glide around the prisoner's neck, and he ties a monstrous knot and puts it right behind the right ear. When the man falls, the neck snaps like a bit of celery."

The gruesome information disgusted Sabrina, but her neighbor was not through. "He makes up two hundred pounds of sandbags like they use to dam up the Arkansas River. He ties those ropes, and he throws the trap. You can hear 'em *squee-thump* almost day and night like he takes pleasure in it."

Maledon wore two guns at his side and was a small, sour-looking man with a pair of dead eyes it seemed. He did not speak except to say, "You fellows can talk."

All five of the men had something to say. The Mexican said, "I am not afraid to die. I have found the Lord Jesus Christ as my personal Savior, and He will take me right to heaven."

His was the only gentle speech. The rest of the men were angry. One of them who stood next to the giant said, "There's worse men than me I see out there in that crowd. Some of you ought to be here hangin'. Not me."

As soon as the last man had spoken, Maledon moved down, putting a hood over each man's head and arranging the hangman's knot behind his ear.

Sabrina began to grow a little sick and wished she were not there, but she was. When the last knot was tied, Maledon, without further ado, caught Sabrina off guard. He simply turned and pulled the lever, and all five men dropped through a trapdoor.

She distinctly heard the popping of necks, and then she heard the most horrible sound of her life. One of the men had not died but was strangling and kicking. Blindly she turned and made her way out of the crowd. *I can't stand this anymore,* she thought and went directly toward the courthouse.

⁂

"I'm sorry, ma'am, but you can't see the judge until after the court has dismissed."

Sabrina stood in the judge's courtroom. Now she looked around with disgust and saw that the courtroom was as plain as art can make it. There were rough-hewn benches made from warping pine.

Judge Parker, the presiding judge, stood upon a slight platform behind a desk. She stood there while he went through the process of handling the business at hand, and he seemed to be a man without feeling. He appeared to be in his early fifties, and there were white hairs in the brown hair that he kept neatly combed. She noticed that Parker had dark smudges under his eyes that looked like bruises. He was a dignified-looking man, handsome in a way.

Finally the last case was dismissed. The judge got up and left, but Sabrina hurried after him. "Judge Parker," she said, catching him, "my name is Sabrina Warren. I've come all the way from Memphis to see you."

Parker turned and bowed slightly in a courteous manner. "Why yes, Miss Warren. Come on up to my office." He led Sabrina up to the second floor and down a hall then opened a door. There was a man seated over to one side, and Parker said, "Heck, would you excuse us, please."

"Sure enough, Judge." The man got up, an ordinary-looking fellow wearing a gun as most did. There was a marshal's badge on his vest.

As soon as he left, Judge Parker smiled. "That was Heck Thomas, the best of my marshals. Would you have a seat, Miss Warren, or is it Mrs. Warren?"

"No, I'm not married."

Parker waited until Sabrina was seated.

She took a quick look around the room. It was barely large enough to contain a black walnut desk as large as most dining tables, several chairs, shelves, and a credenza, but every flat surface was piled high with papers and bursting portfolios. The air was stagnant, redolent of tobacco long since chewed and expectorated and murky with the exhaust of cigars. A revolving bookcase to one side leaned drunkenly, threatening to fall, and mustard-colored bound case histories filled one complete bookcase.

"Now, what can I do for you, Miss Warren?"

"I've come to get your help, Judge. My sister's been kidnapped. She's in the Indian nations, and I've come to enlist your help in rescuing her."

"Tell me all the details," Parker said.

Sabrina went on to tell how her father had hired private detectives, but they had not been able to find her sister. "Finally," she added, "Marianne managed to get a letter brought out. I received word from my father on my way here. Apparently she gave all the money she had to a traveling cowboy. He promised to mail the letter, which he did. In the letter Marianne said she is being held captive by a man named Trey LeBeau."

Parker sat watching his guest with a pair of steady, warm brown eyes, and finally he said, "You've come at a rather awkward time, Miss Warren. At the present time I only have a single marshal, and I have to keep one here. I don't have anyone to send after your sister."

"But I thought you had two hundred marshals."

Parker shook his head sadly. "No, I did have at one time, but over fifty of them are gone. Some killed, some turned outlaw."

"Marshals turning outlaw?"

"Oh yes, ma'am. The Dalton boys, they were marshals. Now they're out robbing trains and holding up people. If I catch them, they'll see the end of a rope."

"But you must have somebody."

"Well, it's like this. This very day I might have five or six rangers come in, but there might not be one for a month. They have to follow the outlaws until they catch them. And that takes longer. There's no schedule to it."

Sabrina grew angry. "I've come all this way to get help. You're the man in charge of law and order in this territory. You've got to help me!"

"I can't help you, Miss Warren, not now. I will as soon as I get some men who will go, but I wouldn't send one man out to capture LeBeau."

"Why not?"

"Because he's got a band of armed outlaws at his beck and call. One man wouldn't stand a chance. It will have to be a posse, maybe at least a dozen men, and I honestly can't tell you when we'll have that kind of personnel."

Sabrina stood up. Her temper, which had gotten her into trouble before, flared out. "Well, I'll find some men who will do the job if you won't do it!" She turned and started for the door.

Judge Parker got up and said with alarm, "Ma'am, you don't know these men. I advise you to wait."

"I won't wait! I'm going to get my sister!" She left the room.

Heck Thomas was sitting outside. He grinned as she stormed by.

She knew he was "laughing" at her expense, but she didn't take the time to stop and upbraid him. She was determined to find her sister and get out of this territory for good.

❦

Sabrina was not accustomed to having to wait for anything. Her father's money and the family's position had always made it possible for her to get her own way. This, however, was not working in Fort Smith.

She knew no other way to find help than to simply stop men on the street and ask them. She received many indecent proposals, for men in the frontier of Fort Smith assumed that when a good-looking woman stopped them on the street, she had something special on her mind. They simply grinned and said things like, "Well honey, let's you and me go somewhere, and we'll talk this thing over."

On the third day she was seated in the restaurant having a lunch consisting of a greasy pork chop and a limp salad when two men came in. They were both tall and well built. When they identified themselves as brothers, she saw the resemblance.

"I'm Asa and this is Roy. Denvers is our name. I hear you are looking for someone that will go into the Territory and do a chore for you."

Instantly Sabrina grew excited. "Yes. I haven't been able to find anybody. Men in this part of the world evidently don't need money or else they're afraid of the Indians."

"Well, that's a shame," Roy said. He had the same pale blue eyes of his brother, and both men were sunburned. There was a lupine aspect in the two. They looked rather like hungry wolves, but Sabrina had expected this.

She said, "Sit down." The two men sat down and drank coffee while she explained about her sister being kidnapped and being held by a man called Trey LeBeau.

"That's bad news," Asa said. He was evidently the older of the two. "LeBeau's a bad man."

"Are you afraid of him?" Sabrina glared at him, waiting for his answer.

"It pays to be afraid of rattlesnakes and men who'll kill you for a quarter."

"Well, then you can't help me."

"Wait a minute." Roy Denver, the younger of the two, seemed to be the brighter. "We can do the job, but lady, it's gonna cost a lot of money. We've got to buy horses, equipment, supplies, ammunition, and guns. Pretty expensive."

"I've got the money, but you've got to guarantee me that you'll get my sister."

"All we can do is say we'll find her and we'll try to get her back from LeBeau. He don't let go of things easy." Roy Denver shrugged. "It'll take some persuading."

"Yes," the older Denver said. "A man could get killed."

"Well, how much money do you want?"

"To buy the equipment? Well, we'd have to have at least five hundred dollars just to get started."

"All right. Let's go to the bank, and I'll get a check cashed." She thought for a minute then said, "When can you leave?"

"Oh, we can buy the equipment today and leave at first light," Roy Denver said.

"All right." She went with them to the bank and gave them the money.

Roy said, "We'll be leavin' in the morning before you get up."

"No, I'm going with you."

The Denver brothers stared at her and then at each other. Roy Denver shook his head. "Ma'am, that is a terrible idea."

"I'm going, and that's all there is to it."

The two argued halfheartedly, but finally they said, "Well, it's going to be a rough ride."

"I don't care how rough it is. I'm going."

"Well, then you'd better get yourself outfitted. You can't wear a pretty dress like that on the trail."

"I'll take care of that. Come and get me at the hotel when you're ready to leave in the morning." She watched the two leave then went at once to buy some rough clothes. She found a riding skirt, for she knew she would have to ride a horse astride, a white lightweight shirt, and a vest with silver pesos for buttons. She found a black hat that had a small brim and a low crown but would be good for heading off the sun.

As she went back to the hotel with her possessions, she glanced up at Judge Parker's office. "I'll show you, Judge Parker, you're not the only fish in the ocean!"

❧

Sabrina was absolutely exhausted. She had ridden for two days now, and the Denver brothers seemed to be made out of leather and steel. They never seemed to be tired.

At the end of the second day, she said, "I can't go any farther."

Asa Denver shook his head. "Got to go a little further, missy."

"No, we'll camp here."

"All right. If you say so."

She stared at him. "I'm not happy with your work. You don't seem to know where you're going."

Both men grinned broadly. "We know where we're going, but I hate to tell you we're going without you."

Sabrina stared at them. They looked like two lean timber wolves at that moment. "What—what are you talking about?"

"We're going to leave you here, and you better count yourself fortunate. Worse things could happen to a nice lady like you with a pair of men like us."

"You can't leave me here!"

"Why can't we?" Roy Denver grinned. He dismounted, came over, and pulled her off her horse. She carried her money in a leather pouch. He reached down, snatched it, and said, "You have a good time out here."

Horrified, Sabrina watched the two get on their horses that contained all their equipment, her money, and all she had. Roy Denver was leading her horse. "You can't leave me here!" she cried out.

"Just go back to where you came, honey. You'll find it."

Sabrina watched them go, and for the first time in her life, real paralyzing fear seemed to grip her in a frozen clasp. She wanted to cry out, but she knew those two men would never return. Slowly she turned and started walking back. She had not paid particular attention to the landscape or the signs and the hills and trees that could have been landmarks.

By the time the sun was low in the sky, her legs were trembling. She sat down on the ground, drew her knees up, and held them with her arms. She put her forehead down on her knees and began to weep.

CHAPTER 14

Sabrina awoke and found she was shivering. The two villains she had placed her confidence in had taken everything, even the heavy coat that was tied behind the saddle on her horse that they had stolen. She hugged herself and shut her eyes tightly, aware that the sky was beginning to light up the east. A sharp pain came to her when a stone that she had lain down on penetrated her thin jacket and the white shirt she wore. She tried to escape into sleep again, for the moment she woke up, at least partially, her plight came to her.

I'm lost in the middle of the desert. I don't have any horse. Nobody knows where I am except the two men who put me here. I'm thirsty, and I'll starve out here in this desert unless someone finds me.

Shifting around, she found that she could not hide in the pavilions of sleep anymore. With a groan she sat up and hugged herself to try to control the shivering. The light indeed was breaking, and she saw the landscape as a ghostly affair with cacti casting hideous shapes, or so it seemed to her. From far off a coyote howled, a lonesome song that somehow made her feel even worse.

She sat for a moment then turned to face the east.

Suddenly an icy hand seemed to run down her back, and fright came with such a powerful force that she could only sit and stare at the Indian who stood no more than ten feet away watching her. *He's going to kill me!* The thought seemed to freeze her mind, and she stared at the savage, waiting for him to come forward and cut her throat or worse. She had heard of the cruelty of the Indians and had never given it any thought. Now, however, a black veil of fear and dread seemed to envelop her.

The silence ran on, and when the Indian did not speak, Sabrina climbed to her feet. She was sore from head to foot from the cold and the hard ground, but she did not take her eyes off of the Indian. He was a handsome enough fellow, judging from the sorry specimens she had seen hanging around Fort Smith. He was no more than medium height, and he wore a pair of white man's jeans and a green-and-white-checkered shirt. His face seemed to be carved from steel. He had a prominent nose and wide lips now compressed, but it was his eyes that held her. They were obsidian, blacker than any eyes she had ever seen, and they stared at her unwaveringly. He had a rifle in his left hand, and ten feet farther off was a horse with a red blanket tied to a mesquite tree. He wore a wide-brimmed hat, but the black braids of his hair hung down his back, red ribbons tied in each of them.

Finally Sabrina tried to speak and found that her throat was dry. She cleared it, coughed, licked her dry lips, and said, "Hello."

Whatever she expected did not happen. She had no idea that the Indian would speak English, but he said, "You are lost."

Glad that he could speak English and that he made no move to threaten her, Sabrina nodded violently. "Yes, I hired two men to help me, and they took my horse and everything I had."

"What two men?"

"Their names were Denver. Asa and Roy Denver."

A slight movement of the Indian's lips might have been a smile. "Bad men," he said simply.

"I—I need to get back to Fort Smith. Could I hire you to take me?"

"My name is Gray Wolf. You were foolish to come with those two men. Everyone knows they are not good."

"I know that now, Gray Wolf, but I'm helpless. If you'll help me get back to Fort Smith, I'll see that you're well paid."

Gray Wolf was examining her from head to foot. He came forward, and she stiffened up for she could not read his intentions in his features. He came and stood in front of her saying, "Yes, I can take you to town." Without another word he seized her by the arm and began to pull at her.

Sabrina's first impulse was to resist but she knew that would be useless. He was strong as an animal, she felt, and for the first time in her life she was completely at the mercy of another human being, one whom she did not know and who owed her nothing.

Gray Wolf stopped beside the horse, which had no saddle. "Get on," he said.

There was only a woven leather bridle around the horse's neck, not even between his lips as a proper bridle would be. "I—I can't get up there."

"Here. Put your foot here." He locked his fingers together and stooped over, and she tentatively stepped in. He heaved her up, and she managed to throw her leg across. There was nothing to hang on to, for the bridle he used, such as it was, was tied to the tree. Gray Wolf said nothing but untied the bridle and began to walk toward the east.

Sabrina felt a great gush of relief flow through her. *He's not going to kill me!* She was not a praying woman, but at that moment she felt that if she were she would give thanks for her deliverance. *I'm not going to die,* she thought, and the thought gave her a sensation of relief such as she had never known before.

For the next four hours the Indian moved steadily forward, tirelessly so, it seemed to Sabrina. She had nothing to do with her hands, no horn to cling to, no bridle to hold, so all she could do was sit there. She recognized none of the territory that they were passing through, but finally she said in a voice that was a croak, "Do you have any water?"

"Over there." Gray Wolf pointed over to the right and turned the direction of the horse that way. He led her two hundred yards on. He stopped, tied the horse, and said, "Water here."

Sabrina slipped to the ground and saw a tidy rivulet of water running over rocks.

"Spring here. Always cold no matter how hot," Gray Wolf said. "Drink."

Awkwardly Sabrina leaned down and, cupping her hands, waited until they filled up. She drank noisily, awkwardly, and thirstily, and repeated that several times until she rose up and wiped her lips with her sleeve. "Thank you. That was good."

Gray Wolf shrugged, reached on his back, and pulled out what seemed to be some kind of a canteen. He filled it up then leaned over and drank himself. "We go now."

Sabrina was exhausted. She had had nothing to eat all the previous day except a small breakfast, and she was beginning to feel the pangs of hunger. "You have any food?" she asked timidly.

"Soon." The monosyllable was all that Gray Wolf offered her, but he put her astride again and walked away.

They had traveled about thirty minutes when suddenly he lifted the rifle in one smooth motion and fired.

The sound of the shot startled Sabrina, and she looked wildly around but saw nothing.

She sat there as Gray Wolf led the way, leaned over, and picked up something. "Food."

It was, Sabrina saw, a large rabbit.

"Get down." She got down, Gray Wolf tied the horse, and then, picking up some small twigs, he pulled some matches from his pocket, struck one, and touched it. The fuel was dry, and he kept adding wood until there was a blaze, its crackling a cheerful sound.

Gray Wolf pulled a knife, stripped the fur off the rabbit, and skillfully cut it into two pieces. He found two sticks and impaled half on each stick. He handed her one, and without another word stuck his own half over the flame.

Almost instantly the smell of cooking meat caused Sabrina's stomach to knot. She quickly followed Gray Wolf's example.

Five minutes later Gray Wolf pulled the rabbit out of the fire, tore off a strip, and put it in his mouth. "Good," he grunted. "You eat."

The meat was only half cooked, but she was ravenous.

He saw she did not know how to eat it. He took it from her and, pulling out his knife, stripped off small portions.

The food was better than anything Sabrina, who had eaten at the finest hotels in the country, had ever tasted. She ate hungrily, and then when they were finished, they both drank.

"We go now."

"How far, Gray Wolf?"

"Another hard day's travel. We get there in the morning if we travel at night. If not, later."

That was all the conversation Sabrina had with him for the rest of the day. The pony seemed to be tireless, as did Gray Wolf. She herself was exhausted by the time dark fell.

Seeing this, Gray Wolf pulled off and said, "We'll rest here." He pulled the blanket off the horse and grunted, "Sleep."

Willingly Sabrina wrapped herself in the blanket and lay down. As sleep descended on her exhausted body, she once again had an impulse that she should give thanks, but she was not a woman of God and knew that she was not a fit subject to ask God for anything.

The sun was high in the sky when Silas Longstreet, who was sitting in a chair tilted back against the outer wall of the courthouse, came to his feet and said, "Well, by gum, I ain't seen a sight like that. That woman's had some trouble." He knew a bit about Sabrina's story, for he was the oldest of Judge Parker's marshals. Parker had told him about the woman and expressed his concern. Now he looked and saw the two, and getting out of his chair, he pulled his hat off. "Howdy, ma'am. My name's Silas Longstreet. Looks like you had some trouble."

Gray Wolf laughed softly. "She's a foolish squaw. She hired the Denver brothers to help her, and they took all she had and left her in the desert."

Silas, who was a small man with a shock of white hair and pale blue eyes, said, "Ma'am, you had some luck there. They could have done a lot more than let you go. Let me take you to the hotel. You can get some rest."

"I can find my way." She turned and said, "Gray Wolf, you saved my life. I have no money here, but I'll get some from the bank. Later on today I'll see that you're well paid."

"Good." Gray Wolf watched the woman go and seemed amused. "She's a proud woman but not so much anymore."

"You'd better keep an eye on her, Gray Wolf. She ain't got much judgment. She's a city woman obviously. She could get mixed up with somebody worse than the Denver boys."

"Yes. Give me money. I want something to eat. All I've had is a stringy jackrabbit."

Silas stood before Judge Parker, who was seated at his desk, and was just finished telling him the story of Sabrina. "So, sure enough, she got cleaned up and she gave Gray Wolf fifty dollars. More money than he's ever had in his life, I reckon."

"He's probably drunk by now."

"No, he ain't drunk. He went to the mission school. He's a Christian Indian. Don't act like it sometimes, but he is."

"Well, she could have been raped and killed out there. I'm glad Gray Wolf found her. I don't know what she's going to do."

"What did she come here for?" Silas listened as the judge repeated the story of how she had come to get her sister free from the clutches of Trey LeBeau and his band.

Silas shook his head then whistled softly. "Well, that's a bad one."

"I told her I didn't have no marshals to send. You're the only one here."

"We don't need to send one man out to get LeBeau. He's got at least a half dozen killers."

"That's right, but I've got an idea. She's not going to quit on this thing, Silas. She's going to hire somebody, but I think her only hope is one she'd never meet if we didn't help her."

"Who's that, Judge?"

"Waco Smith."

Silas was surprised and showed it. "Why, Judge, he's in the penitentiary at Yuma."

"I know it, but I've got a plan. I'm a good friend of Warden Crawford, the warden of Yuma Penitentiary. He wrote me a letter and told me how there was a breakout and he could have been killed. There was a man ready to do the job when Waco jumped in front of him and killed the man with a gun he'd taken from one of the guards. He got shot a couple of times, but he made it. Warden Crawford is right grateful to him."

"Well, I don't see how he can help her if he's in prison."

"He's the only one I know who would even have a chance against LeBeau. Let me have a talk with that young woman. Have her come by my office."

"I'll do that, Judge."

"I think I may have found a possible man for you to hire."

"Just one man?"

"That's all we've got right now, but this one can help if anybody can. His name is Waco Smith."

"Well, I'd like to talk to him. I'll hire him if you say he's a good man. Where is he?"

Parker smiled slightly. "You won't like this. He's a prisoner in Yuma."

"He's a criminal?"

"I guess he was when he went in, but sometimes prison changes a man. He's the only man I know who's tough enough to go with you into the Territory. We can maybe find some more, but you'll need one man like this."

"I can't hire a criminal."

"You don't know the Territory, miss," Silas Longstreet said. He had brought her in and now leaned against the wall. "Waco knows it like the back of his hand. He's a hard man."

"I can't hire a criminal! He's a dangerous man, I'd think."

"Yes, he is, but he may have changed since he's been in prison. Prison either makes a man better or worse or kills him. From what Warden Crawford says, I think we might work something out."

"How could he help me if he's in prison?"

"Well, he saved the warden's life. I think I could let him out on a conditional pardon, and the warden would agree to it. Then you can talk to him and see if you want to take him on."

Sabrina nodded slowly. She was not happy about the decision to hire a criminal, but yet the opportunity was the only one that seemed to be opening its way up.

"All right. I'll talk to him, but I can't imagine going into the Territory running around with a criminal."

"You need to get rid of that idea," Silas said. "You don't need to be going into the Territory with Waco or anybody else."

"I'm going," Sabrina said flatly and put her eyes on Silas. "There's no argument about that. It's settled."

"You are a stubborn young lady, but the Territory changes folk."

"Well, I'll talk to the man."

"We'll have to go to the prison."

"How long will that take?"

"Just a day's ride from here. It ain't far."

"All right. When do we leave?"

"We'll leave first thing in the morning. We may have to stay overnight."

"Silas, you go along with Miss Warren and see she's all right."

"As you say, Judge." Silas nodded. "We'll be ready first thing in the morning. You want me to rent a buggy?"

"That might be best, or a wagon in case we bring him back with us. But I don't think that's likely."

The sun beat down on the men who were working clearing rocks and breaking them into smaller chunks where necessary. Waco swung the sledge, struck a rock, broke it in two, picked it up, and threw it to one side. He was covered with dust, as were all the men out working on the road, and as always, he was hungry and thirsty. He drew his forearm across his face. He was working without a shirt and had sunburned at first, but now he was burned a bronze color almost like an Indian. He did wear a cap with a bill that shaded his eyes, and now he looked over and said, "Cecil, you okay?"

"Doin' fine, Waco."

The young man, Waco saw, was about past going. He was frail, and the road work was more than he could handle. Fortunately the guard, a man named Roberts, was one of the gentler ones at the prison.

Waco had said, "Mr. Roberts, I'll do some more work if I need to, but Cecil there. . .he's just not fit for this."

"Yeah, I'll try to get him a job in the office somewhere out of this heat. You're right. He ain't fit to be breakin' rock."

Waco had thanked him, but he still kept a close watch on Cecil.

The two worked until noon, and then the whistle blew and the water wagon came with the noon meal, which was bread and slices of ham that made them thirstier, but the water was worth it all.

"I sure hope there ain't no roads to do in heaven." Cecil sighed. He had eaten the bread but had only nibbled at the ham, knowing that it would give him a raging thirst.

"I expect they got angels doing that." Waco grinned. He had resented Cecil's preaching at first, but now it merely amused him. "The Lord wouldn't let a good man like you break rock in heaven. Besides, I heard the streets were made of gold. Like to have a shot at that."

"That's right, and the gates are all pearl, bigger than you'd think. Imagine a pearl big enough to make a gate out of."

"Sounds sumptuous."

"Oh, it is, Waco. Heaven's a good place. I'm going to see you there one day."

Waco smiled. "I doubt that. God wouldn't want a maverick like me dirtyin' up His heaven."

"He's gonna do things for you. He's gonna make you all clean and pure and clothed in the righteousness of Christ as the Bible says."

"Well, I've always heard God could do anything, so I reckon if He wants to do it, He could do that for me."

The two went on until the whistle blew again. Waco got to his feet, pulled Cecil up, and said, "Don't try to break any rocks. Just go through the motions. I talked to Mr. Roberts. It's okay with him."

"Why, that wouldn't be right."

"He's gonna try to get you a job inside. I'm kind of a favorite of Warden Crawford now. If Mr. Roberts can't do the job, I'm gonna ask the warden to do it."

"Well, he owes you a favor. You saved his life."

"Yeah, he hasn't said anything about it except thank you when

I was first comin' out of it. Men forget, I guess."

"Maybe not. It just takes time."

Ten minutes later Roberts came out and said, "Waco, come on with me. You've got to go see the warden."

"Well, what have I done wrong this time?"

"Nothing, I don't think. It might be somethin' good."

"You think that, do you, Mr. Roberts? I've about given up expectin' on something good."

"You've had it tough, Waco, but Cecil's givin' you the right advice. I ain't much of a Christian myself, but he is. I've seen the real thing enough to know that it can happen."

"Well, you sure been a gentleman and a Christian to help Cecil out. I appreciate it."

"Nothin' to it. Come along now."

Sabrina was sitting in a chair in Warden Crawford's office. She turned when the door opened.

"Here he is," the man in the blue uniform said. "Call me if you want me, Warden."

"I'll do that, Roberts. Thank you."

The door closed, and Sabrina fixed her eyes on the man who stood there. He had on a shirt and wore a pair of worn jeans. He had black hair and eyes almost as dark as those of Gray Wolf, her Indian rescuer. His face was broad at the forehead and tempered down to a determined jaw, and a slight scar on his right cheek went down to his neck. He was burned by the sun and had wide shoulders and a narrow waist. His eyes went to the warden then came over to take her in. He said nothing but simply stood waiting.

"Waco," Warden Crawford said, "I've been talking with this young lady. This is Miss Sabrina Warren. She needs some assistance, and Judge Parker and I think you are the man that could help her."

"She's not going into the prison, is she?" Waco smiled slightly.

Sabrina saw that he had very white teeth. The teeth of most of the men she met were stained with tobacco from chewing and smoking.

"No, I'll let her tell you what her problem is, and then we'll talk about it. Have a seat."

Waco dragged a chair over and sat down facing Sabrina. He was alert as a wild animal, Sabrina saw, and there was a toughness and a wildness about him that she recognized would be excellent qualities in a man-hunter, which was what she wanted.

"I have one sister, Mr. Smith."

"Just Waco, ma'am. I lost my mister along with other things when I came to Yuma."

"Well, Waco then. She's very fragile and naive. She ran off with a man named Trey LeBeau and is being held captive." She waited and said, "Have you ever heard of him?"

"I know Trey."

"You know him? How do you know him?"

"Well, I had dealings with him a few years ago. He did me a bad turn. He's not exactly a friend of mine. What do you want me for?"

"I need somebody to go into the Territory and get my sister away from him."

"Well, that's Judge Parker's job, or his marshals'."

Crawford said, "You know how many marshals he lost, and those he has left are just bogged down, Waco. He just doesn't have anybody to send. He's the one who suggested we might get you to help Miss Warren."

"How can I help her in prison here?"

"You can't, but here's what Judge Parker came up with. He said if I agreed, the two of us together could give you what is called a *conditional* parole."

"Never heard of it."

"Well, that's because it's never been done. What it means is this. We release you to Miss Sabrina's custody. You will help her get her sister back. When the job is done, if you've been faithful and done your best, we'll make the parole a full-fledged parole. You'll be free."

Sabrina was interested in the workings of the man's face. She saw at once that he was interested and said quickly, "I'll also be willing to pay you to help me. My father has means, and we can pay almost any fee."

Waco was quiet, and finally Crawford said, "What's the matter? Don't you like the deal?"

"Not that. I just can't believe it."

Silas spoke up. "It's true enough, son. You've had some jolts along the way, but this woman's the real goods. We checked into her family. You do what Judge Parker and Warden Crawford ask you to do, and you can get a new start."

"Well," Waco said, sighing deeply, "I can use a new start. Sure, I'll do it, Miss Warren. Can't guarantee anything, you understand. LeBeau's a tough hairpin."

"Well, one man doesn't seem like enough," Sabrina said.

"It won't be one man. You're gonna have three men," Silas spoke up. "I'm going along and so is that Indian that saved your life, Gray Wolf. He can track a buzzard over the desert floor. I swan he can. We'll be going along so that'll give us three guns. Maybe pick up some more."

"The odds are still against us. He's got a rough bunch, Miss Warren," Waco said. "I've met most of 'em, all killers, and they might not be as nice to you as the Denver brothers. Might not be enough to just rob you."

"I'm going along, Waco, so don't argue with me."

"Just sayin'." Waco closed his mouth and nodded. "I'll take the deal, Marshal."

"Good. I'm releasing you right now. Go get changed into some decent clothes."

"I don't have any."

"Well, we'll find you some. You can't go looking like a tramp."

"Thank you, Warden."

Sabrina smiled, went over to the warden, and offered her hand, which Crawford rose hastily and took. "I wish the good Lord to help you."

"That's kind of you. I'll thank Judge Parker when I see him."

"We brought a buggy, so I guess we'll take him back."

"Might be best."

CHAPTER 15

"You think you'll be able to get along with that woman, Waco?" Silas asked. He had come to the general store and found Waco buying supplies.

The tall man turned to him and grinned suddenly, which made him look much younger. "No, I don't reckon I can—and I don't reckon anybody else can."

Silas could not contain his smile. "Well, you read her about like I do. She's had her own way pretty much. Comes from a rich family. Her parents probably spoiled her to death. I been tryin' to talk her out of this fool notion she's got of traipsin' around the Territory."

"So have I, but she's stubborn as a blue-nosed mule, Silas." Waco shook his head and looked up at the ceiling for a moment. His face was relaxed, and he was silent, staring at a hornet's nest that was built in the ceiling. "We had a hornet's nest in Grandpa's house where I grew up. I offered to get rid of it for Grandma. She said, 'No, let 'em alone. They catch flies.' I never did get to feeling easy around hornets though." Taking a deep breath, he said, "I'm gonna have one more try at talking some sense into her, but don't hold your breath."

"Well, we need more men. Just me and Gray Wolf ain't gonna be enough, even with you along."

"I talked to Judge Parker about that. He's pretty stubborn. He said he won't have any more men for at least six months. Not enough to send a band out to get LeBeau."

Silas studied the tall man carefully. "You ever meet LeBeau?"

Something crossed Waco's face. It brought a tension, and his eyelids half dropped as if he were staring at a specimen that he didn't particularly care for. He reached up and ran his hand through his black hair and said briefly, "I've met him."

"You didn't take to him, I guess."

"No, I didn't. I owe Mr. LeBeau something. It wasn't only to help Miss Warren get her sister back. I've been promising myself when I got out of prison to pay LeBeau a visit. I figure he owes me something. I'm gonna take it out of his hide."

"Men have tried that before and didn't make it. He's quick with a gun. Quick as a snake they say, and no more feelings in him than a snake either. He'd be a good one to decorate Judge Parker's gallows. Let Maledon have a hand at him. He could break his neck with one of them big knots of his."

"That'd suit me fine," Waco said flatly. "Here. Finish getting this list together, but watch it. I figure we'd take a light wagon. Don't know how long we'll be gone. Won't have time to run down to buy groceries every day."

Silas took the list and shrugged. "Well, go have a shot at it, boy. Maybe you'll have luck."

⟡

Waco left the general store and walked down the main street of Fort Smith. It was a busy day. The streets were crowded with wagons of all sizes, buggies, horsemen, and mule trains. The sounds of voices filled the air, some acrimonious and angry and others laughing. Getting to the hotel, he turned in and went to the desk. "I need to see Miss Warren."

"Well, she's upstairs."

Waco got the room number and walked up the stairs. When he got to the door with the number he was seeking, he knocked, perhaps harder than he had intended.

The door opened, and Sabrina Warren stood facing him. "What is it, Waco?"

"Can I talk to you?"

"I don't see any point in it, but come on in if you must."

Waco came in, took his hat off, and turned to face her. "I am gonna make one more try to talk you out of going on this hunt, Miss Warren. It's not like you think it'll be."

"I'm a good rider. I've been riding since I was twelve years old."

"I'm sure that's true, and I admire that in a woman, but there are other things besides riding a horse. It's gonna be a hard trip, and when the marshals go out it wears them down, and they're about the toughest men on earth."

Sabrina shook her head. "I'm not going to argue about this. We've settled on a price. I'm going, and you can just move on out now and let me get some sleep."

Waco, for a moment, seemed inclined to argue, but he saw the hopelessness of it. He stood for a moment staring at her, wondering what it would take to break her spirit down. He knew that there was a pride in this woman that could sweep her violently and set off a blaze in her eyes. He had already seen it more than once. He, more or less, admired the fire in Sabrina. It brought out the rich, headlong qualities of a spirit otherwise hidden behind the cool reserve of her lips. She had an enormous certainty in her, a positive will, and if things had been different, Waco felt he could have been drawn to her. But he had a job to do and he was not interested.

"We'll be leaving early." He turned without waiting for a word, stepped outside, and shut the door. He put his hat on, walked downstairs, and crossed down the street until he found Silas making the last purchases. "Well, that ought to be enough, Silas," Waco said. "It looks like we're going on a vacation instead of a manhunt."

"Never know how these things will turn out. We might be out there two months just huntin' for LeBeau. He's harder to find than a flea on a long-haired dog."

"You got that right. All right. We'll pull out real early."

"Gray Wolf is movin' around town here. I'll see if I can find him. We'll be ready when you say, Waco."

❧

A voice broke into Sabrina's sleep, and at first she did not know where she was and thought perhaps she was home again with her father speaking to her.

And then the voice spoke again. "Time to get up, Miss Warren."

Instantly Sabrina sat up, all ideas of sleep gone. Moonlight filtered through the window, and she saw the tall form of Waco Smith standing beside her bed.

"What are you doing in my room?"

"You told me to get you up when it was time to leave."

"Can't be time to leave. I haven't slept more than a couple of hours."

180

"Well, we're leavin'. If you want to stay and sleep, that would probably be a good idea."

"You get out of my room!"

"Are you goin'?"

"I'll be there. Give me time to get dressed, and don't you ever come in my room again!" Sabrina waited until the door closed behind Waco, and then she leaped out of bed and began dressing. She was angry that he had intruded her privacy. "He's a beast! No more manners than a grizzly bear!" she muttered. She dressed, got her personal things in a small canvas bag, and went downstairs. She was hungry but knew that the restaurant would not be open.

The three men were standing beside the wagon, three horses tied to the back. "Well, you ready to go this nice, cheerful morning?" Silas asked.

Sabrina still felt the gritty sensation in her eyes that came from a sleep interrupted. "Why are we leaving at this ungodly hour? What time is it?"

Waco answered her. "It's about two o'clock, I reckon. I got a lead on LeBeau and his bunch. We're gonna go check it out. May be a false alarm. You could just stay in town here, and when we find out if it's true or not we'll come back for you."

"No, I'm going, and I don't want to hear anything else about it."

"Well, all right. Get on board then." He climbed up into the driver's seat of the light wagon.

Sabrina scrambled to get into place, tossing her bag in the back. She saw the wagon was filled with supplies, including extra rifles.

"Be mighty nice if you stay here and rest up," Waco suggested.

She did not answer him. She knew he was trying to discourage her, but she was determined not to complain.

The trip was harder than Sabrina had planned. She wished she had brought a pillow or a pad, for the hard seat paddled her rear. She was sore before they had ridden for an hour. The road was nonexistent, nothing but potholes and ruts throwing her from one side to the other. Once she was thrown over against Waco.

He grinned and put his arm out. "Maybe I'd better hold you in before you get thrown out, boss."

"Take your hands off me!"

"Just tryin' to be a help," Waco said.

Turning, she looked back and saw that Silas was practically asleep in the saddle. "It's cruel of you to make an old man like that keep a schedule like this."

"I didn't invite him, boss. I told him it would be rough, and he said he'd been on rough hunts before. Tell you what. I could let Gray Wolf take you and him back, and then he could come back and meet me. We could go on this hunt then. You two can wait, and I'd come and get you in time for you to watch me kill LeBeau."

"Kill him?" Sabrina bounced in the seat and grabbed to hold on. When she turned to face him, her eyes were large with shock. "What do you mean kill him?"

Waco turned and looked at her with surprise. "Why, I thought you knew that. He won't be taken, Miss Warren. He'd rather take a bullet than hang." He saw the truth sinking in and realized that this was the first time that she had thought that far ahead. "What did you think would happen when we caught him? What was your plan to take care of him?"

"Why, to capture him and take him into Fort Smith. He could

go to trial in Judge Parker's court. He'd pay for kidnapping."

"He's got a lot more than kidnapping to pay for," Waco said. "He's killed four men that I know of. Two of them in a robbery where he's been identified. There's been a paper out on him a couple of years now. None of the marshals have been able to catch him."

"All I want to do is get my sister back."

"You think all you have to do is face Trey LeBeau and say, 'Mr. LeBeau, would you please give me my sister back?' Nothing like that is going to happen."

"He might. I'll offer him money."

"You could offer it if he gave you a chance to talk. But when he sees me he might start shooting."

"Why would he do that?"

"Because we didn't part on the best of terms. I owe Mr. LeBeau something."

"You're not hired for that. I would just ask him to give me my sister back."

"You might as well ask a hungry wolf to give up his dinner." He slapped the lines on the team and they sped up.

Sabrina noticed that his eyes were never still. He looked from point to point and each side constantly. She had seen Gray Wolf do the same thing and even Silas. They were men on edge. She realized she was in a world that she had never imagined.

Finally Waco said, "These men are killers, boss. They'd think no more of killing a human being than killing a deer."

The day wore on, and finally, when it was just before dark, they pulled up beside a small stream that Gray Wolf knew about. It was all Sabrina could do to climb out of the wagon. She felt like she had been beaten with a flat board, her muscles were so sore.

She had missed practically an entire night's sleep and now she was so groggy she staggered when she hit the ground.

She leaned up against the wagon and watched the men quickly and efficiently go to work. Gray Wolf gathered up some sticks and built the fire, adding dry wood to it that he found from a fallen tree. Silas was busy with the supplies, getting out some food to be cooked.

It was only half an hour later that she was offered a pancake in a tin plate. "I make the best pancakes in Fort Smith. Better than the restaurants," Silas said. "Try these, missy."

All of them had pancakes, and Silas suddenly said, "I reckon we'd better ask a blessing on this food."

Sabrina was watching Waco and saw a smile turn his lips upward. "My cellmate at the prison in Yuma always said thanks over the meals. Personally, I didn't think some of 'em were worth thankin' anybody for, but he was real faithful."

"Well, he was a child of God, I take it," Silas said.

"That's what he said."

"Did he try to make one out of you?" Sabrina asked.

"He tried, but it was a hopeless task."

"Let's eat these pancakes. I brought some sorghum molasses to make 'em sweet."

They all sat around eating pancakes and eating the bacon that Gray Wolf had fried, and when they were through, they washed their tin plates in the small stream that was fed by a spring.

"I'm gonna hit the sack. I'm plumb played out," Silas said. He got up and limped over to the wagon, pulled a blanket out, moved away, and rolled up in it. He seemed to go to sleep almost instantly.

Gray Wolf watched him and said, "He is one tired man."

Silence reigned for a time, until Waco looked to Gray Wolf, who stood peering out in the night, and said, "Why'd you leave your tribe, Gray Wolf? You never told me."

The Indian turned and gazed down at the two of them, who were still seated on a log. "I was too pretty. The squaws wouldn't leave me alone."

Waco suddenly grinned and winked at Sabrina. "Well, I've had that problem myself."

Suddenly Gray Wolf turned and loped out into the darkness. He was soon hidden, and Waco said, "That's an Indian for you. That's what they like. Prowling around looking for something to shoot or skin or scalp."

"But he's a Christian Indian."

"Well, that may be so. Gray Wolf's a Christian, I think, but he'd kill his enemies quick enough. Mission school can't take that out of him."

Overhead the stars began to come out in a magnificent fashion. Sabrina noticed that Waco was looking up at them and asked, "What did you do to get yourself put in prison, Waco?"

He turned to face her, and a serious expression swept across his face. "A woman put me there, boss. I guess that's why I don't put too much stock in the breed. They always get a man in trouble."

Sabrina stared at him. "Did you—did you kill her?"

"No, I didn't kill her. I might have, but I didn't have a chance."

"Well, how did she get you put in prison?"

"I had a friend. . .or at least a man I thought was my friend. I left town for a while. When I came back, my friend and my woman were gone. Took everything I had. Left me with nothing. A thing like that takes the strength out of a man. I didn't care what

I did, so I got into trouble. Got in with a bad bunch. I was charged with train robbery. Lucky I didn't get charged with murder. Came near to gettin' killed."

"One woman hurt you, and now you hate all women?"

"Tells the story completely," he said, allowing admiration to shade his tone. Then he asked, "You married?"

"No."

"Why not?"

"That's none of your business."

Waco leaned back and stared at her. "Might be." The solid moon was bright, and the flaws on it were obvious. "Why boss, we might fall in love just like in the romance books. You've read them stories. Rich, beautiful city girl falls in love with a handsome outlaw; then she makes a man out of him. Then they get married and live happily ever after."

"That's something in a book. That'll never happen, especially not with you and me."

"Just a minute." He got up, walked over to where she had put her blanket down on the ground, picked it up, and shook it.

"Why'd you do that?" Sabrina demanded.

"Well, to get rid of scorpions or rattlesnakes."

His words sobered Sabrina, and she looked fearfully at the blanket. "Do—do they get into a bed?"

"Pretty often. Some fellows believe if you put a rope in a circle around a campfire, snakes won't cross it."

"Does that work, Waco?"

"Nope." His answer did not cheer her up. He came over and handed her the blanket, and as she reached her hand out to take it, he held on to it. "You should be scared right now, boss."

"Why?"

"Snakes and scorpions aren't as dangerous to you as a man like me."

Instantly Sabrina grew angry. "I'm not afraid of you!"

Waco stepped a little closer, still holding the blanket. He could see the fear in her eyes and said so. "Yes, you are, boss. I can see it in your eyes." He reached out with his free hand and held her by the forearm. "You need to learn to be afraid of things, Sabrina Warren."

Fear touched Sabrina, for although Silas was there and Gray Wolf was somewhere around, she knew that this man had the power to hurt her if he chose. Suddenly he smiled and said, "Go get some sleep. I'll keep the snakes off of you."

Snatching the blanket from him, she went back away from the fire, laid it down, and rolled up in it. But as she lay in the darkness tired, weary, and sleepy, she remembered the strength of his hand. "I'm not afraid of him," she whispered, but she knew deep down she had been afraid.

By sunup they had risen, eaten pancakes, had coffee and bacon, and started in on a day's ride. Sabrina did have judgment enough to make a pad out of her blanket and affix it on her seat.

"These hard seats sure hurt a woman's bottom, don't they?" Waco asked.

"Some things seem impolite. Don't talk about that."

"About what?"

"About my bottom."

"Well, you've got one, I take it, and I know what it is to get sore."

"Just don't talk."

"All right."

He kept his word, and as they traveled all day, stopping only once for water and some beef sandwiches, they finally reached the outskirts of Hayden, a small town.

"We'll pull up here and stay for the night. I'm going into town. I've got a fellow here who might know where LeBeau is."

"He wouldn't tell you, would he?"

"With a little persuasion he might."

Silas said, "Bring some good grub back. Maybe some good candy."

They had a good supper with beans and bacon and the last of the fresh bread they had bought. Sabrina went to bed but was awakened at some time in the night by a horse whinnying. She sat up and saw that Waco was stepping off of his horse and tying him to a mesquite tree.

She got up at once. She was dead tired. She said, "Did you find out anything?"

"Maybe. Silas, get up."

Gray Wolf had been awakened by Waco's coming. "You know that man's too old for this kind of thing."

"Yes, but he's here and he has to come along."

"Let the old man sleep a little longer," Sabrina said, putting a gentle note in her voice.

"Sure."

"You will?"

"Yeah. I'll go do some poking around and see what I can stir up. You all stay here and wait for me."

"No, I'm going."

"You are the stubbornest woman I have ever run across."

"And you are the hardest man I've ever met. Don't you feel anything for anybody?"

Silas was not yet up, and Gray Wolf was hitching the team. They were on the far side of it. Suddenly he moved toward her. When she saw something in his face she said, "You stay away from me."

"Well now, boss, in those romance books at a time like this it gets real romantic. The hero kisses the girl, and she just can't resist him."

Suddenly she drew the .38 she had brought and carried in a holster and pointed it at him. "Stay away from me or I'll shoot."

Waco said, "Well, our romance isn't making much headway, but it'll pick up." He nodded and added, "And that gun isn't loaded."

Sabrina looked down at the gun, and suddenly he snatched it from her. "That was your best chance to shoot your lover. Here. The gun's loaded. Just don't believe everything I tell you." He laughed at her, and she shoved the gun back in her holster and started making a fire for breakfast.

CHAPTER 16

As Marianne stood on the front porch of the house, she lifted her eyes and saw that sunlight burned against the earth, catching at the thin flashes of mica particles in the soil. The day was already hot, the heat dropping on the tin roof layer on layer until it was a substance that could be felt even in the bones. Heat was a burning pressure in this country, she had discovered, and sometimes the gray and burnt-brown desert and heat rolled back from the punished earth to make an unseen turbulence. She took a deep breath and noticed that the smell of the day was a rendered-out compound of baked grass, sage, and bitter dust.

This was one of the few times she could relax. As she stood there, over in the east the land at first had been only a looming in the darkness, dim and vague, but now night was leaving, and the features of the land began to show themselves. At first it was only a darkness beneath the shine of pale stars. Finally low clouds began to appear, and timber far off stood massed solidly with a brooding atmosphere that seemed to haunt her. Slowly the light arose as she stood there, and the earth began to take on form. She waited until the sun rose and the whole eastern sky was alight. Far down by the creek, birches stood whitely in their cleanliness, and squirrels trilled high up in the oak trees. It was a time she had learned to steal from her situation. Now she glanced overhead, noting that the stars, gold and brilliant, were disappearing, nothing but faint pulses of light. Daylight then flowed over the land. The smell of dust lay rank and still upon the earth, and Marianne could not help but let the memories, bitter as gall, come to her.

The worst memory always came, bringing with it something almost like a physical pain. The day that she had arrived at the ranch, she and the man she now knew was Trey LeBeau had gotten off a train. He had obtained a wagon and a team, and they had left Fort Smith in the early hours. Even then it had seemed to her he was anxious and was somehow careful and stealthy in his movements.

She remembered how excited she had been when they left town and began crossing the prairie. She asked him questions along the way. What kind of tree is that? Does that river have a name? He had smiled and answered her. She did not notice at the time, but there was a sharkish, dangerous look about him. However, she had not the experience to see it.

After two days' travel, he pulled up and said. "There it is. Your new home, Marianne."

That moment came back to her now, and she felt all the keenness of the disappointment. She had seen pictures in books of fine ranches with corrals, barns, and cattle browsing in the background.

There was none of that here. High on the rise stood a house with a tin roof that was red with rust and almost past reflecting the sunlight. It was a small house with a porch running along the front with windows in the upstairs. Perhaps it had been painted at one time, but now the rain and the wind and the blowing dust had rendered it a pale gray so that there was nothing artful, beautiful, or romantic about it. She remembered how her heart had sunk and how she was aware that he was looking at her strangely. "Not what you expected, is it?"

She had managed to say, "Not exactly."

He had laughed and then driven the horses down, and as they approached the house, men came out. She remembered running her eyes from one to the other, and when they pulled up the team he said, "Boys, I want you to meet my new wife. That small fellow there, he's Al Munro." A short man with pale blue eyes and prematurely silver hair stared at her. There was something deadly about him.

"That big fellow there. That's Zeno Shaw. Don't ever get him mad at you. He'll crush you like a bug."

Shaw was a man whose face was scarred with the memories of many fights. He grinned at her and said, "You got you quite a good-looking woman there, Trey."

The use of the name, she remembered, was the first time she had found out that this was Trey LeBeau.

The other three men were introduced. Rufo Aznar, a Mexican with a terrible scar on the right side of his face, Breed Marcos, a muscular half-Apache, and Boone Hagerty, a big, fine-looking man, but with a cruel look about him.

"Well, this is Marianne. Marianne LeBeau for a while anyhow."

As she stood on the porch watching the sun slowly illuminate the land, she felt again the keen pain of that revelation that had come to her like a bolt of lightning. She remembered thinking,

Mother and Father were right, and Sabrina was right! I've been a fool!

Unable to bear the memory, she went out to where someone had put up a wire fence and a few chickens cluttered around. She opened the gate then opened the cabinet, took out some chicken feed, and began to scatter it, calling to them. They came clucking and fluttering around her feet, and she watched for a moment as they were fed.

"Let's have one of them for lunch."

Quickly Marianne turned and saw that the man she had once loved but now hated, Trey LeBeau, was leaning against a post grinning at her. The sight of him that once had pleased her so much was now hateful, and now he said, "Come on out of there. I'll have Zeno pluck a couple of those chickens."

She hesitated, and Trey's smile disappeared. There was a lupine expression in his face. "Did you hear me, Marianne? I said come out here."

She came out slowly and locked the gate, and he came over to her, threw his arms around her, and held her figure against his. He kissed her roughly, and she could do nothing.

"You ain't got much spirit for a bride. I expect a little action out of a good-lookin' woman like you. Sleepin' with you is like sleepin' with a dead woman."

Marianne was used to such talk. It had pained her to the heart when she had first heard it, but she had to learn to endure it.

He said, "Come on in the house."

She followed him in, and the fetid odors of male sweat, tobacco, and alcohol were rank. The place was a wreck. "Clean this place up. Make yourself useful."

"Looks like a man could get more use than that out of a good-lookin' woman." Breed Marcos, the half-Apache, was grinning.

He was thin and muscular and carried a knife that he constantly whetted when he was sitting still.

Al Munro was the smallest of the men. He had pale eyes, and there was something carnivorous about him. Marianne realized he reminded her of a panther she had once seen in a zoo.

She began to clean the house, knowing it was futile. LeBeau seemed to get pleasure out of tormenting her and found ways to do it. Her mind was dull, and she tried to make it so. Whenever she got close to one of the men, he might reach out and grab at her until LeBeau said, "Find your own woman. This one's mine."

❧

Sunset was approaching, and a visitor had come to the house. He was a half-breed, but the Indian side of him did not show. Marianne did not know what business he had with LeBeau, but she knew it was something dirty. Desperation had caused her to think up the only plan that seemed at all possible. She had written a letter and sealed it and taken what money she had, thankful that LeBeau had not found it. When the man left, she could hear the cursings and laughing of the men inside. They were engaged in a wild poker game.

"Please wait a minute."

The half-breed turned and stared at her suspiciously. "What do you want?"

"I have some money here and a letter. If I give you the money, will you mail the letter for me?"

"Why don't you get Trey to do it?"

"No, I can't. The letter's to my father, and then I asked him to send you five hundred dollars more. All you have to do is post the letter at a post office."

"I'm not gonna get LeBeau down on me. He'd kill me like a snake."

"He will never know. I'll never talk. There's nearly two hundred dollars here, and you'll get five hundred more. My father's a wealthy man. It says in the letter he's to mail it to you if you'll write your name on it. You could pick it up at the post office in Fort Smith."

The half-breed hesitated and glanced at the house. The noise was increasing. It seemed they were all getting drunker by the minute. He took the money and the letter and said, "This could get me killed, but I need the money. Don't ever say nothin' to nobody."

"I promise I won't. My father will be happy to give you the money. He would give you even more if you asked for it. You'll just have to wait until the letter gets to Memphis, and he'll probably wire you back. Just tell him your name."

The half-breed stood irresolutely then turned and walked away. She watched him go, knowing that this was her only hope. Looking back, she remembered that LeBeau had left no trail. He had used a false name until they got back to the Territory, and now she watched the man ride away. She found herself praying that he would mail the letter and not drink it up as she feared.

᠊᠊᠊᠊᠊᠊᠊᠊᠊᠊

Calandra Montevado had been angered by Trey's action in bringing another woman. "I thought I was your woman," she said acidly.

"Why, you are. This one's just for fun."

When he came over to put his arms around her, smiling, she

suddenly produced a knife and held it poised over his stomach. "You take one more step, and I'll open you wide, Trey. You keep your hands off of me. Have all the women you want, but don't be comin' to me."

Trey knew that the woman was totally capable of cutting his heart out. He had seen that in her, and he had said, "It's your call, Callie."

Later on Callie found the captive young woman sitting in a chair. The men were gone on some errand, and Trey had told her to keep an eye on her. She sat down and studied the girl, who looked about sixteen years old. "What's it like to be rich?" she said.

Marianne blinked with surprise. "I don't know what you mean."

"I've never been rich, but I'd like to be. I think it probably beats this life."

"Have you been with— Have you been here long?"

"Too long." Callie continued to stare at the girl. "I'm not surprised Trey was able to win you. He can do things like that, win women, me for one."

"Why do you stay here? You could get away."

Callie Montevado's lips turned bitter. "Where will I go?" she asked. "Who would have me now? Don't try to get away. They'd find you and make it worse for you." She got up and left the girl. Actually she felt sorry for the young woman, but her life had not left much room for grief or sorrow.

❧

The sun had been sharp and bright and blazing all day. Now it was settling westward and seemed to melt into a shapeless bed of gold flame. Far off the mountains broke the horizon, and the desert seemed to cool off instantly. The sun slanted down to the west, and the late summer's light was golden, and already the night birds were beginning to make their lonesome calls.

Gray Wolf had gone hunting and come back with a fat young deer. He and Silas were cutting it up. Silas grinned. "This will go down pretty good. I'm about half-starved."

"Where did Waco go?"

"Oh, he said he had an idea. That man don't talk enough. I don't know what's going on in his head half the time."

"Well, probably out looking for LeBeau." He glanced over and saw that Sabrina had put her blanket down and was lying there curled up sound asleep.

Silas shook his head. "That girl's in bad shape. She's wore plumb out."

"She's had some good years." Gray Wolf shrugged. "Now she has some bad years. You know, at the mission they told us about a story in the Bible about a man called Job."

"Yeah, I've read that book."

"One thing I read in it I agreed with," Gray Wolf said as he stripped the flesh from the bones of the deer. "A man is born to trouble as the sparks fly upward. I ain't sure about the rest of the Bible, but that's true enough."

"I guess we all know that. You know," Silas said thoughtfully, "I heard an educated preacher once say that Job was the oldest book in the Bible, but I never really liked it."

"What's not to like?" Gray Wolf looked up with surprise. "It's a pretty good story."

"No, it's not. Job was a good man. As a matter of fact, the Bible says he was a perfect man and upright."

"You can't get no better than that. I expect he went straight to heaven when he kicked off."

"Well, it always bothered me that Job was probably the best man on the face of the earth, and God experimented with him. The devil told Him, 'The only reason Job serves You is because You're good to him. You made him rich and gave him a family. Who wouldn't serve You?' "

"I remember that." Gray Wolf grinned. "God said to the devil, 'Well, that ain't so. You just take it all away from him. Just don't touch his body.' And that's what the devil done."

"Stripped him down to nothin'. He had everything in the first chapter and from then on out he had nothin'."

"Makes you think, don't it?" Gray Wolf bit off a chunk of the raw venison, chewed it thoughtfully, and swallowed it. "That's good, tender venison. Let's get some of it to cookin'."

They built a fire quickly, and as they were cooking the steaks, Silas said, "You know, makes you wonder about LeBeau. He's got everything. All the money he wants, and does what he pleases. He's a wicked, evil man, but he's got everything most men want."

Gray Wolf looked up, and his eyes seemed to glitter. "Well, he'll lose it all one day."

"You're right," Silas said. "He will. We got to remember that, me and you. Them two with us, they're not Christians."

"You figure to convert 'em?"

"Gonna do my best, Gray Wolf. You might give it a try, too."

The sound of hoofbeats awoke Sabrina. She sat up and saw that Waco had come in. She watched as he tied his horse to a mesquite tree and got up and went to meet him. He was weary to the bone she saw, and she asked, "Are you hungry?"

"Yes."

"Well, sit down. Gray Wolf killed a fat deer. The best thing we've had."

"I can use it." He moved over toward the wagons and slumped down cross-legged, leaning back. Fatigue was in his every movement, and she knew that he was exhausted. He had slept less than any of them, and now she was well aware of the discipline that he imposed on himself. She studied the shelving jaws of his big-featured face. His eyes, she knew, were sharp with a light in them, but there was a recklessness and something in him like a hidden heat. He was a tall man, and his shoulders were broad. His high, square shape made an alert form against the shadow of the wagon. There was a toughness to him and a resilient vigor all about him. He had discipline, she knew that, and as she pulled a chunk of meat off of the grill and put it before him, she said, "There's two biscuits left from breakfast."

"Sounds good."

Sabrina watched as he ate the meat, hungrily tearing at it with his strong white teeth, and saw that he had plenty of water. Finally she asked, "Did you find anything, Waco?"

"Not really." He gave her a sharp look. "Are you wantin' to give up?"

"No."

"I didn't think so." He finished his meal, put it to one side, then came to his feet. He moved slowly at times, but there was a hint of speed and power in him. "Come along." He walked out of the camp, and she followed him with some trepidation. He walked quickly for all his fatigue. Finally he stopped and said, "Look at that."

It was growing darker, but she moved closer and saw a stone

flat and upright. "That looks like a tombstone," she said.

"That's what it was, but the wind and the sand and the rain have eaten it all away. Look. Whoever buried him made an outline of where the coffin is." He pointed down, and Sabrina saw that there were a few stones that marked a rectangle. She watched as Waco suddenly moved forward. He began to pull his boot through the line of stones, digging a little trench. When he had gotten all around it, he kicked the stones back in the trench.

She could stand it no longer. "What are you doing, Waco?"

"Don't know. Maybe trying to put off what has to come."

"Like what?"

"Whoever this is, they had the same kind of dreams I have, I expect. Maybe a husband that found a wife and loved her. Maybe a wife that found a husband, but she only made it this far. I don't know. It makes me sad."

"You didn't know whoever it is."

"No, that's true," he said slowly, and she could see he was thinking deeply. "But whoever it is, when they were alive, they have the same hungers I do and the same problems probably. Maybe it was a husband whose life was cut short. His wife had to bury him out here in this wilderness."

"Could have been a woman."

"That would be even sadder to me." He began to move away from her and traced the line of small stones that marked the grave into a trench with the toe of his boot. Then he carefully put the stones back in there.

When he stood up, she asked, "Why did you do that, Waco?"

"Don't know. Feel sort of down, I guess."

Suddenly she said, "Waco, I wish you could put that behind you. If you don't, you'll be like those men who took Marianne.

Like you say LeBeau is. I wouldn't want you to be that kind of a man. Don't nurse grudges and hate until you are rank inside. You'll be your own worst enemy. You weren't meant to snarl at the world, be against people, be cruel."

He took her hand and looked into her face. "When you lose something it hurts."

"You're thinking about the woman who ran out on you."

"Guess I'll never forget her. How she betrayed me."

Again a wave of pity came as Sabrina was very much aware of his hand, the warmth and the strength of it. "I'm sorry, Waco."

He shook his head. "Funny thing, Sabrina. I haven't been thinking much about the hurts of other people. Too busy pitying myself—but I hate to see you hurting over your sister."

Sabrina did not know what was happening, but she waited there, saying nothing, when suddenly he reached out and pulled her to him. He put his arms around her, and she looked up at him. The feeling of his kiss went through her, and it was a goodness without shame. She was stirred and did not know why it was, but it was what she wanted. She felt the luxury of it as well as he.

She felt that Waco was on the near edge of rashness. His impulses were clear. He was a strong man, and she was a beautiful woman. She saw the battle take place, and then with some sort of joy, she saw him shake his head and step back. "I'll do my best for you, Sabrina, to find your sister. . .even if I have to die for it."

The deer meat was about gone, and that night it was Waco who said, "We're going to have to go get more grub. We're worn down to nothing."

It was night, and they had just eaten the last of the canned beans they had brought along with the last small chunks of bacon. They hungered for bread, for something solid.

Silas had been quiet, and as they sat there finishing their meal, he said, "You know, I still miss my wife, Lottie."

"How'd you meet her, Silas?" Sabrina smiled.

"Well, I was no good, but I took one look at her and fell in love with her just like in the storybooks. She wouldn't have anything to do with me. I'm glad she wouldn't. She was a pure woman."

"Well, how did you ever get her to marry you?"

"I went off and I looked for God. I had some trouble there," Silas said thoughtfully. "I signed a trade with God. I'll be a good man if You give me that woman. I found out pretty soon you don't do business with God like that. Finally I said, 'God, whether You ever give me Lottie or not, I'll serve you.' So I got saved out behind the church with the service goin' on. I was too ashamed to go in, so I listened to the singin' and the preachin'. When the preacher made an altar call, I went in. Been servin' Jesus ever since." He turned and said, "Gray Wolf, how'd you find Jesus?"

Gray Wolf had been listening carefully. He grinned, and it softened his features. "I was a real bad man. I was on a horse-stealing raid and got captured. The chief was a tough hombre. I was on the ground tied, and he had a spear in his hand. He lifted it up, and I knew he was going to run it through my heart." He grew quiet then.

Finally Waco said, "Well, he didn't kill you obviously."

"No, he didn't. He stood there looking at me, and something came into his eyes. He had hard eyes, I tell you, that Indian did! But after a while he threw his spear down and walked away. I couldn't understand why he let me live. For a long time I wondered about it, but I know one thing. . .only God could have made that man spare me. So I promised I'd live like a Christian."

Silas said, "I'm going to tell you two sinners how to get saved."

"That's what I like. You're a real Southerner with your preachin'." Waco grinned. "Go ahead. Turn your wolf loose."

Silas began to quote Scriptures, almost all of them about the death of Jesus. "It's His blood that washes us from sin. The Bible says God puts our sins behind His back. He blots 'em out of the Book. We become a part of His family, and all you have to do is give Him everything you've got, which most people can't do," Silas said.

He spoke for a long time, and finally Sabrina was forced to admit, "I don't know what he's talking about. I've been going to church all of my life, but I don't have anything in me like Gray Wolf and Silas."

❧

The next day they pulled out, and as they did, Sabrina turned to Waco and said, "What did you think about what Silas said?"

"Funny you should ask," Waco said. "I'm a pretty hard nut, but I can't forget what he said about Jesus."

"Do you think you'll ever be a man of God?"

Waco dropped his head. "I hope so," he whispered.

CHAPTER 17

Heat lay like a thin film in the windless air as Sabrina stood with her back to the campsite looking out into the distance. The sun was a white hole in the sky, and the deep haze of summer had lightened so that the land was a tawny floor running immeasurably away into the distance. The Territory frightened her, for it was not the kind of climate or the kind of world that she had been born into. There was no security in this land. None by day and none by night. It was a country of extremes, of long silence and sudden wild crying, a bone-searching dryness followed by a sudden rush of cloudburst torrents down in the narrow canyons. It was raw and primitive, and she had already seen it scoured the softness out of a man and made him into something sometimes frightening.

"I've been wanting to talk to you, Sabrina, about Marianne."

Instantly Sabrina turned to him, for she heard a somber tone in his voice. "What is it? What do you want to tell me?"

"I don't think you're going to be happy, Sabrina, even if we find her." There wasn't the faintest hint of tension in his body or voice.

"I think we'll find her," he said finally. "But you come from a family that's well off, and your parents are religious people. Well—"

"What is it?" Sabrina asked. "What do you want to tell me, Waco? Just say it."

"All right. I know LeBeau. He's using your sister like he uses all women. That's what he does, Sabrina. He never loved a woman in his life. To him they're something to be used and thrown aside. He'll throw her aside, too, as soon as he gets tired of her."

Thoughts of this nature had come to Sabrina in many forms, but she refused to agree. "I don't care. I don't care what's happened or what she's done. Marianne's my sister."

"You may love her, but what about the way she feels? You think she can just walk away from this? When these things happen they leave scars."

"You're wrong." She held her hand up and said, "See that scar?"

Waco nodded.

"I almost cut that finger off, and it bled and it hurt. Even after it was bandaged it hurt for weeks, but look at it now. Touch it. See? It doesn't even hurt. I know it's there. I know that something happened that day, but the pain's not there anymore. Just the memory. And that's what it'll be when we get Marianne back. We'll take her home, take care of her and love her, and she'll be all right."

Waco smiled slightly. "You always think the best, don't you, Sabrina? Well, I'm glad you do, and I hope you always do."

Their talk was interrupted when Gray Wolf rode up on his pinto pony. He slid off of the horse, walked over, and grinned at the pair of them. "I found them!"

Waco looked up and exclaimed, "LeBeau!"

"Yes. My cousin, he come from the north. Cherokee nation.

Says he saw LeBeau three days ago close to Grand River."

"Come on. Let's tell Silas."

Quickly they held a council of war, and when they heard what Gray Wolf had to say, Waco said, "Why, I know where that is. I'd forgotten about it. LeBeau doesn't use it much. Sometimes he goes out and robs a train; then he ducks back in there. It'll be hard to get at," he sighed. "They can see for miles in every direction. If too big a bunch comes after them, they split up and fade in the hills. Then they'll come back together somewhere else."

"What do you think, Waco?" Sabrina asked. "You think we can go after them?"

"Yeah, we can. We'll travel tonight. Be cooler that way."

The party pulled out shortly before dark, just as the air was beginning to cool, and traveled most of the night. Waco called a halt just before dawn. The horses were beginning to tire. They rested there all morning then started again after eating at noon. They traveled hard all that day, making quick camps and taking short rests.

Waco was glad to see that Sabrina was standing the trip better than he had hoped. "I believe we're going to make it," he remarked to Silas. "She's doin' better than I thought she would."

"I guess so." Silas nodded. He took off his hat. A slight breeze lifted his fine white hair.

Waco saw that the old man was tired and looked even more frail than ever.

"I wish she weren't here, Waco," he said. "This ain't no place for a woman like that. She could get killed."

"I've thought of it, but I don't know what to do with it. That woman's got more determination than a hungry mule." The two stood there for a moment looking off in the direction they were headed. "What do you think of her? Sabrina, I mean."

"A good-looking woman. Stubborn though."

"Always liked a woman with grit in her," Waco remarked.

They rode hard, and the next day Waco sent Gray Wolf ahead to scout. The Indian left at three o'clock while the others made camp. Darkness fell as they were finishing the evening meal, and Waco lifted his head. "Somebody's comin'," he said in a low voice. He picked up his Winchester and moved over to a large rock, listening carefully. After a moment he lowered the rifle and said, "Gray Wolf." The Indian rode in, excitement lighting his smooth face. "Found them!"

"You saw him? LeBeau?"

"No, LeBeau's not there, but a woman is there and Boone Hagerty."

"It's them then." Waco nodded.

"A woman?" Sabrina asked curiously.

"Yes." Gray Wolf grinned. "Name is Calandra Montevado. I always liked her name. People just call her Callie though."

"Did you see my sister?"

"Small woman with blond hair?"

"It's Marianne. We found her!"

Silas was excited. "Found 'em at the right time, too. If there's only two men there, the rest of 'em must be out on some kind of a raid. What do you think, Waco?"

"Sounds good. We'll take 'em in the morning. Tonight might be better. Catch 'em off guard."

"I'd say morning," Silas said. "You get to shootin' in the dark, no tellin' who could get hurt. Tomorrow we get there and we surround that cabin at daylight. As soon as the men come out, I'll take one, you take the other. With only two, we can kill 'em the first thing. They won't be causin' no trouble."

His words seemed to send a chill over Sabrina. "You mean kill them without warning?"

Silas stared at her. "You didn't think we'd get your sister back without shootin', did you?"

"Well no, but don't we need to give them some warning? Give them a fair chance?"

"You're thinking like a woman that lives in a fancy house in Memphis," Waco said. "Don't you understand? We let 'em know we're here and one of 'em will grab a pistol and put it to her head, threatening to kill her if we don't leave, and they'd do it, too, Sabrina. They don't think any more of taking a human life than you think of taking a drink of water." He hesitated then shook his head. "I know it sounds rough to you, but out here it's different. These men you have to treat like wild animals."

Sabrina walked away and began cooking over the fire.

Later on Waco came and sat down cross-legged in front of her. He put aside his hat. "You all right?" he asked.

"I'm worried about tomorrow."

"Yeah. I knew you would be, but Silas is right. The important thing is to get Marianne out of there. If you give those men one chance, they'll kill her, Sabrina."

A heavy stillness seemed to hang in the air, and as Sabrina stared into his face, he knew she was wanting comfort. "I—I just can't think straight," she whispered. "It goes against everything I've ever thought that I know."

He stood up then and stood before her, his face impassive. She was very beautiful as she stood close to him, and the vulnerability of her spirit was reflected in the troubled lines of her face. Her eyes were enormous, and they glistened in the ghostly light of the moon. She was trembling, and Waco muttered, "I wish you didn't have to go through with this."

Suddenly Sabrina stepped closer to him. Finally she whispered, "I just don't know what to do." Unconsciously she reached out and touched his arm as if to gather strength from him.

Waco was starkly aware of her closeness and the aura of femininity that seemed to emanate from her. Sabrina was a woman, shapely, beautiful, full of vigor, and her nearness made him desire her in a way he had never wanted a woman before.

Seeing desire in her eyes, Waco put his hands at her hips, pulled her upright against him, and kissed her full on the lips. His mouth bore down hard and heavy on hers, and he could feel her wishes joining his. Her response touched the deepest chord within him, and he had never known such exhilaration.

Suddenly she drew back. "I don't know why I let you kiss me." Her voice was distraught. "This must never happen again."

"It probably will," Waco said calmly. Then he shrugged his shoulders. "You've got to decide, Sabrina. What will we do?"

She stood absolutely still for a moment, and then she whispered, "All right. Do what you have to do. I want my sister back."

❧

"I know you don't want to shoot nobody, Sabrina," Silas said. He handed her a rifle and said, "You just point this up in the air. Make a racket with it. Here are some more shells. Make it sound like we got twenty marshals out here."

209

The small group stood facing Waco, and he said suddenly, "Sabrina, you sure you want to go on with this? We can back off right now. We can take you back, and me and Gray Wolf and Silas will get at it another way."

"No, I want Marianne back now."

"All right," Silas spoke up. "We're going to surround the house. If anything happens, remember you just fire off as fast as you can in the air. We want to make 'em think they're outnumbered. Waco, let's you and me and Gray Wolf take up a position beside them rocks. As soon as those two birds come out, we'll pop 'em, and it'll be all we need to worry about. You think we need to worry about the woman?"

"No, she's an old friend," Waco said evenly. "I think we can leave her alone. What if the men come out one at a time?"

"No good," Silas said. "We've got to get both of them. They'll have to come out together sooner or later."

The plan seemed simple enough. They arrived, and at first light a lantern came on inside. Almost at once a man stepped outside. "That's Boone Hagerty," Silas said. "He's as bad as the rest of them, but his mother was a fine Christian."

Time crawled on, and Hagerty did nothing but smoke and stare out across the desert. Suddenly the door opened, and Marianne came out. Sabrina almost cried out. She seemed to devour her sister with her eyes. Finally she went back into the house, and for nearly an hour Hagerty sat on the front porch smoking and staring out at the desert. Finally he rose and got a drink of water.

"I wish that other bird would come out," Waco whispered.

He did not, but the woman came out. Sabrina, who had stayed beside Waco, saw a strange expression on his face, and then her eyes went back to the woman.

She was very attractive, with black hair and a shapely figure. She went to the barn and came out ten minutes later mounted on a beautiful black mare. Calling out something to Hagerty, she spurred the horse and rode off into the west.

The time dragged by. It was now close to dark, but the two men never appeared at the same time.

Waco moved over closer. "What do you think, Silas?"

"I don't know. I never could stand waiting."

"Always that way, I reckon. I remember once before that charge at Gettysburg. I was as nervous as a June bride."

The two spoke quietly, and finally Gray Wolf called out, "They're coming back. Callie and another one. Now there's three men for us to worry about."

"That's not Pratt. That's Al Munro. He's the worst of the crew," Waco said. "We can't hang around here, Silas. That bunch could come back at any time."

"You're right," Silas said with finality in his voice. "Here's what we'll do, Waco. I'll sneak down front. You go around the back. You peep in the window, and if you can see the men in there, you break the glass and let 'em have it. I'll rush the front door when I hear your shots. It's risky, but so is hanging around like this."

"I don't like it, Silas. Those men are quick on the shoot."

"Well, let's try to get closer anyway. They've got to come out sooner or later."

As they crept closer, Waco said, "You stay here. I'm going to go catch a look at the layout of the cabin. If it looks bad, we'll pull back and wait for morning."

"Go do it, son."

Waco moved toward the cabin, taking a roundabout way. He moved carefully across the ground until he reached the side of the house and flattened himself against it. He could hear the muted voices inside, and removing his hat he cautiously lifted his head. He saw the girl he had been seeking. Boone Hagerty, Al Munro, and another man were sitting at a table playing cards. He didn't see Callie anywhere. He assumed she was in one of the bedrooms. It was almost pitch dark now, and Waco decided he couldn't take the risk.

Suddenly he started, for the sound of gunfire screamed through the night somewhere in front of the house. He leaped to one side, cleared the window, and saw several men shooting. *They're back!*

The men inside burst out the door, and Al Munro shouted, "Over to the side, Boone. They're over there. Get 'em!"

Waco ran forward and the men opened fire on him. He heard the shots whistling through the air and tossing up dust almost at his feet. He laid a heavy fire but knew he had missed because he was shooting blindly. As he neared the hiding place, he said, "It's me. . .Waco. Don't shoot!"

Instantly Gray Wolf was at his side. "No good! No good! We leave now!"

"Yeah, let's get out of here. Let's move, Silas."

"I'm comin'." Suddenly Silas said, "We can still—"

Waco's heart seemed to sink. "I think they got Silas. You wait here, Gray Wolf." He found Silas. "Are you hit bad?" he asked.

"Don't—know. Somewhere low down."

Waco knew he couldn't help him there. Crouching down in the darkness, he picked up the old man and slung him over his shoulder. "This is going to hurt, but we've got to get you out of here." He ran across the open spaces. "Don't shoot!" he called. "They'll know where we are if they see the muzzle flashes. Come on. Let's get back to the others."

They made their way back, and Gray Wolf helped carry the old man. Waco saw vague outlines, and he let off a round. Instantly he heard a shout of pain and someone yelled, "This way! Come on, we got 'em, Trey!"

LeBeau's voice ordered, "Spread out now! Surround 'em!"

Waco grimly lifted his rifle and began to lay down a heavy fire, but knowing he was being quickly cut off, he retreated. The two men made their way stumbling, and they found Sabrina.

"What happened?" she asked.

"LeBeau got back," Waco said. "He surprised us. Silas got hit. We've got to get out of here and get Silas to a doctor." They lowered the old man into the wagon, and he said, "Sabrina, you'll have to drive. Just head on out. We'll find you."

"I'm staying."

"You get going. We'll take care of this end."

Waco and Gray Wolf reloaded their rifles. "We'll hold 'em for a while and give her a chance to get a clean start."

"Too many." Gray Wolf shook his head. "No."

"We'll have to hold 'em just for a little while."

The fight began in earnest, and at some point, after they loosed a volley of shots, Waco heard someone call out, "I'm hit! I'm hit!"

"We've got to get out of here," he heard another voice say in panic. "We've got to get out of this. There's too many of 'em. They got Hagerty. He's a goner."

"Pull back then!" LeBeau's harsh voice called.

It was the moment Waco and Gray Wolf had been waiting for. "Let's go," Gray Wolf gasped. "Let's get back to the others. They won't be coming after us."

"They'll be after us as soon as it's light enough to track us. We can be clear by then. I want you to stay here, Gray Wolf. There's no way LeBeau will stay at this place. They'll go to a new hideout. You find out where it is and meet us in Fort Smith."

"Yes, now go. Back soon." Gray Wolf melted away into the night, and Waco hurried, his heart heavy as he realized that Silas was badly hurt.

❧

"We've got to get back to Fort Smith," Sabrina said desperately. She had drawn Waco aside near where Silas was lying flat on a blanket. They had taken him out of the wagon. The sun was now high in the sky, and the horses were pretty well winded by the fast pace of all last night and half the day.

They reached a small creek and decided to rest the wounded man. "How far is it? How long is it going to take?"

"Best part of two days." Waco shook his head. "And we can't go too fast. It'd shake him to death. But you're right, we can't stay here."

"Do you think Silas will be all right?" Sabrina asked.

"I don't know, Sabrina. He wasn't too strong to begin with, and that bullet hit something in his lower back. Last time he woke up he said he didn't feel any pain. Bad sign."

They stood paralyzed by indecision, and finally Waco said, "All right. We'll rest here until it cools off. We've got plenty of food but no grain for the horses. I'll take 'em out and find some graze and rub 'em down and let 'em rest tonight. We can make it in two days, I think." He turned and looked at Sabrina. "I'm sorry we didn't get your sister. I made a bad play."

Sabrina looked at him. "No, Waco, it wasn't your fault."

They stayed beside the cool trickle all day. Early in the morning

214

they loaded up and headed out.

They had not gone far when Waco said, "Pull up! Stop the horses!"

As she obeyed, Sabrina said, "What is it?"

"I don't know. We need to check on Silas."

He pulled the stretcher down and looked at his face. "Something's gone wrong. I'm not even sure he's breathing."

Holding his breath, he put his hand over the frail chest of the old man. Silas did not move. "Heart's beating like crazy. Real fast and not at all. I don't know what that means."

"Let's get him in the shade," Sabrina said. "I'll bathe his face with some cool water."

When they got him into the shade and she had bathed his face, she whispered in anguish, "He looks awful."

"I always feel so blasted helpless. If we only had a doctor."

Sabrina turned to him. "I'm not sure a doctor would help now." She continued to bathe the old man's face.

Waco pounded his hands together in a gesture of helplessness. "Well, I guess we'll stay here until he comes to. Or maybe I'll ride on ahead and bring a doctor."

"No, don't leave us," Sabrina said. She was more afraid of the country and the predicament than she let on.

The afternoon passed slowly, the burning raw heat changing into a cooling breeze. Waco did not get far away from the wounded man. He fed the fire, and they made a pot of coffee. It was black and bitter, but it was hot and refreshing.

The hours passed, and finally a faint sound came from Silas Longstreet. Like a cat, Waco sprang to his feet, and almost as quickly Sabrina was there. "Can you hear me, Silas?" Waco asked.

At first there was no answer; then Waco saw the old eyes

slowly open. He cried out, "Silas, can you hear me? Are you in pain?"

"Water."

"Here." Quickly Sabrina knelt at his side and held the canteen. He managed to drink a little as most of the water ran down his chin.

"That was good." He stared at Waco and then at Sabrina. "Well, I guess I've torn it this time."

"You'll be all right. We'll get you to a doctor."

Silas shook his head slightly. "Can't feel nothin' except my head. Ain't that somethin'? It feels like my whole body has gone to sleep." His eyes began to droop, and they were afraid he was drifting into unconsciousness. "Sorry about your sister, missy."

"Don't worry about it." Sabrina reached up and gently brushed a lock of his white hair back from his forehead then lightly wiped his forehead with the handkerchief she had dampened. "We'll find her, Marshal, and you'll be all right."

"No, not this time," Silas whispered.

Waco glanced at Sabrina then said, "Sure you will, Silas. You've taken bullets before."

"No," Silas said, "this is it for old Silas." There was a peacefulness on his face and in his eyes. "I'm on the receivin' end this time." He looked up and said, "Don't you cry now, missy. Don't you cry for old Silas."

"I can't help it," Sabrina sobbed, biting her lip. "It was all my fault."

"I was here 'cause I wanted to be, missy. I've been on lots of hunts that I wasn't proud of, but this time I was proud. Wish we could have done it."

The dying man was silent, and finally he said, "I ain't been the man I should have been. Hard to be a Christian in this line of work. I tried to be fair and honest, but I had to handle some rough characters. That takes rough ways, don't it, Waco?"

"That's right, but everybody knows you're a good man," Waco said gently. He felt helpless kneeling beside him. He loved the old man. He had known him and respected him, and now he saw life slipping away like sand through an hourglass.

The moon crept fully across the sky; the stars twinkled and burned quietly against the velvet black curtain of night. The desert silence was broken from time to time only by the cry of a night bird or the howl of a coyote. As the old man's life flickered weakly and seemed to be fading away, Waco was struck dumb by the awesomeness of the moment.

Finally Silas roused and whispered, "One thing—one thing." He faltered, but then his voice returned stronger than before. "One thing I done a long time ago. I took Jesus as my Savior. I ain't been faithful to Him always, but I always loved Him, and I always studied His Word. And now I guess when I go to meet my God, all I'll be able to say is Jesus died for me."

The old man's voice trailed off, and then he opened his eyes. "Son, I'm going. I'd like to know if you are going to find God, and you, too, missy." His faded blue eyes closed, and for a moment there was silence.

"He's gone," Waco said angrily. "One of the best I ever knew shot by a no-good dog!"

Very carefully Sabrina lay Silas's head down, crossed his frail arms across his chest, stood to her feet, and walked away to stand in the darkness.

Waco walked over to her. "We'll leave as soon as you're ready, Sabrina. I know how hard it is. You loved that old man, didn't you?"

"Yes, I did."

"Me, too. I've known lots of men but never known one more faithful. He was the kind of man I wish I was. The cards didn't turn up that way."

Sabrina turned and looked at him, wiping the tears from her cheeks. "Not too late, Waco. Maybe this all happened so you can see what it's like. I know it's made me see. I call myself religious, but I couldn't go out to meet God like Silas did. I'd be scared to death."

Waco searched her face, his expression puzzled and questioning. He was disturbed by her confession, but he muttered, "I can tell you one thing. I'm coming back, and I'll get LeBeau. I'll put a bullet right between his eyes, and I'll get your sister."

"No, don't talk like that," Sabrina said quickly.

"Why not? It's what you want, isn't it?"

"I want Marianne, but if you turn out to be a man who does nothing but kill—why, it's all for nothing, Waco."

"I don't know any other way to get the job done."

They put Silas back in the wagon and headed for Fort Smith.

Waco did not say so, but he had been moved and shaken by the old man's death. Not just the loss of his friend but thinking of his own walk before God. . .or lack of it. He had tried to avoid thinking about things like this, but now it had happened, and he knew he would never forget that moment. "Maybe it's my time," he muttered as he rode forward into the darkness.

CHAPTER 18

The journey back to Fort Smith was a terrible time for Sabrina. The farther she and Waco went, the blacker the pall seemed to become as it hung over her heart. She still grieved terribly for her sister, but now she knew that the price that had been paid was terribly high, and it wasn't fully paid yet.

As they finally entered Fort Smith and headed down the main street, Sabrina was shocked to see her parents coming toward her. Both of them rushed forward and surrounded her, and Sabrina saw that her mother was weeping.

"You're safe," her father said, his voice tight. He held on to her, squeezing her. He was not a demonstrative man, as a rule.

"Are you all right, Sabrina?" her mother asked.

"Yes, but we didn't get Marianne back. It almost worked, but it didn't."

"Did you see her at all?"

"Yes, from a distance. It broke my heart."

Father turned to face Waco, and seeing the question in his eyes, Sabrina said, "This is Waco Smith. He's the man who set out to help us."

"I didn't do the job, Mr. Warren. Sorry."

They were interrupted then when Judge Parker came out, accompanied by Heck Thomas. The two men had waited until the family had greeted Sabrina, and then Judge Parker paused and said, "What happened, Waco?"

"We got ambushed, Judge. They got Silas."

The judge's eyes flew to the still form on the wagon. He turned to say, "Heck, take him down to Roberts. He'll take care of him."

Heck climbed up into the wagon, and it moved away.

"I'd like to hear all of the story," Judge Parker said. There was pain in his voice. "I hate to see it. Silas was a good man. Who did it?"

"Can't be sure." Waco shrugged. "Most likely LeBeau. If it wasn't him, it was one of his men. All the same."

An ominous light glowed in the eyes of the judge, and his lips drew into a thin white line. "We'll nail his casket shut." He turned to her father and said, "If I can do anything, Mr. Warren, let me know."

"I expect it's going to take you in this thing, Judge. I'll be depending on you."

Parker turned and walked away.

Her father turned back to Waco. "So you're Waco Smith. I've been looking into your character. Asking around, you know. Way I hear it you're a rangy wolf with long teeth and whiskers of metal shavings. Scare little children in the night, do you, and make the girls scream and run for cover? That's what they say. What's the other side of you?"

Waco replied, "Isn't any."

"Well, just as well you think so then." Her father had an ability to make decisions about people. When he did, he seldom changed his mind and almost never made a mistake. "I know you feel bad about your friend Marshal Longstreet."

"He was straight. Never let a man down. Never broke his word." Waco shuffled his feet then said, "Well, I don't guess you'll be needing me anymore."

"Oh no, you're not getting off that easy, Smith," her father said calmly. "We're going to get that girl of mine back, and you're the one who's going to have to do it. I can't go because I can't sit on a horse and can't shoot. So let's make some plans."

"Come on into the café. I imagine you're hungry." They all went inside, and for some time they discussed the possibilities.

Finally her father said, "There's nothing else we can do now. I know you're both dead tired. So let's eat, and then I'll get you a room here, Waco."

"No need spending your money on me, Mr. Warren."

"Got more money than I have good sense. You're going to do this job. I want you to be fresh. You go get some rest. When you get up in the morning, we're going to get together and decide what to do. I'm going to ask the good Lord for an answer, and if you know how to pray, you might do the same." He got up abruptly and walked away, her mother following him.

As soon as they were gone, Waco stared after him, saying, "He's quite a fellow, your dad. Is he always like this?"

"Yes, he's the kindest man I've ever known, but it's taken something out of him. Mother's suffering, too."

Waco's expression suddenly went grim. "The best thing would be to get twenty marshals and throw a chain around that bunch."

"But what would happen to Marianne? Could she get hurt?"

"She can get hurt any way we go about it, but you're right. The first sign of something like that, and LeBeau's going to threaten to kill her." He looked at her and saw her weariness. "You're worn out. Go to bed."

"All right, but do you think we have another chance, Waco?"

"Always a chance," he told her. "Your dad said something about praying. He's a praying man?"

"Yes, he is, and my mother, too. Do you ever pray, Waco?"

"No, wouldn't be right."

"Not right? What do you mean?"

"A fellow like me, I never think of God, never do anything for God, then out of the blue I start beggin'. Seems pretty small to me."

Sabrina chose her words carefully before she spoke. "I think all of us have to reach some point where the only thing we can do is ask God. Until we get there, we're pretty likely to stay stubborn— at least that's what I've been. I'm turning in. We have a lot facing us tomorrow."

"What do you think about this fellow Waco, Sabrina?"

"Think about him? Why, I don't know." She had come to her father's room early in the morning to talk to him, and now he said, "Well, you must have some thoughts, girl. You trusted him enough to go gallivanting around the desert with him."

"I—don't really know, Dad. He's a strange man."

Charles Warren knew this elder daughter of his. She never had acted like this about a man before, and her difficulty in speaking of Waco Smith made him want to ask more, but he decided not to press her. "Well, I've discovered one thing. He's tough as a boot heel. Far as I know he's not vicious."

"He's had a hard life," Sabrina said. "I think if he'd had more chances, he would have made something out of himself. He's very quick. Not educated, but he knows things. He's what you used to call 'country smart.'"

"He's quick-witted all right. You know, he looks kind of like a wolf. His eyes are sharp, looking right through you."

"I dread the funeral. I don't do well at funerals, but I've never lost anyone that I was close to like I was to Silas."

"Well, funerals are never happy affairs."

Waco accompanied the Warrens as they left the hotel and went to the small, weather-beaten white church. The funeral was heartbreaking.

The minister was a well-built man with greenish eyes and curly blond hair. He had known Longstreet for many years, and he preached a sermon about how wonderful it was that Silas Longstreet had stepped from one world into another one. "In an instant's time," he said, "he stepped from earth to heaven. And however many problems he had, he doesn't have them anymore."

The mourners left the church after the sermon, went out to the cemetery, and gathered around the grave. "Would you care to say a few words, Judge Parker?" the minister said.

Parker cleared his throat. "I'm not a preacher, but I am a believer, and I want to say something about Silas my friend. Well, that's what he was to me. He was more than a marshal, you know. He had a hard job, and he always did his duty, but even when he was doing the hardest things, he stood by the way of Jesus Christ. He was a faithful servant, and his greatest desire, as he told me many times, was to stand before God and to be with his faithful wife, Lottie." He hesitated and then looked around the crowd. "One of the last things Silas said to me before he went on this trip concerned some of you standing here. He was worried and concerned about your souls."

The preacher then read Scripture, and the wooden coffin was lowered.

Waco turned and left, but Sabrina caught up with him. "I've cried myself out, Waco."

"I wish I could cry. I know I'd feel better."

Waco heard someone call his name, and he turned to see Judge Parker approach him. The tall man's face was grave, and he said, "I didn't want to call any names in public, and it was you, Waco, and Miss Sabrina here, that Silas was concerned about. Before he left, he asked me to pray for you, and if I had a chance to give you an encouragement to turn to the Lord."

"How kind of you, Judge," Sabrina said. Tears filled her eyes again. "He was such a good man."

Waco escorted the Warrens back to their hotel. He began to walk a bit aimlessly down the street. He was hard hit by the death of Silas Longstreet, and his grief was mixed with a bitter, fiery anger against LeBeau. He finally encountered Heck and said, "I don't think a posse will ever catch up with LeBeau."

"No, he's pretty sharp. When he sees a bunch comin', he'll kill that girl or threaten to."

"Somebody's got to pay for Silas," Waco said, then turned and walked away without another word.

❧

Later in the day, Charles and his family were seated on the front porch of the hotel.

"There comes Waco," Sabrina said. "He has that serious look on his face. He's thought of something."

"You think so?"

"I know that look, like he could bite an iron spike in two. He's stubborn about things like that."

"Hello, Mr. Warren. Mrs. Warren. Sabrina."

"Sit down. Tell us what you've been doing, Waco," Charles said. Now he saw what Sabrina meant about the steady look on Waco Smith's face. His features seemed to be set in metal somehow. There was a dark preoccupation in his face, and Warren saw that he was a man taller than the average, heavier boned, more solid in chest and arms. His life, perhaps even the life in prison, had trimmed him lean. Exposure to rain and sun and cold had built within him a reserve of vitality. Warren knew without being told that never in his life had he known real peace. *There is a sorrow shining through this man,* Warren thought, *guiding him into strange ways.*

"I've been thinking, and I have a plan for getting your daughter back."

Instantly all three members of the family straightened up. "What is it?" Sabrina asked quickly.

"Well, we've talked about how it's hard to sneak up on LeBeau. He's ready for that. But you know if somebody was there on the inside, a member of the gang, well, he could make a chance to get your daughter away, Mr. Warren."

"Are you thinking about yourself?" Charles Warren spoke sharply.

"I can't think of anybody else," Waco replied offhandedly. "I know LeBeau. All he really knows about me is that I've had my share of run-ins with the marshal. As a matter of fact, we rode together for a while. He trusted me then."

"That will be pretty dangerous," Mr. Warren said. "If they found what you're there for, they'd kill you in a blink. You think he knows you were in that shootout when the marshal got shot?"

"No, it was dark. I didn't say anything. I was hid real good."

Sabrina said plaintively, "Waco, how could you do it? I mean, even if you were there, they'd be watching you. They'd be suspicious, wouldn't they?"

"They're suspicious of everybody, that bunch is." Waco shrugged. "But like I say, if I was right there, I could make a chance for Marianne. They'd ride out sometime and leave just a man or two with her. I might be one of those men they leave. Then I'd just take Marianne and ride out with her."

Silence fell over the group, and every face except Waco's was troubled. After a while Charles Warren said, "I've thought of everything in the world, but not one idea that would have a chance. Maybe, just maybe, this one would, but it's dangerous. I'd pay you for it though. Real well."

Waco did not act as if he had heard.

"How could the rest of us help? You can't go out alone."

"Better that way." Waco looked at Sabrina and said, "So if you agree to it, I'll pull out as soon as Gray Wolf comes in. Probably a couple more days."

"But we've got to make a better plan than this," Sabrina protested. "You propose just to disappear into the desert. You can't get in touch with us. We won't know what's happening." The vehement flow of words stopped, and her eyes narrowed.

Charles Warren knew his daughter's determined expression. "What's going on in that head of yours, girl? I know that look."

"I just had an idea, but I'll have to think about it." She got up suddenly and left without another word.

"Well, there she goes. We've seen her look like that before, haven't we, Caroline?"

"Yes, we have."

"I don't know what she'd be able to think about in this kind of a situation." Waco shook his head. "Anyway, I'll see you again before I leave."

The sun lit the tips of the eastern mountains, touching the ragged rim of the hills. Then livid red balls began to break out, spilling over the spires and peaks and rough-cut summits of the mountains far to Waco's left. He looked quickly as light flashed a thousand sharp splinters against the sky, creating a fan-shaped aurora against the upper blue. He had watched the mountains since he had left Fort Smith an hour earlier, and now hot silence covered the summit as he stared. He heard only the staccato beat of a woodpecker pattering rocking waves of noise out in the distance.

Suddenly, as if he had received a clearly spoken warning, a sense of danger overtook him. He had had this sense before, and it had saved him more than once. He drew his horse in sharply and took shelter behind a large outcropping of rocks. Dismounting, he tied his horse to a small sapling and crept back. Inching his way on his belly, he worked his way up to the top of the outcropping of rocks. He lay flat, his outline invisible to any onlookers, appearing only as a darker part of the stone. There was enough light to see, and now he heard what he thought he had heard more than once that morning, a sound of hoofbeats coming from the same direction he had traveled.

Lying as motionless as the rock beneath him, every nerve in

Waco was tingling with a familiar sensation, one he had always felt at the approach of danger. More than once since he had left Fort Smith he had sensed that someone was following, but never until now had he heard the sound of pursuit.

The hoofbeats of a single horse sounded along the trail that wound directly beneath the rock. With extreme caution, Waco moved into a crouch, his legs gathered beneath him, his boots gripping the rough surface. He could have used his gun, but he was wary of the sound of gunshots carried to other ears.

Suddenly a horse appeared with a single rider. Waco tensed his muscles. The animal slowed to a trot. Waco's nostrils flared as he tried to judge the distance. The rider would pass within five feet of him. He could easily ambush the stranger without having to arouse any unwanted attention.

When the shadowy figure appeared directly in front of him, he released himself in a powerful spring, the muscles of his legs thrusting him forcefully, his arms outstretched. Knocking the rider from the saddle, the two of them hit the ground. The horse reared and neighed shrilly, and from underneath Waco heard a muffled grunt. He pinned the rider down, and his hand went down the side of the coat looking for a weapon.

"Who are you?" he demanded. "Why are you following me?" Even as he spoke, he caught the faint wisp of delicate scent. He whirled the rider around and knocked the low-brimmed hat back, then stood in shock. "Sabrina!"

Sabrina was gasping desperately for breath. "You didn't have to do this."

Hot anger coursed through Waco, and a chill of fear gripped him over what might have happened. "You crazy, fool woman!" he shouted. "I almost shot you!" Clutching the lapels of the jacket she wore, he pulled her to her feet and bellowed, "What are you doing out here? Don't you know you could get killed? Assuming I didn't shoot you first, there are Indians and outlaws around here."

Sabrina was finally able to draw a deep breath. "I was following you."

In disgust Waco muttered, "Fool woman! You could have gotten killed." He looked up at the sky in disgust and then asked, "Are you hurt?"

"No, just the breath knocked out of me. I know you are furious with me, but I had to come. I had to. You're going into danger, and I didn't like—I mean, I didn't think it would work."

"Does your dad know you're here?"

"Yes, I left him a letter telling him what we're going to do."

"What *we're* going to do?" Waco jerked to a stop. "*We're* not going to do anything. *You're* going back to Fort Smith."

"Wait a minute. Please, Waco," she begged. "Just let me tell you my idea. Just give me a minute, please."

"Oh, for crying—" Waco blew an exasperated breath. "Well, let me go catch your horse. He's probably halfway to the next territory by now."

He turned and scrambled up the steep rock outcropping, went to his horse, and swung into the saddle. It was an easy job to catch her mount, for the little bay had not gone far before she stopped. Waco found her dawdling around nibbling at some scrub brush. On the next rise he could see the form of a rider, and he recognized Gray Wolf's familiar mount. Grabbing the reins, he went back to Sabrina. "Well, let's go riding. Gray Wolf's up ahead."

"All right," Sabrina said meekly. She swung up into the saddle.

Waco relentlessly searched the horizon. "I hope Gray Wolf doesn't shoot us. Now what's all this about?"

Eagerly Sabrina began to speak. "I thought of a way that would be better. You were going in blind without any plan at all, and I don't think it would have worked, Waco. You could have been found out. They could watch you every second. You know they're suspicious."

"Well, what's your plan, Miss Sabrina Warren?" He was still angry at her and couldn't keep it from his voice.

"All right. I thought about this a lot." She took a long, deep breath and then spoke rapidly. "You take me into the outlaws' camp. You tell LeBeau that I'm the daughter of the manager of the Western Express Company over at Durango. I was in New Orleans when LeBeau came to our house, and he won't know who I am. We never met. Anyway, they ship gold coins usually by train."

"How do you know that?"

"Some of the men were talking at the hotel. That's what made me think of it."

Waco thought then said, "What's next?"

"You tell them that you kidnapped me and you're going to make my father give you the number of the train and when it's due to leave with a big shipment of gold, a million and a half dollars or something like that."

Despite himself, Waco smiled. "Well, that ought to be enough to get Trey's attention. So how does this work?"

"We'll locate some place out here in the desert and plant a sealed bottle there. Your story will be that my father's going to send us a message about the train."

"And what then?"

"You tell him that you've got this big shipment of gold located, but you don't have a gang to hold the train up. Trey's got the gang; you know when the gold will be shipped. You see?"

"What will Marianne say when she sees you? Won't she accidentally reveal who you are just because she is excited to see her sister?"

"I think if you tell everyone who I am before she has a chance to speak that it will work. She catches on to things pretty quickly."

Waco couldn't help himself and muttered, "She didn't with LeBeau."

"She was blinded by his loving attention."

Waco had an active imagination. He rode along without speaking, the clopping of the horses' hooves on the dusty ground the only sound. The dust rose in the air, and Waco could sense the spicy aroma of sagebrush and the thousand other indefinable scents of the desert that he had grown to love. His mind toyed with what Sabrina had told him, and at length he said reluctantly, "Well, it might work. It has possibilities anyhow. Look, there's Gray Wolf. I guess I'd better ask him not to shoot us." He called out, "Gray Wolf, come in here."

"Will you try it, Waco?"

Waco was of a divided mind. It did sound like a good plan, but it would put Sabrina into danger, and the last thing in the world he needed was for her to get hurt or even killed. He said, "I'll think on it as we go. If I decide it won't work, I'll have Gray Wolf take you back."

"You can't do that," Sabrina said, and suddenly there was that streak of stubbornness that Waco had noted many times. "I'm going to help with this, and you've got to let me do it."

Waco suddenly grinned. "I probably will. Tell me, woman, was there ever a time when you didn't get your own way?"

"Yes." Sabrina smiled brilliantly. "I think it was when I was six years old. Let's go. I'm anxious to get started."

PART FOUR

CHAPTER 19

A storm seemed to hover over the land late in the afternoon. The air was filled with streaked lightning and long, booming drums of sound. The sky itself was gloomy and dark, and the wind made a howling noise to accompany it.

This kind of storm Sabrina had never seen before. She lived in a city where the buildings made barriers to cut down on the wind, and she was always indoors when the storms that they did have came. Now the thunder clapped loud and sharply because there was nothing to serve as a barrier, and the sound reverberated endlessly, rolling off into the distance. The thought came to her that this must be something like battle, cannon shots, suddenly deafening and shattering then clattering on, dying by slow degrees. The sound left her stunned, and her ears were dull. The shock seemed to rock the earth.

Lightning suddenly reached down from out of the dark clouds and seemed to fork and branch and grab the ground. The lightning flashes burned and leaped upward, crackling and vivid, dangerous it seemed to her. It almost seared the eyes, and she wanted to cover her ears when the thunder boomed and the white streaks blinded and burned.

She clung to the pommel of her saddle, and slowly the storm seemed to move on. The wind was still there, sounding like the tearing of soft silk, and then without warning rain fell fiercely in slanting lines of light. Glancing over at Waco, she saw that he sat upright in the saddle, appearing to ignore the rainstorm. The fat rain came down on both of them. She noticed it was soaking his clothing, and her own clothing was sodden and uncomfortable.

Waco walked the horses at a medium pace, but now the afternoon was so dark it could have been night. The sky was thick and furred like a blanket. To her the air seemed heavy just to breathe, and there was still the sharp, metallic taste of the storm. For the next half hour the rain did not slacken, and the wind continued to blow, sending before it, high in the sky, vast swollen cloud rollers that slashed earthward in crusted, gravel-core sheets and then in ropey gouts and then in whirling balls of wind.

"Are we ever going to stop, Waco?"

She saw Waco turn to her. He wore a wide-brimmed Stetson with the top creased and filling up with water then running down over the brim. "We're not far from where I told Gray Wolf to meet us." He gave her a slight grin. "You ready to stop and rest?"

"Who could rest in rain like this?"

"It'll stop pretty soon. Look. The clouds there, they're about blown away."

His words came true. Within half an hour the air cleared, and it smelled clean and pure, unlike the dusty smell she was accustomed to in the rolling plains of Oklahoma. She was wearing a lightweight divided skirt that had soaked through, and the rain had now run down into the tops of her boots so that she was miserably uncomfortable.

She was glad when he finally lifted his arm and said, "There's where we're going, right over there."

Sabrina lifted her gaze to follow his gesture and saw, no less than a mile away, a rising cone-shaped hill. The hills of Oklahoma were rough and irregular, but this one seemed to be shaped by human hands. "That's a funny-looking hill."

"Yes, everybody travels this way uses it for a landmark. Come along. We'll try to get some dry wood to light a fire and dry ourselves out."

They rode at a slow pace, the horses' hooves making splashes in the puddles left by the driving rain.

Waco looked around and said, "You know, this'll be pretty in a couple of days. Rain like that always brings out the wildflowers. You wouldn't know this place. The prettiest time of the year, I do think."

The rain had stopped completely, and finally they reached the foot of the cone-shaped hill. It was much larger than it seemed in the distance, and there were lower hills around the base of it.

"We've got to get dried out," Waco said. "We'll freeze to death. You got any dry clothes?"

"Yes."

"First we'll fix a fire. I'll rig something to dry these wet ones out. The blankets are pretty well soaked, too."

For the next hour they gathered firewood, such as could be located. Waco found an old tree, broke it open with his knife, and dug out the inside. "This is called punk. It burns real good. You see if you can find some small branches. Shake 'em out until they're as dry as we can get 'em. I'll look for something larger."

That was the way they built the fire. She found a double handful of small branches that seemed to be fairly dry, and he came back with several larger chunks. He laid the punk on the ground, surrounded it with the branches she had, then took a box of matches out of his saddlebag, struck one of them, and held it to the punk. The yellow tongues of fire leaped up immediately. He carefully added wood, and finally they had a large fire going. Taking his knife, he trimmed off two of the saplings that were close to the fire and tied a piece of string to each of them. "There. We'll tie the blankets on these and get them dry. It's gonna be cool tonight."

After they had hung the blankets up, he dug into his saddlebag and pulled out two cans of beans and then reached into her saddlebag and got a large chunk of bacon. Taking out his knife, he sliced it into thick portions, put the frying pan on the fire, and let it all begin to simmer.

The odor of the cooked food hit Sabrina almost like a blow. She had not known real hunger, but they'd had only a small breakfast and nothing for lunch. She watched eagerly as the bacon sizzled and the beans began to smoke.

He stirred them occasionally with his knife, adding a little water from his canteen. Finally he said, "Okay, let's eat."

"I'm starved."

"Pretty hungry myself. Here." He dumped half of the beans in a tin plate, added some of the crisp slices of bacon, then handed her the plate and a fork. He fixed his own, and Sabrina did not wait but began eating at once.

They had finished eating when suddenly a voice scared Sabrina. "Food." She looked up and saw that even Waco was startled as

Gray Wolf stalked in. "You better start givin' some warning before you walk into a camp, Gray Wolf." Waco grinned. "You might get shot."

"You white eyes can't hear anything. You don't have any ears. I want something to eat."

"Well, we have to fry up some more bacon and beans. Sit down, and while it's cookin' I'll tell you what the plan is."

Waco prepared more meat and beans and handed them to Gray Wolf on a plate. "Here. I'm gonna write some notes. I've got a jug hid where only you can find it, a glass jug with a top, but I've got to write some notes."

He took out a pencil and a small pad of paper and began to scribble. He looked up once and said, "Here's the first one. I want you to put this in the glass jug as soon as we leave."

"What does it say, Waco?" Sabrina asked.

"Says I won't pay until you give me evidence that my daughter is safe."

"I see. That'll give us some time, won't it?"

"Yes, we take that note in and prove to LeBeau that we've got a good thing going. The second one is supposed to be written from her father. It says the gold will be shipped on August 3 on the 2:20 train out of Lake City. The gold will be in a locked car, and you won't be able to get inside. I'll have one man on the train. He's short, stocky, and will be wearing a gray suit and a white hat. As soon as you turn my daughter over to him, he'll go and tell the man inside to open the door. Then he and my daughter will leave and you can get the gold." He folded it over and said, "We'll put the other one in before we leave. They'll send me out with somebody to find it, but then after we get this one out, you put the second one in."

239

Gray Wolf listened stolidly but ate furiously like he was a starved wolf indeed. He got up and said, "Sleep now." He lay curled up away from the fire, wrapping up in a blanket that looked sodden, but it did not bother him.

Sabrina looked at Waco. "You think this will work?"

"It better. It's the only chance we've got."

"What if something goes wrong?"

"Nothing we can do to make sure everything is right." He got up, felt the blankets, and said, "Well, these are nice and warm. Better wrap up, and I'll keep the fire going pretty well all night." He got up and came back with some larger wood and built the fire up so that it blazed, sending golden sparks like stars into the sky.

She sat there thinking what a strange thing it was that she would be out in a place like this with a man she ordinarily would not trust for a moment. She stared at him, but he was looking at the fire and appeared to pay no attention to her. He sat with his elbows on his knees, his head dropped forward, and his lip corners had a tough, sharp set. She watched him with the closeness that could come only of deep personal interest. Everything about him fascinated her, his expression, his mannerisms, the way his long fingers hung down. He had a man's resilience and a rough humor she had seen at times. She was relatively sure she saw in his face the marks of old wounds and a white scar from some encounter with horses, cattle, or even men.

She picked her blanket off the string, and moving back a little from the fire, she rolled up in it. She was exhausted. She continued to think about him as her eyelids grew heavy, and she knew that for some strange reason she could not explain, she was attracted to him in a way that no man had ever drawn her. *It's just that he's*

240

different, she thought wearily. And then she thought no more but fell into sleep.

🐉

It was one of those strange dreams when consciousness is there. . .but not there. Sabrina felt herself dreaming of a huge man coming toward her, his hands held out, a cruel smile on his face, and she cried out, "No, leave me alone!"

Suddenly she felt hands on her arm, and when she opened her eyes, she was instantly awake. She saw Waco bending over her. Freeing one of her hands, she clawed at his face and raked her fingernails down his cheek.

He grabbed her wrist and said, "Wake up! You're having a bad dream."

Waco released Sabrina, and she sat up at once, trembling and staring around her wildly. "I—I thought somebody was—"

"I can imagine what you thought. No wonder. Not many women would try what you're doing. You're a nervy one all right, Sabrina."

She glanced over and saw that the light from the fire was enough to reveal a bloody track down his left cheek where her fingernails had raked him. "I'm sorry," she whispered. "I didn't mean to do that."

"No problem. You just had a nightmare." He got up, went to the canteen, washed his face off, and dried it.

"I'm so sorry," she whispered again.

"Don't worry about it, Sabrina. If we get out of this with no more damage than that, I'll be happy. We got enough grub left for breakfast. I gave Gray Wolf the notes he's supposed to put in the jar and told him where to find the glass jug. Let's eat a bite, and then we'll get on our way to find Mr. Trey LeBeau."

They had made their way across the broken land until they finally came to a deep valley that sloped downward and then rose again. Up on the top of the hill was an ancient house made of unpainted wood and capped by a tin roof that was red with rust.

"Well, there she is. You sure you want to do this, Sabrina?"

Sabrina gave Waco a steady glance. "That's my sister we're talking about."

"Okay. Just remember I'm gonna have to treat you roughly. We'll be lucky if they give us a chance to say anything. I didn't make this plain to you, but LeBeau and I didn't part on the best of terms. He did me a bad turn, and I expect he knows I haven't forgotten it."

Sabrina suddenly wondered what would happen if they killed Waco. She had no other source of safety. "Be careful," she said nervously.

"Okay. They're not going to believe me. The only thing we can do is convince them that we've got a scheme that'll make them money. Money is all they care about."

She nodded, but he could see she was nervous. Suddenly he turned and said, "What would you do if I slapped you?"

"I—don't know. Nobody ever slapped me."

"Well, I may have to do that. You can't be what you have been, Sabrina. You're a young woman who's been protected all your life. Now you fear for your life. That's the role you have to play. You're not strong. You're weak, and you're scared to death of LeBeau, and I don't think that's all bad. If you're scared enough, you won't have to do much acting. You've got to convince these outlaws you're terrified."

"I'll do it, Waco. I'll do it."

"All right. Let's go." He spurred his horse, and the two of them rode down the slope. When they were halfway across the bottom of the valley, Waco said, "There they come. I told you we wouldn't sneak up on 'em."

They started up the hill, and when they were halfway up the rise, a group of men rode quickly down and framed them in by forming a half circle around them.

Waco spoke first. "Well hello, Trey. I haven't seen you in a while."

Trey LeBeau scowled. "If you've come to get even with me, you picked a bad way to do it. We'll shoot you out of the saddle if you make one move, Waco."

Waco shook his head and grinned. "No, I'll admit I had a pretty bad feeling about you. You left me in bad shape on that train robbery."

"Didn't plan it that way. It just happened."

Waco shrugged his shoulders. "Water under the bridge."

"Who's the woman? You haven't up and got married on me, have you?"

Waco laughed. "Not likely, and if I did, it wouldn't be this one. We're pretty hungry."

"You didn't accidently come this way. You knew about this hideout," LeBeau said. "What do you want?"

"I want to make you a business offer."

Suddenly LeBeau laughed. He was an attractive man and could charm anyone when he wanted to. "That's like you, Waco. Come in makin' boasts that you can't carry out. What kind of business could you throw my way?"

"Not just you. All you fellows." Waco leaned back in his saddle,

243

shoved his hat to the back of his head, then said, "I've got a good thing that I need help with."

"What kind of help do you need?" LeBeau demanded.

Al Munro, Trey's most trusted man, suddenly drew his .45. "I say kill him here. He's just trouble."

"I guess you just don't want to be rich, Al," Waco said. He looked around and saw Zeno Shaw, Rufo Aznar, and two men he had not met. Both of them were large men, and one of them appeared to be half-Apache. The other one was a strong-looking man who watched Waco steadily.

It was Rufo Aznar, a trim man with an olive compexion and dark eyes and a terrible scar on the right side of his face, who said, "Hold on, Al. Maybe you don't want to be rich, but I do. We ain't had no luck lately."

"I heard about that train, Trey," Waco said. "Didn't you get rich off of that?"

All the men suddenly looked disgusted, and LeBeau said, "We got some gold watches and a few wallets, but there wasn't any gold."

"Why don't you invite us in, and we can make some medicine together."

"Take his gun, Al." Al spurred his horse forward. He reached out and plucked Waco's gun and stuck it in his belt.

"Okay. We go up to the house, and we'll listen to what you have to say."

Waco and Sabrina had both been worried about Marianne. The sight of her sister might be the end of the plot. If she called out Sabrina's name and showed that she knew her, there was little chance for any of them to get out of this alive.

As they rode up to the house and dismounted, Waco saw a

young woman come out and knew this was Marianne. He held his breath, but after one glimpse at him and then one no longer at Sabrina, she just stood and watched.

"Get off that horse, Helen!" Waco said. Sabrina/Helen did not move, and he reached up, grabbed her by the arm, and cuffed her. "Didn't you hear what I said?"

"You're not treating her like a lady friend," Trey said. "Who is she?"

"That's part of the business deal, but we need something to eat."

"All right."

"But I've had to take a quirt to her once or twice."

"Take it easy, Waco," Al said suddenly. "If you really got somethin' that'll make us rich, let's have it."

"After we eat."

"We'll have to cook somethin' up." At that moment, a woman left the house and walked toward them. She stopped dead still and stared at them. "What are you doing here, Waco?"

"Hello, Callie. Maybe just came to visit you."

"You're a liar! Who's the woman?"

"We'll talk business after we have a little something to eat."

Trey watched the scene between Calandra Montevado and Waco with obvious interest.

Waco knew Callie had been Trey's woman until he had come along and she had turned from Trey.

Trey's eyes narrowed. "We'll get something to eat, and then we'll know what you're here about—and whether we let you live or not."

Waco laughed and seemed totally relaxed. "You love money too much to let anything happen to me. I'm your one shot at getting you enough money where you can live like you want to instead of out here in this hole."

After they entered the house, two of the men started stirring up the fire, and Marianne began cooking a meal.

"That's a good roast," Zeno Shaw said. He was over six two, a brute of a man, with scars of fights of the past on his face. "Got some taters left over here, too."

Soon Waco started to sit down and said roughly, "Sit over there, woman." He was glad to see Sabrina had somehow, although she had not spoken a word, showed her fear. It wasn't all acting he knew. She was afraid. He reached out, grabbed her by the arm, and threw her into a chair. "Eat something."

"I'm not hungry."

He reached out and grabbed her by the hair and said, "Eat something or I'll shove it down your throat."

Callie was watching all this. "She's not your woman, I take it."

"Well, in a way she is. I'll introduce you to her after we eat."

The cabin seemed to be charged with electricity. Only Waco seemed to be at ease. He kept slicing pieces of the roast off and eating it with great enjoyment. "Your woman is a good cook, Trey. We've been eatin' prairie dog lately. About ready to eat a hawk."

Calandra was watching Sabrina carefully. "She's scared to death of you. What are you doing with her? Did you steal her?"

"Now Callie, don't be hasty. This is going to be a long night. I've got lots of business to talk to you."

They ate, Waco eating heartily and Sabrina picking at her food.

As soon as Waco was finished, Callie sat down across from him and said, "All right. What's all this about, Waco?"

"He's threatenin' to make us rich," LeBeau said. "I think he's just a lot of hot air."

"You won't think so after I tell you the whole story. Let me have some of that coffee, and I'll lay it out for you." Waco smiled as if he had not a care, but he saw the hatred in Trey LeBeau's eyes, and understood that with one false move he and Sabrina would be doomed.

CHAPTER 20

From the moment she had faced Trey LeBeau, Sabrina had been truly afraid. It had occurred to her for the first time that since LeBeau had been in her home, he might well have seen one of the pictures of her, for there were many in the house. But when he stared at her with no sign of recognition, she suddenly realized, *I don't look much like I did then.* Indeed, the trip had worn her down and her hair was now stringy and she looked very little like the Sabrina Warren who had come on this quest.

She noted that Waco, after one glance at Marianne, paid her little attention, but finally he put his gaze on Marianne and said, "Well, Trey, I see you got yourself a new lady friend." His glance went to Callie, who merely smiled at him. "It looks like you got your time beat, Callie."

"No, nothin' like that, Waco. I picked this little girl up back East. She's got a rich daddy, and you don't have to talk about makin' me rich. As soon as I get tired of her, I'll sell her back to him. I expect he'd pay a pretty good ransom for you, wouldn't he, honey?"

He had spoken to Marianne, who refused to answer.

"Not very talkative, is she, Trey? Well, this one of mine's not either."

"You two aren't on a honeymoon. I can see that, Waco."

"Why, it is kind of a honeymoon. She's not used to the idea yet, but she'll be fine when she is."

Trey was watching Waco carefully and said, "Well, this ain't exactly a hotel for honeymooners, Waco. Was you thinkin' to stay the night?"

Waco drank from his coffee and leaned back and nodded with sleepy satisfaction. "Good meal. Thought we might, Trey."

LeBeau said, "You're losin' your bedroom tonight, Breed. We'll let the lovebirds have it. You go sleep in the shack."

All the outlaws were waiting to find out what Waco was up to, and finally Trey said, "Well, what's this all about?"

"So you didn't get rich on that train robbery?"

"No, I've told you we didn't. It's not my fault."

"We wasted our time. It wasn't worth the trouble," Zeno Shaw said. He stared at Trey with discontent in his eyes.

"I can't guarantee what a train's carrying," LeBeau snapped.

Waco studied Callie carefully and openly.

She held his gaze and said, "What's on your mind, Waco? We've got no secrets here."

Waco said, "All right with me. How about you, Trey?"

"Just say what you got on your mind," Trey said. "For all I know Parker might have got you out of jail to be one of his marshals. You might be wearing a badge under that vest."

"No badge," he said, pulling his vest away from his shirt, "but if Parker wants me to work for him, that shows you what a good cover I have, doesn't it? I've got a job coming up, Trey, but I'm not sure your bunch is able to handle it. You're down a few men, aren't you?"

"We're able to handle any job you come up with, Waco. What is it? Spit it out."

"All right." Taking a deep breath, he said, "Here it is. My lady friend is Miss Helen Richards. Her father's name is Charles R. Richards. That mean anything to you?"

Nobody spoke, and Waco grinned. "Mr. Richards is in charge of the Express Company over in Durango."

Suddenly everybody in the room grew alert. They obviously were well aware that the Western Express handled large amounts of gold and silver. There were no mines where the offices were located, but they received shipments of gold and silver coins from the Treasury in Washington and transported them over different parts of the country.

Al Munro's eyes gleamed. "Western Express! You're not dumb enough to hold that place up I hope, Waco. They've got enough guards to furnish an army."

Waco grinned at Munro. "No, nothing like that. What I've got in mind is helping the 'transport' end of things."

Trey said impatiently, "You know every train robber in the country has tried that, Waco, but they're clever. They ship out empty boxes one day. Then boxes loaded with rocks the next day, and any day they might or might not ship the real stuff. Anything to throw us off. Nobody ever knows what or when."

Waco leaned back in his chair and ran his fingers through his dark hair. He glanced over at Trey and said, "That's right. We don't know—but Helen's dad knows." The silent tension built up in the room. "Her dad's in charge of the shipping. He always knows."

An electrifying current went around the room. Rufo Aznar

said, "Why, if we knew which train to hit, we'd all be rich."

"Shut up, Rufo!" Trey snapped. He leaned forward and stared at Waco. He was silent for a moment then stared at Sabrina. "That's right, is it? Your daddy runs that express?"

Sabrina said, "Yes, but he'll never tell you about the shipments. Men have tried to get at him before. You wouldn't believe how much money he's been offered just to tell them when things are shipped."

Waco laughed broadly, his eyes gleaming in the twilight. "But they didn't have his only daughter held in Indian Territory away from the law, did they, honey?"

"He'll see you hanged if you do this!" Sabrina muttered. "You won't get away with it."

An excited babble rippled through the room, everybody talking at once. Sabrina watched them. Each one of them was visibly excited. *This is going to work,* she thought triumphantly. *They're going for the bait.*

Suddenly Callie's voice commanded the attention of the room. "And how do we know all this is true?" Her dark eyes were a feline glow in the lantern light, reflecting its yellow flame. Coolly she stared at Waco and Sabrina. "These two come out of nowhere and have this big scheme, and I don't believe a word of it."

LeBeau gave Callie a thoughtful glance. "You may be right," he said. He turned back to Waco. "You've never done anything like this before. You may have done a little holdup work, but you've always been a lone wolf."

"What have I got to show for it?" Waco shrugged. "A horse, a gun, and a blanket." Every eye in the room was locked on him. This was the moment in which they would stand or fall. His voice grew rock hard as he said to LeBeau, "I'm not proposing to join

251

you, Trey." Looking around scornfully, he went on. "I don't want to live in a shack out in the desert somewhere running from Parker's marshals. Not me! I'm gonna do one job, make a pile, and buy a ranch somewhere far out of this forsaken territory." There was a loaded silence in the room, and Waco banged his cup down on the table and told the group curtly, "But I can see you're more interested in listening to Callie than anything I've got to say." He rose to his feet and said, "Come on, honey, let's get a little sleep. Tomorrow we'll pull out of here and see if we can find somebody else. I've been thinking about Jack Chambliss."

"Jack could do the job," Callie said.

Callie's words infuriated Trey.

"We can do anything Chambliss can do!" LeBeau snapped. "But we don't need you, Waco."

LeBeau was on the verge of pulling his gun and shooting Waco, at least so it seemed, but Al Munro said, "Wait a minute. We can do this job, Trey."

"All right, put these two in the room, Al."

Munro led them to a room at the end of the hall. "You two can stay in here tonight."

"Get in there, Helen!" Waco said and pushed Sabrina through the door. He shut it at once and took a deep breath. "Well, all right so far."

"Oh, Waco," Sabrina whispered. She was feeling weak, and she put her hand on his arm. "I was so scared."

"That's good. I wanted you to look scared."

"I think they all believed you. . .except that woman." She watched his face as she mentioned Callie, but Waco's expression didn't change. She thought for a moment then said, "I saw how she stared at you. She hates you."

"How do you know that?"

"A woman doesn't have that kind of animosity unless she loved a man once."

Waco ran his hand through his hair and wiped his forehead. "We were friends at one time," he said briefly.

From that one sentence Sabrina knew what she had suspected was true. *Waco and Callie were lovers. That's why she hates him. He must have walked off and left her or done something awful.* Bluntly she asked him, "So you were lovers?"

Strangely enough, her words seemed to embarrass Waco. He looked into her eyes and asked, "Why do you care, Sabrina?"

"I don't care." Even as she said it, she realized that she *did* care. Resolutely she thrust the thought away from her. "But she was in love with you once. You may have to use her to get us out of here."

"No."

The refusal was so flat that Sabrina knew instantly there was no use in pursuing it. She was embarrassed by the scene and agitated by her own show of jealousy when faced with Waco and Callie's relationship. Confused and conflicting thoughts crowded her mind. She said, "Well, Marianne's here and she's all right, so we have a chance."

Waco breathed out heavily. "Yeah, we got a chance, and I don't want to mess this up, but it's going to be tough. They're gonna be watching us like hawks no matter what we do." He pushed himself away from the door, walked to the window, and looked outside. "They've already put a man out front. We've got to be careful because they could sneak up here. He's probably watching through this window, and someone will be watching it all night. They're not about to let us leave here unexpectedly."

Sabrina's shoulders drooped. The hard ride and the immense

strain of the past few hours had begun to affect her.

Waco glanced at the single bed. "You take the bed, and I'll take the floor." It was early, and they were both tired. "I'll blow out the light, and you can get undressed."

"I'll just sleep in my clothes," she said hastily.

Waco didn't reply. Finding a blanket in the gear they had brought in, he made a bed beneath the window, took off his boots, and started to lie down. Instead he rose, walked over to the single chair in the room, carried it to the door, and shoved it underneath the doorknob. "Somebody might want to come bustin' in here, Sabrina. They'd expect us to be in the same bed."

Sabrina didn't reply as Waco lay down. For days now she and this man had slept within five feet of each other beside a campfire, but somehow being in a bedroom with him was totally different. She was apprehensive, almost afraid. She lay down on the bed, pulled the blanket over her stiffly, and lay unmoving and tense until she heard his even breathing. Then she relaxed.

Sleep didn't come all at once though. Sabrina lay quietly thinking of the strangeness of it all. Her other life, her life of teas and parties and balls and fancy dresses—those all seemed a million miles away. With a mental start, Sabrina realized that she could not easily go back to such a life. It would seem so tame after all she had gone through.

She began to worry about the next day, when suddenly Waco's voice came quietly. "I'm glad Marianne's all right."

"Yes, I was afraid. She's going to have a hard time even when we get her away. She's ashamed of what she's done."

"Never easy to get over your bad deeds."

His words intrigued Sabrina. "You're speaking from experience."

Waco didn't answer her for a few moments, but finally he

said, "We're not on this earth here for very long, and sometimes I think it doesn't mean anything. But then once in a while I meet someone who's found more meaning and purpose than I ever thought about. Like Silas." His voice grew soft as he spoke of the marshal. "I've thought a lot about him. He was a good man, and his life meant something."

"He did die well, didn't he? I've admired him very much." When Waco didn't reply, Sabrina turned over and allowed sleep to claim her.

"All right. Tell us how this thing works. How are we supposed to know when that train with the gold moves?" LeBeau said.

They were all in the main room, even Sabrina and Marianne.

Waco said, "All right. Here's the way it will work. I've got a man out there, an in-between sort of fella. But I don't know about your bunch. It's going to take all of us. What about these women?"

"I'll take care of mine. You take care of yours."

"Who will take care of me?" Callie grinned like a cat.

"Here's what'll happen," Waco said. "I got us a man between me and Helen's father. As soon as her father finds out she's all right, he'll send the information about the shipping."

"So he's got to have proof that she's alive. How will we do that?" Trey demanded.

"All she has to do is write her dad a letter. Tell him to send the money. That she's been treated good."

They were talking for some time about the plan, and finally Trey said, "How are you going to contact him? You're stayin' with us until we get the job done."

Waco leaned back and said, "Well, Trey, if I told you everything I know, you might not need me. So I'm not telling you, but I've got a meeting place and I'm not telling who he is, but I will tell you this. When I get the lowdown, which is what train to hit, I know the place to hit it."

"They're bound to be carrying plenty of guards with a big shipment," Al Munro said.

"Nope. That's one thing I found out about Richards. They don't send out a whole lot more guards when they ship the real stuff. They figure it'd be sort of like posting a sign saying that gold and silver are on this here train." Amused laughter ran through the room. "Sometimes they don't even send out one guard more than usual, and that's what's going to happen this time."

No one said anything for a time. Waco was leaning back in his chair, and he dropped it with a crash and slapped the table. "Come on, Trey, look at it! No guards, lots of money, one train. Hit it, we're gone, and that's the last you'll see of me. Any of you."

A thick silence fell over the room, and Waco knew they were greedily weighing the possibility. His eyes surveyed all their faces. "What do you think, Al?"

"I put no trust in any man," Munro said. "But I think Waco's hungry enough to pull it off." Then his voice changed slightly, and his heavy lips twisted with cruelty. "We're going to watch you, Waco. You're going to be in the crosshairs at all times. One thing goes wrong, you get a bullet in the brain. You got that?"

"Sure, Al. I know that. But don't you forget. I want to be rich more than any of the rest of you." His tone couldn't have been milder, but every person there recognized the seriousness in his words.

"All right. Let's do it then," Rufo Aznar said. "I'm tired of penny ante stuff."

LeBeau said, "All right, but one thing more. I get some cash out of this girl. I'll get word to her man to lay his hands on some cash and give it to me or I'll send her head in a sack."

"That'd be hard to do two things at once," Zeno Shaw said.

But Trey was adamant. "I'll send a telegram to her old man. Tell him to have the cash in Fort Smith and we'll hand the girl over."

Finally LeBeau turned to Callie. "You've been awful quiet, Callie. What about it? You for it?"

"It's all right with me. I think it'll work."

"When's this message coming?" Callie asked.

"I got a spot staked out. I'll have to ride out and check it every day until we hear from the old man."

"You ain't goin' alone," Trey said.

"No, he's not. I'll go with him," Callie said.

"I don't think I trust you either."

"Shut up, Trey," Callie shot back. "You do your job, and I'll do mine. That's the way it'll be."

"Might as well ride out today," Waco said. "I don't think it'll be there, but I don't want to risk missing it." He nodded to Callie. "Whenever you're ready, Callie, we'll take a little ride."

"All right, Waco."

The two were ready at once, and as they left, Marianne came up to Sabrina and said, "I can wash your clothes if you need some help."

"Oh, thank you," she said.

As soon as they were alone, Marianne fell against the other woman, crying out, "Oh, Sabrina, I'm so glad you're here! But what are you doing here?"

Sabrina was holding on to Marianne and felt the tears come to her eyes. She was so glad to see her sister, and there was at least a hope of getting her away. "We've come to get you out of here."

"Who is that man that's with you? He looks like an outlaw himself."

"His name is Waco Smith. He's been made into one of the marshals, and his job is to get you out of here."

"Just one man?"

"We have another man outside there, and we've got a scheme. But you and I, we're going to have to be sure that they don't suspect that we're sisters."

"I don't see how anybody can do it, especially with that man. He looks so rough."

"He's a good man, Marianne. He's been—well, a little wild, you might say, but now he's risking his life to get us out of here."

"I'll have to lock you in, but I've got to go clean up. Why don't you lie down and get some rest, and we'll have time to talk tonight."

Marianne clung to Sabrina fiercely and began crying. "I'm so glad to see you, sister. I thought I was lost forever."

"No, we're going to get out of this. You lie down now."

Marianne said, "I'm afraid. What if Waco goes away and doesn't come back?"

"He'll be back," Sabrina said briefly.

Looking sharply at Sabrina, Marianne said, "Well, who is he? What kind of man is he? The others talked about him and Callie being sweethearts once."

The words cut Sabrina much deeper than she cared to admit, but she gave no answer.

"I suppose he's just another hired killer like everybody else around here," Marianne said bitterly.

"A man should learn to fight or let him put skirts about his knees," Sabrina rasped, trying to hold her anger in check.

Marianne had never seen her sister so passionately defend a man. "I'm sorry, Sabrina. I didn't mean it, but I'm so scared."

Sabrina closed her eyes and forced herself to calm down. Finally she said, "Don't worry about Waco. He's a hard man, and in this situation I think that's a good thing. He will get us out of here. He will." She stared at the two riders disappearing into the distant shimmer of the heat on the horizon. "I don't know what he'll do after that, but I know he'll never quit until he does what he sets out to do." They continued washing, and all Sabrina could think of was the long ride that Callie and Waco would take and what that ride would entail.

᷎

Waco said little as he and Callie rode steadily east, but her presence had a powerful influence on him. From time to time he turned slightly, and vivid memories came trooping through his mind.

She broke the silence, saying, "Well, Waco, do you ever think of when we were together?"

Waco was startled and could not come up with an answer. He was shocked when Callie laughed, and when he turned he saw that her dark eyes were alive with an emotion he couldn't name.

"It's an easy question," Callie said and waited for an answer.

"Sure I do," Waco said slowly and faced her as he added, "but it's ancient history, Callie."

"Is it?"

"I don't think people can go back where they once were."

"You're wrong about that."

Her blatant reply startled Waco, and he demanded, "Would you want to go back to that time?"

"It was a good time, wasn't it?"

For a moment he was silent and confused, then he said slowly, "I remember the good times."

"We could go there again."

"You're Trey's woman."

"I'm not his woman. I'll never belong to any man as I did to you."

The cry of a far-off bird came to Waco, and he could not remember a time when he'd been so shaken. He had never once thought that he might find what he'd once had with Callie, and now she was offering him herself.

"I don't think it would be smart to go back to that time—not with this job in front of us. It's going to be tough, and no matter what you say, Trey won't let anything of his go."

"Maybe he is, but you're a strong man, Waco. I'm a strong woman." She kneed her mare, and when they were close, she put her hand out and gipped his arm. Her touch startled Waco, and she whispered huskily, "We had something once—and we can have it again. . . ."

At that moment, Waco Smith realized he was not as strong as he had thought himself to be. *She can stir me up—and I don't know if I can say no to her!*

CHAPTER 21

Waco Smith had always considered himself to be basically a simple man able to make up his mind quickly and then follow through. But something had happened to change all that when Callie had urged him to pick up their love affair where it had left off years ago. It had caught Waco off guard so that he spent long hours simply walking alone out on the territory surrounding the hideout house, and he did so now this Tuesday afternoon. He glanced up and saw the horizon fading as the late afternoon sun seemed to be melting into the earth. He had always had an appreciation for the world of nature and had taken an unspoken delight in the sky, the woods, the animals and birds, but now they seemed to give him no pleasure.

"Waco, just a minute."

Quickly Waco turned to see Sabrina, who came walking toward him. She had some wet clothes in her arms, and she was headed for the wire stretched between two posts to dry them out. Waco glanced toward the house and saw that Breed Marcos, the Apache halfbreed, was watching carefully. Turning quickly, he walked toward her and said, "Be careful, Sabrina, you're being watched."

"I know. I'm always being watched. I feel like I'm an animal in the zoo."

"You better start putting those clothes on the line or they'll send somebody out here to see what we're talking about."

"All right. I will."

Waco stood back, ignoring the hideout and Breed watching from the porch. He knew what she was talking about, for he himself had been under surveillance ever since he had arrived with her at LeBeau's house. He turned so that he seemed to be facing away from Sabrina and said softly, "Are you all right?"

"Yes. I'm just afraid."

"I guess we all get afraid of some things."

She was pinning a dress on the line and she didn't turn, but after a moment she said, "I wouldn't think you'd be afraid of anything."

"You'd be wrong there."

"What are you afraid of?"

The question caught Waco off guard, and for a moment he had to stop and think. "Lots of things. Afraid of growing old and nobody with me, nobody to take care of me. Afraid of getting crippled so that I can't take care of myself."

"Are you afraid of death?"

"Well, not so much death. I face that pretty often. It's what comes after death that scares me."

She continued to hang up the clothes, and finally she picked up a petticoat and, hanging it on the line, said, "You're worried about your soul, then?"

"I never put it like that, but I guess that's right."

"I know what you mean, Waco. I've been so selfish all my life, and now that I've hit something really hard, I just don't know how to handle it."

"We have to take it as it comes, Sabrina."

Suddenly her voice changed, and he turned to face her fully. He had always considered her a weak woman, softened by the life that she had led, but now he saw that there was something different. In her eyes and lips lay flexible capacities carefully controlled as though she was determined to do something, and Waco felt he had a view of the undertow of her spirit. For that moment she forgot her reserve and was watching him with the fully open eyes of a woman momentarily and completely engrossed. The lines of physical fatigue showed in her face, and the hard usage that she had taken had made her shoulders sag, but he saw in her, despite this, a fire burning that had not been there when he had first met her. Her skin was lightly browned by the sun, and her lips were broad and on the edge of being full, the lips of a giving woman but not a pliant woman. He asked her, "Sabrina, have you ever been truly in love with someone?"

"No," she said, and bitterness tinged her voice. "I've been in love with myself. I didn't know it until I lost Marianne. What about you?"

"I thought I was once."

"With Callie?"

"Her and the other woman who betrayed me. I guess I don't learn very quickly."

"You have a distrust for women. Two women were dishonest, and you're afraid to trust any other woman."

"I guess you're right. I don't like to admit it."

"Do you think you'll ever find a woman you can trust?"

"I don't know, Sabrina. Sometimes when I'm riding along and

dark is falling, I pass a cabin, and I can see the yellow glow from the fire inside. Sometimes I can see people laughing, can hear them, and it never fails to make me sad."

"Why should that make you sad?"

He shifted his shoulders, and his lips tightened. "Because they have everything, those people, and I don't really have anything."

She continued to hang clothes, and finally she asked, "But you thought you loved Callie."

"It wasn't the kind of love you could build a marriage on."

"What kind of woman would that take?"

Waco suddenly had a moment's insight. "I thought it might be you, Sabrina."

His words startled her, and she exclaimed, "Me? Why, we're as different as night and day!"

"I guess so, but still, who can explain what a man sees when he looks at a woman? I guess," he said slowly, "every man carries a picture in his head or in his heart or wherever things like that take place, and they carry a picture of a woman, the one they want. But I thought that sometimes it was a picture built up of many women, not just one."

"Well, that's not very fair for the woman a man finally gets. How can a woman be everything a man wants?"

Suddenly Waco smiled. It made him look much younger. "I guess when a man finally gets the right woman, he sees all the things in her that he wants to see."

"That's a whole lot like saying that love is blind."

"No. I'd say it's like a very strong light. It makes a man see things he otherwise wouldn't. There's some sweetness, some honesty in the woman and things that he always admired, and he suddenly realizes that this is the woman he's been looking for, although he didn't know it."

"Until she hurts him."

"That goes with love, I guess."

"Even people in love hurt each other, don't they?" She hung up the last garment and now picked up the basket and said, "I'd better get inside."

He said suddenly, "I never would have imagined that you had thoughts like this, Sabrina, and I guess I embarrassed you by telling you that I have feelings for you that I never thought I'd have for any other woman."

Sabrina was shocked. She had felt the masculinity of Waco Smith. It was the kind of strength that a woman loved to see, but she had not featured herself being in love with this man so different from herself. "I guess we're both surprised then."

Suddenly he caught a glimpse of movement on the porch and saw that Trey and Callie had come outside. "They're watching us," he said. "I'm going to have to treat you rough. I'm going to have to push you around. Act like you're hurt. I'm going to tell 'em you won't write the letter."

"Go ahead. Do what you have to."

Without looking toward the two who were approaching suddenly, Waco reached out and seized Sabrina by the arm. He saw her eyes open wide, and he swung his open hand and slapped her on the face. She cried out slightly, and then he slapped her again. "This has to look good," he muttered.

"What's going on here?" Trey asked.

"This woman's getting some kind of religion. She said she wasn't gonna write that letter, but she knows now she will or she'll be sorry."

"I'd hate to have you mad at me." Callie laughed. "Of course, if you slapped me around, I'd shoot you."

Waco suddenly grinned. "I expect you would. Well, let's get that note written, and I'll take it."

"I'll go with you."

Waco shrugged. "That's fine." He went inside and found a piece of paper, had Sabrina write a note simply saying to her imaginary father that she was well but that she was frightened and needed him.

Waco took the note and shoved it in his shirt pocket and stepped outside. "I've got it."

"I'm going with you this time," Trey said.

"You stay out of it," Callie said. "We'll do what we've been doing."

Temper flared in Trey LeBeau's features, and he glared at her, but she merely laughed at him. "We don't need you along. I'm not your woman anyway."

"You will be when we get out of this," Trey said.

"Come on. Let's go get this note in the bottle, Waco."

The two left at once, and as they were riding out, Waco said, "You're going to go too far with LeBeau. He's capable of hurting any woman bad."

"He'll never touch me. He knows I'd kill him if he did."

They rode slowly, and she asked finally as they approached the site of the bottle, "Did you think about what I said?"

He was silent for a while, and then he said, "You know, a friend of mine was kind of a scholar. He liked to read the old Greek writing. He read about one Greek philosopher that said you can't step in the same river twice."

"I don't understand that."

"Well, it means the rivers are moving all the time. You step in them and ten minutes later that river's gone and another's come. I always took it to mean you couldn't start all over again with anything that's dead."

She pulled her mount up close, reached out, and grabbed him, and he leaned toward her. She kissed him and laughed. "I'll show you what's dead! What we had wouldn't die. It may have been asleep for a while, but it'll come back."

The two found the bottle, and she watched as he put the note in it. He concealed it and said, "Now we just have to wait until we get the information we need on that train."

"Let's take our time going back. That place depresses me."

During the ride back, more than once, Waco was aware that she was trying him out. She made several allusions to the love they had had, and despite himself he had memories, sharp and keen, of how she had come to him in a way that a woman comes to a man that he never forgets. He tried to shake it out of his mind, but he found himself instead thinking of Sabrina and their brief conversation. *I don't see any good in that,* he thought. *No matter what I try to do she's above me.*

🐍

Judge Parker looked up, for the door to his office had opened with no knock and Charles Warren and Frank Morgan entered. "We need to talk to you, Judge."

"Sit down," Parker said at once.

"This is Frank Morgan."

The judge saw that the young man looked soft but had a determined look in his eye. "Sit down and we'll talk about this thing."

For the next half hour, Parker managed to get both men

calmed down as he told them of the plan he was working out with Waco and Sabrina. "We've been exchanging notes. Waco and Miss Sabrina have convinced LeBeau that she's the daughter of one of the officials of the railroad in charge of shipments of gold and silver. They've told him that they can find out which train the shipment will be on and that there'll be no guard."

"You think they'll believe that?" Frank Morgan demanded.

"Depends on how good a front Sabrina and Waco put up."

"So what we're doing now is waiting on a signal," Warren pressed.

"Well, it's farther along than that. There's an Indian that's been helping them out. He brought this in yesterday." He opened his desk drawer and pulled out a piece of paper much folded.

Warren took it and stared at it. It said:

Daddy,

These men are going to kill me if you don't help me. I'm all right now and they say they'll let me go, but you have to tell them the time for the next gold shipment. Please help me.

Helen

"There won't be any gold on that train. Instead of that, we'll have every marshal, and I'll hire some new posse members. We'll load that train up with men who are good with guns. We'll stop Trey LeBeau's clock."

"I'm going along," Warren said.

Instantly Frank Morgan nodded. "Get me a gun. I'll go, too."

"Could be dangerous. You could get shot."

"I don't care. I've got my wife here, and I'm staying until we get both our girls back. If I get shot in trying it, it won't bother me.

I've got to do what I can for my family."

Parker studied the two and finally said, "Well, we can always use more guns. I've already written the answer and sent it by way of the Indian." Parker studied the two men and said gently, "I'm sorry for your trouble, but I'm hopeful that it will come out all right."

❦

LeBeau looked up and saw Callie and Waco coming back. It had been three days, and they had sent the letter from Helen, and now he got up and said, "Well, at last here they come. They better have somethin'.

"Sometimes I think this whole thing is gonna blow up in our face," Al Munro said. "There's something I don't like about it."

"The one thing I don't like about it is Waco Smith." The anger and rage had been building up in LeBeau, and when the two got off and entered, he said, "What did you find?"

"Answer to the letter." Waco handed him the bottle with the paper inside. "Won't need to be any more letters passed."

Taking the bottle at once, LeBeau fished the paper out. He read it out loud. " 'Two ten out of Lake City will be carrying a huge shipment of gold. There will be no guards on the train. There will be one man on board wearing a blue suit. You give my daughter to him. He will get you into the gold car. They'll open the door for him. Please let my daughter go.' "

"I know that train," Waco said. "And I know a good place to hold it up. There's some sharp bends in the road there, so they can't make much speed."

"What are we going to do with these women while we're doing the job?" Al Munro demanded.

"I know what we can do with them," Waco said. "I don't want

any murders in this thing. None of you need it either. There's a deserted cabin not far from where this hook in the railroad is that makes the train slow down. It's less than a mile away. It's empty now. We can lock 'em in there while we're doing the job and then we can turn 'em loose."

Trey was staring hard at Waco, but finally he nodded his head slowly. "All right. That's the way we'll play it, but I'm telling you, Waco, I'll kill you if you even blink."

"I won't be blinkin'. I want this gold as much as you do—more, I think."

"Well," Trey LeBeau said, "the note says it'll be in two days. We'd better get everything ready and be on the spot."

❧

The gang spent most of the time getting their guns oiled and polished and packing ammunition. There was a sense of expectation about it, and Rufo Aznar moved close to Waco saying, "Don't think you can pull anything on us, Smith. You're tough, but you're not tougher than the whole band here. Everybody will be watching you."

"They better be watching that train."

"We can do both at the same time."

❧

The hours crept by. Marianne and Sabrina found a few moments alone to talk in whispers about what was going to happen.

"I'm afraid it won't work," Marianne said. "Even if it did, they may just kill us. These men are all murderers."

"Waco won't let them do that."

"He's only one man."

"I know, but he can do things. I have confidence in him."

Marianne stared at Sabrina. "Why do you feel like that about him? You've known him only a short time, and you know he's a criminal."

Sabrina could not answer. She dropped her head and said, "I don't know, but there's something in him that I trust."

The next day as they were pulling out, Waco was saddling Sabrina's horse. When she came to mount up, he whispered, "There's a way to get out of that house. If you can get out, fine. There's some woods over to the north of it. I'll come for you if I make it."

"Don't take any chances."

He suddenly grinned. "Life is a chance, but if I don't make it, I want to tell you, Sabrina, I've never felt about any woman like I have about you. I know it's useless. We have no future together, but if things were different, I could see it would be great for me."

"Maybe for me, too. Oh, be careful!"

As the band rode off, Callie rode up to ride beside Waco. "We're going to get that gold," she said quietly so that it could not be heard over the sound of the horses' hooves hitting the hard ground. "I mean we'll get all of it."

"Your plan could get us both killed."

"No. We'll get that gold. We'll leave, and we'll find a place where we can spend the rest of our lives doing whatever we want. We'll have a new life." She suddenly looked very young, and there was something like joy in her face that Waco had never seen. "I can change, Waco."

"I guess you can. I guess any of us can."

"I'm tired of being what I've been all my life, a bad woman."

She laughed and said, "Wouldn't it be something if we got married and had a house full of kids? Can you see me changing diapers?"

"Can you see me doing that?" He grinned and said, "Both of us need a change, but we'll have to be careful. If LeBeau even suspects either one of us, he'll kill us in cold blood. Stick close after we get the gold."

"We don't have much of a plan."

"Impossible to plan for a thing like this." Waco felt a sharp pang as he realized that he was being as deceitful to this woman as a woman had once been to him. He knew he did not love Callie, never had really, but when he saw the joy in her eyes, he felt like a traitor. He said no more. The troop headed steadily toward the site of the holdup.

CHAPTER 22

The room was crowded, but Heck Thomas, the chief marshal, wanted to see all of the men he had chosen at one time. He looked over the room and saw that at least four regular marshals were there plus six more that he had recruited. These were men who he knew were tough and could shoot and would not hesitate in a fight to take Trey LeBeau and his bunch down.

Thomas started to speak, and then his eyes fell on Charles Warren and Frank Morgan. They stood out blatantly against the other members of the posse. Both were wearing suits and looked like what they were, businessmen ready to go to work in an office but hardly fitted to go up against hardened, cold-blooded outlaws who would kill them without a second thought.

Shaking his shoulders in a gesture of dismissal, Heck spoke up in his husky voice. "All right, you men, we've been over this war plan, I like to call it, several times. Let me repeat. There will be no passengers on this train. This a special train designed to do one thing—to wipe out LeBeau and his band once and for all. Now I put most of the men in the car next to the mail car where the gold and silver is usually hauled. Nothing in there now, of course, except two of you who will be ready in case LeBeau does get the door open. They think only one man will be waiting for them, but I think they're going to come with all guns blazing. That's the way they always do, and they're convinced that they've got the inside track on the biggest train robbery since there were trains. All right. Any questions?"

For a moment there was silence; then one of Isaac Parker's marshals, Ted Summers, said, "You want us to try and keep 'em alive, Heck?"

"No. Put them down any way you can. If they live, they'll be hanged. If they get shot in the heart, that'll just save the judge an extra trial. All right. If there are no more questions, we'll meet at the train. I've already assigned you your places. When the train slows down, that'll be when they'll send a man to go up and stop the engineer. The train will stop, and that's when they'll come in. All right. Let's get at it."

The men started to leave, but Heck said, "Mr. Warren, you and Mr. Morgan, just a word."

Charles Warren and Frank turned and faced Heck. "What is it, Mr. Thomas?"

"Just Heck will do. I'm gonna tell you one more time. This ain't a good idea."

"Don't try to talk us out of it, Marshal. We're going. Those are our folks that LeBeau is holding. We're going to get them back." Frank's face was paler than usual, but his jaw was set. He glared at Heck Thomas, daring him to reply.

"Well, I can see your mind is set on this, Mr. Warren, and you, too, sir, but let me bring this up. How would you feel if I came into your business office and tried to take over your duties there? You wouldn't permit it for a minute."

"Not the same thing," Charles Warren said abruptly. "This is a matter of family, and you know it."

"Can you shoot?"

"I can shoot this." Warren reached over to the wall and picked up a double-barreled shotgun. "I've got plenty of extra shells. If they get within range, I can blast their heads off."

Despite himself, Heck smiled. "That'll do the job, I guess. What about you, Mr. Morgan?"

"I spend my winters hunting ducks. Not the same as hunting men, I know that's what you're going to say. But I've been in several shooting matches. I've got this rifle. I don't think I can hit anything with a handgun, but with this rifle I won't miss."

Heck paused and tried to summon another argument, but one look at their stern faces and the determined light in both their eyes and he finally shrugged and said, "Well, some of our men are liable to get shot, and you may be the ones."

"We're going to get our womenfolk, Heck," Charles Warren said grimly. "Whatever it takes."

"All right. When the shootin' starts, just be sure you shoot one of them and not one of us."

❧

The mounted party arrived at the cabin where the women were to be kept. It was set back in deep woods, and the path had almost grown over. "This house hasn't been used in a long time," Waco said. "Nobody ever comes here."

"I still don't like it," Breed Marcos said. "They could get loose."

"No, they can't," Waco spoke up at once. He stepped off his

horse and saw that LeBeau had done the same and the outlaw was eyeing him with a hard look.

"Why'd we bring all these extra horses?" Rufo Aznar said. He required a big horse himself since he was over six two and weighed well over two hundred and thirty pounds.

"We want fresh ones," LeBeau said, not taking his eyes off Waco. "When this is over, they'll be sending a posse after us. We've got to outrun everything."

Waco said, "That's good thinking."

Le Beau said, "Well, let's see the inside of this place." The men all dismounted, and Waco stepped up to the door. It was a solid door made of two-inch-thick oak. "They're never gonna break this down," he said. He shoved the door open, and they stepped inside. LeBeau saw that there were only two windows, and a large fireplace dominated one side. The furniture was simply a battered old table, a few chairs, and what was left of a bed.

"This won't do, Waco," LeBeau said. "All they have to do is shove the door open. It locks from the inside."

"We're going to nail it shut on the outside. I already thought of that," Waco said. As a matter of fact, he had not, but he could not show a moment's hesitation. The men were walking around, and Zeno Shaw said, "They must have been expecting Indians or something. This place is like a jail."

"That's right. They can't get out of here. That's why I thought of this place. We can fasten them in, come back after the job's over, and turn 'em loose."

Waco walked over and pulled Sabrina off her horse. "Come on, sweetheart," he said.

Marianne slid off her own horse, and the two walked inside.

Waco said, "Don't be tryin' to bust out of here. If you do, it'll be bad for you."

"We won't do anything," Sabrina said, staring at the rough outlaws.

"No, you won't," LeBeau grinned. "I'm leaving a guard here."

"You can't do that," Munro protested. "We need all the fire-power we got."

"No, Callie will watch these women."

Callie said, "No, I won't do it."

"Do it or I'll shoot you in the leg," LeBeau snapped. "Somebody has to watch these two, and you're the right one."

Waco said, "That's a good idea, Trey." He was facing Callie and winked at her. She caught his meaning and nodded, saying, "All right, I'll do it."

Waco said, "Let's get out of here. We don't have all that much time."

They started out, and Waco saw to it that he was last. He said, "Oh, I forgot something." He turned and came to stand before the two women. "You two women don't try anything funny. You'll be all right if you do what we say."

Sabrina was watching his eyes, and he winked at her, his back to LeBeau. "If you try anything funny, you could get killed, both of you."

"We won't do anything," Sabrina said quietly.

Waco turned and walked outside.

"We'll leave the horses here in that corral right there, tied out back here," LeBeau said.

It took a few minutes to get the extra horses tied out so they could get to water in a trough, and then they all mounted up. "Let's do it," LeBeau said. He turned to Waco and said, "This better work, Waco, or you'll pay for it."

"It'll work." Waco nodded and said, "Go this way." He led the band to the place that he had selected. He pulled up and said, "There. You see that steep curve. Every train that goes through here has to slow down to no more than ten miles an hour."

"Why'd they make it curve like that?" Breed Marcos asked.

"Because they couldn't run it through that big rock formation over there, so they just laid the tracks around it. It slows the train up, and then they have to get up speed again."

"Where are we going to hide out where they can't see us?" LeBeau demanded.

"Right over there in that patch of trees. By the time the train slows down, it won't be going over more than fifteen or twenty miles an hour. So all you have to do is put one man on that train; he goes up and puts a gun on the engineer and makes him stop the train. As soon as the train stops, go for that gold, LeBeau."

"Well, you're always wantin' to show off, Waco." LeBeau smiled, but it did not reach his eyes. "It'll be your job to stop the train."

"I can probably do that better than anybody I see here," Waco said, holding LeBeau's glance.

"All right. Let's get the horses hidden."

"I'll stay here, and the rest of you get on down about a hundred yards. It'll take that long for the train to stop. You can hide out behind those oak trees."

"If anything goes wrong, I'll put a bullet in you, Waco."

"Nothing will go wrong." Waco stepped off his horse, tied it up, and said, "All we have to do is wait."

LeBeau stared at him for a moment then said, "All right.

Let's get on down there and get ourselves ready. How long will it be?"

"It'll be another hour," Waco said, "but we'll need to stay under cover."

"Don't tell me how to run my business," LeBeau said.

LeBeau led the troop up to the clump of oaks that offered shelter. "Get those horses tied down. When we rush the train we won't need them," LeBeau said.

Breed spoke up. "According to what that letter you got said, there'd only be one man on there, but he's expecting us to give the girl to him."

LeBeau grinned. "Let him wait. He can expect anything he wants, but if he argues, we'll give him a bullet in the head."

"Better not do that," Al Munro said. "According to the letter, he can give the word to get us in to where that gold is."

"We won't kill him, but we'll hold a gun to his head and make him think so," Trey said. "Now everybody knows what to do. Scatter out here."

The others moved to both sides from where LeBeau was standing, all except Al Munro. The two men were silent. LeBeau said nothing for so long that his lieutenant said, "What's on your mind? I know you're thinkin' about somethin'."

LeBeau turned and grinned at Munro. "I tell you what, Al. It grates me to have to split all this money with Waco."

For a moment Munro looked startled, and then he grinned. "I don't reckon we have to do that, do we, boss?"

"One of us will take care of it. Once we get the money, take him out."

"What about those women?"

"I guess we can let 'em out of that house and let 'em walk wherever they're goin'."

"Well, they can identify us. Maybe we ought not to give them that chance."

That Al Munro was suggesting that the women be killed to keep from testifying did not seem to shock LeBeau. "Might come to that. Let me think on it. Now let's wait it out here."

Waco had been waiting impatiently, and finally he heard a faint whistle. He got on his horse and said, "Okay boy, get me on board that train, and then you can do as you please." He checked the loads in his guns and pulled his horse out almost to the clear.

Five minutes later he saw the train appear, puffing black smoke, the drivers churning. It began to slow down as it always did, and as it made the curve, the speed lessened even more.

When it came out at its slowest speed, Waco kicked his mount in the side and said, "Get 'em, boy!" The horse shot out like a racehorse opening a race and soon was galloping beside the engine. Waco looked up and grabbed the handles that led beside the stairway. When he got on he saw that the engineer was a tall, lanky man wearing a marshal's badge.

"You must be Waco Smith. I'm Marshal Fred Gierson. He grinned and said, "I used to railroad before I became a lawman. How's it lookin'?"

"Pull it down to a stop, Fred, right now."

Instantly Gierson threw the brakes on, and the screeching of the brake's steel began to sound like a banshee.

"The men all in place?"

"In every car. Mr. Warren and his employee Morgan, they're there, too."

Waco climbed over the coal tinder and entered the first car behind. The first man he met was Heck Thomas, who suddenly grinned and shouted over the noisy engine. "Well, I thought you might be joinin' us. Are they waitin'?"

"They'll jump us as soon we're up by those trees."

"I got men in every car. As soon as they come out, we'll catch 'em in a crossfire. What do you want to do?"

"I'll wait until the train stops. I'll drop out on the other side. I'm gonna run down to that express car. That's where LeBeau will be. I'll try to nail him. Promise me you'll take care of him. By the way, there's a house about three miles northeast by a big cut, an old stone house. Anybody can tell you where it is. The Warren girls are there. You get 'em out if something happens to me."

"Sure, Waco. We'll take care of it. You watch yourself. That LeBeau is a wolf." Pulling his gun, he looked out.

Waco leaped out on the other side. He had not gone ten steps before he heard shots ring out. *Something's gone wrong. They were supposed to go to the man inside. I think somebody's trigger happy.*

The train ground to a complete jolting stop, and Waco crawled beneath it. Before coming out, he saw that the band, all of the men, were shooting at the car, and fire was being returned.

He looked quickly to find LeBeau and saw him stooping down. He fired a shot but didn't have much of a target.

He could tell that the windows were open and Heck's men were throwing a blistering fire on the outlaws. They were completely unprepared for it, and even as he watched, Zeno Shaw was knocked backward, his face a bloody mess. The next to go down was Breed Marcos. The half-Apache was firing rapidly, but a bullet took him and knocked him backward. He tried to lift his gun, but two more slugs struck him. That left Aznar and Al Munro, as well as LeBeau.

Al Munro said, "Let's get out of here. It's a trap."

Munro and Aznar started to run but were cut down by the withering fire. He could hear the boom of a shotgun and couldn't imagine who would be firing it.

Scrambling out from under the car, Waco met Heck, who was reloading his pistol. "I think we got 'em all."

"All except the one we wanted."

Heck looked startled. "You didn't see LeBeau?"

"No. I got a feeling he might have stayed back and let the other men take the risk. The rest of them are dead or wounded."

The men were piling out of the cars, checking the bodies and putting cuffs on the two who were alive and able to stand up.

Suddenly Waco said, "LeBeau's gone to get those women."

Heck shot him a startled glance. "We'd better get there."

Waco said, "I'll take care of it." He ran back to where his horse was standing with the reins dragging. He moved quickly to the saddle and said, "Let's go, boy. Let's have a fast trip." The big horse strode out with a sudden lurch that nearly threw Waco off, but he leaned forward, and although the fight had caused him no fear, he knew what that was now.

The thought passed through his mind. *LeBeau will kill 'em just to get his revenge.* He leaned forward and urged the big stallion to a full driving run and prayed, "God, let me get there in time!"

⊛

Heck Thomas walked the length of the train, stopping to look down at several bodies. He stopped when he saw Charles Warren holding the 12-gauge shotgun and staring down at the body of one of the outlaws. Warren's face was pale, and he turned to ask, "What's his name, Marshal?"

"Breed Marcos," Heck said. "He was a real bad one. Four murders that we know of."

"I think I killed him."

Heck shook his head. "No, you didn't."

"How can you tell?"

"Because those are bullet holes in his chest, not wounds from that shotgun." He saw that Frank Morgan was standing off to one side, a bitter expression on his face. "He's taking it hard, I reckon. When I was a soldier with Lee, I noticed that most of us felt pretty bad after we killed our first Yankee. Almost made me sick! But as time went on, we learned to live with it." He hesitated then added, "You didn't kill this man."

Warren sighed with obvious relief. "I'm glad of that. I just pulled the trigger and reloaded." He stared down at the bloody corpse. "I know he was a bad man, but it's a tragedy for a man to wind up like this."

"He chose his way, Mr. Warren."

"I know, but I can't help feeling sorry for him. If things had been different, he might have had a better life."

"He would have killed your two daughters and thought nothing about it."

Warren looked up abruptly. "I guess he got what he deserved."

"He would have been hanged along with Rufo Aznar if we'd taken him alive. But the bad thing about all this is that the big fish got away."

"You mean LeBeau?"

"Yes." Heck shook his head, an angry expression on his

sunburned features. "I'd rather we got LeBeau and the rest had lived. He's the kingpin, and he'll get another bunch of outlaws, and we'll have it all to do again."

"What about my daughters?"

"Well, Waco told me they were kept in a cabin not too far from here." Heck's mouth drew into an angry line, and he continued, "Waco had his horse, and he's on his way there now. I hope they're all right. Waco said they left that woman that hangs out with the gang to guard them." Heck suddenly called to one of his men and walked away, and Frank came at once to stand before Warren. His face was strained, and he said, "I'm glad that's over. Did you hit any of them?"

"Marshal Thomas said I didn't, not a killing wound anyway. How about you?"

Morgan's mouth became a tight line, and he said, "I killed the one they call Al Munro. He was LeBeau's right-hand man. I shot and hit him right in the heart."

"I know you feel bad about that."

"Not as bad as if he'd hurt Marianne or Sabrina."

"Well, we've got to go to them as soon as Heck's men locate the horses."

"Charles, I've got to tell you something."

"What is it, Frank?"

"I'm going to marry Marianne." Morgan took a deep breath then said, "I've loved her for a long time, but she wanted another kind of man. She's going to have a hard time getting over this, and I'm going to be right with her."

Warren said, "Why, Frank, Caroline and I have wished for a long time that you and Marianne would make a match of it. We'd be proud to have you in the family."

Even as he spoke, a rider emerged from the timber leading

three mounts. "There's our horses," Heck said. "Mount up and we'll go to your girls. Waco told me how to get there. The place ain't far, but LeBeau is a wolf. He got beat, and he'll try to get even."

The three mounted, and Heck led them out at a driving run. It was all Charles Warren could do to stay in the saddle, but he could only pray that his girls were all right.

☙

"Somebody's coming in. It must be over," Sabrina said.

"I hope Waco's all right and the rest of the men, too," Marianne said.

Sabrina called out, "Waco, is that you?" There was no answer and finally the door itself swung open, but instead of Waco, Trey LeBeau stepped inside. His face was red, and he was furious. "Well, you two pulled a fast one."

"What are you talking about?" Sabrina gasped.

"That train was packed full of lawmen. They got all of us except me, so that leaves me with you."

"Just let us go, LeBeau," Marianne said. "You can't take us with you."

"I can do it all right. Waco Smith will be here soon if I know him. You stand inside there. You make a funny move I'll kill you."

The two women moved back and watched as LeBeau loaded his six-shooter. He put it in his holster but stood behind the open door looking out.

Callie said, "We can ride away from this, Trey. Leave these women alone."

"Not likely. We're leavin', you and me, but not until after I kill Waco Smith."

At that moment Sabrina Warren knew how much Waco meant to her. She had not recognized it until now, and she was convinced that LeBeau would shoot him down without warning. She knew it would be a dark hour for her.

"There he comes. You women get over there!"

"Let me go out and talk to him," Callie said.

"Nothin' doin'. You're all soft on him. I knew it all the time. He won't get you now. We'll get out of here and start a new life." LeBeau suddenly turned and said, "There he is." He watched as Waco pulled up and stepped off his horse twenty feet from the cabin door. He raised his revolver.

Suddenly Callie ran past him. She moved across the yard, calling, "LeBeau's inside, Waco! He's going to kill you!"

Waco stopped and put one bullet through the open door. He could see the shape of LeBeau. No sooner did he fire than LeBeau returned the fire, and he felt it rake his ribs. Not a bad wound. He knew he was a dead target there, for LeBeau was in the shadows of the house and he was afraid to fire for hitting Marianne or Sabrina.

Suddenly Callie put herself against him, and even as she did, Waco felt her body shudder as a bullet struck her. "Callie!" he cried and lowered her to the ground. He saw LeBeau come running out of the cabin, firing as he came. He had time to lift his gun and fired one shot. It caught LeBeau in the chest. It stopped him, and LeBeau stared down at the blood that stained the front of his shirt. He looked up and tried to speak but couldn't. He tried to lift his gun, but it was suddenly too heavy. It dropped from his fingers, and suddenly he collapsed and fell to the dust.

"Are you all right, Callie?" He knew this was a foolish question. He could feel the blood on his hand where he was holding it behind her back. He was aware of the two women who had come out of the cabin, but he leaned forward, for Callie was trying to speak. "What did you say, Callie? I didn't hear you." He put his ear down to her lips and felt her hand on his face. Her voice was feeble, and suddenly she whispered, "We won't be going on that trip, will we, Waco?"

As Waco held her, she died in his arms. When her body went limp, emptiness and despair filled his heart.

CHAPTER 23

As soon as he pulled up his horse, Charles Warren saw the lifeless body of LeBeau and Waco sitting on the ground, holding a woman in his arms. Then he saw Marianne and Sabrina, and crying their names, he fell out of his saddle and ran to where they stood. As he caught Marianne in his arms, she cried out, "Dad! You came for us!"

"Of course I did!" Warren tried to speak, but his throat was tight and he felt tears running down his cheeks. He held her close and felt her body trembling, but she was safe! "Are you all right, daughter?" he whispered.

"I—I'm fine now."

Warren turned to embrace Sabrina. "You did it, Sabrina!" Warren said. "I'm so proud of you!"

"It wasn't me, Dad. It was Waco."

"But you found him and you stayed with him. What happened?"

Sabrina did not speak at once but finally said, "Waco planned the whole thing, Dad. I once thought he was pretty dense, but he's smart! He had to convince LeBeau and all the other outlaws that he had a plan to make them all rich. Some of them wanted to shoot us, LeBeau for one, but he just sold them all on his scheme."

"Were you afraid?"

"I was scared to death, but Waco had told me what to do. He told them I was the key to getting the information about the gold and the train it would come on. Dad, he never showed anything like fear. He has more nerve than any man I've ever seen!"

"How did he treat you?"

Sabrina smiled. "Like dirt. He had to convince them that I was the key to the whole thing, and he treated me terribly. Once he slapped me after asking me if he could for the act, and it helped convince LeBeau."

Warren studied Waco and saw that his features were twisted with grief. He hesitated then asked, "Were they lovers—Waco and that woman?"

"Once they were, a long time ago."

"Looks like he never got over her."

"He did, but he had to use her to get Marianne and me away."

"Use her how?"

Sabrina hesitated then said, "It's complicated, Dad."

"He looks like he's grieving. Doesn't that mean he still loves her?"

Sabrina shook her head. "He used her to keep LeBeau and the others fooled. But he told me that he felt nothing for her any longer, that he had never really loved her. But he never told her that."

Warren shook his head. "I don't understand why he's so shook up over her death if he didn't love her."

Sabrina knew that it would be impossible to convey to her father all that had gone on with Callie, but she had to try. "She saved his life," she said simply.

"How did she do that?"

"When LeBeau came back, he told us he was going to kill Waco. He meant it, too. You could see it in his eyes."

"What about the woman? What's her name?"

"Her name is Calandra Montevado, but everyone called her Callie."

"If she was in love with Waco, wouldn't LeBeau have known it?"

"I think he knew, and it gave him one more reason for killing Waco. I think he planned all the time to kill him."

"But how did she die, Sabrina?"

"When Waco rode up, LeBeau stayed inside, but he had his gun out. We all saw he meant to shoot him down. Callie ran outside, and she was calling out, 'LeBeau's inside, Waco! He's going to kill you!' Then she got in front of Waco, and when LeBeau fired, his bullet hit Callie in the back. Waco caught her, and when LeBeau ran out the door firing, Waco got off one shot, but it killed LeBeau."

Warren turned to stare at the big man holding the dead woman. "So she saved his life and lost her own doing it. She must have loved him greatly."

"Yes, I think she did." Sabrina nodded. "I ran out to where she was lying in Waco's arms, dying, and I heard her say, 'We'll never make that trip now, will we?' "

"Which trip did she mean?"

"She had begged Waco to run away with her. She said she was tired of the life she's been living."

"I see. So that is what's bothering him."

"Yes. He promised her they'd have a life together, but he never meant to do it. And that's why he's sitting there in the dirt holding her. He knows he can never make it up to her."

"Maybe he'll get over it. Most men do."

"I don't know, Dad. He's a rough man, but he feels things more deeply than you can guess. He may not be able to put her death behind him." She turned her face away from him, but not before he saw the stricken look on her face.

❦

"I can't tell you how I feel, Marianne," Frank said. He had come to stand beside her while Warren spoke to Sabrina. "I don't think I've had a full night's sleep since you were kidnapped."

"I wasn't kidnapped, Frank," Marianne said in a spare tone, devoid of feeling. "I ran away with an evil man, and all the time all of you were telling me how foolish I was."

Morgan shook his head. "You were inexperienced, Marianne, and thought you were in love. We all behave foolishly over love." He waited for her to speak, but she said nothing. It was this silence that troubled him, that and the deadness he seemed to see in her eyes. He desperately wanted to take the pain away from her, but he was wise enough to know that only time and true, godly love would make a difference to this woman he loved so greatly. He looked toward Waco, wondering at how he held to the dead woman, and then he noticed how Sabrina was standing a few feet away, her eyes fixed on him. "Sabrina looks terrible," he said. "Why do you suppose that is? She didn't know that woman all that well, did she?"

"She's not grieving for Callie," Marianne said. "She sees what's happening to Waco."

"What do you mean?"

"She's fallen in love with Waco."

"No! That can't be so."

"Why not? He's a strong man."

"But they're not alike, Marianne, not in the least."

"I think they may be more alike than you think. She had no

use for him when they first met, but they went through some hard times, and that changed Sabrina."

"They come from different worlds," Morgan said, shaking his head. "And it looks to me like he cares for that woman. Look how he's holding her."

"She died for him, Frank," Marianne whispered. "When someone dies for you, I don't think you can ever walk away from that unscathed."

"It's all over, Marianne."

"No, it will never be over."

Frank said, "Time will help," but she looked at him with tears in her eyes. He said softly, "You've got a whole life ahead of you, Marianne, and I intend to be in it."

Waco had once been struck a violent blow in the stomach that had taken away his breath and rendered him unable to speak or move. Now as he sat holding the dear body of Callie, he was unable to think or to speak. He was aware of people moving and speaking, but none of it made any sense to him. All he could do was try to think of how he had failed Callie, and a sense of deep hopelessness cloaked him, profound and frightening.

He heard his name spoken and looked up to see Heck Thomas standing over him. "What did you say, Heck?" he asked, his voice thready and uncertain.

"We've got to get back to the train, Waco." Heck squatted on his heels and stared into Waco's eyes. "It's time to get away from here."

Waco turned his head and saw that they had tied LeBeau's body facedown on his horse. "You're not tying Callie on a horse like that," he said flatly.

Heck said softly, "We've got to get her into town, son."

"Not like that."

Waco glanced across at Sabrina, who had come to stand and watch. She stooped down and asked, "What do you want us to do, Waco?"

Her words seemed to confuse Waco, but then he said almost roughly, "Bring me my horse, Sabrina."

At once Sabrina rose and walked quickly to the line of horses that were tied to a rail in front of the cabin. Quickly she loosed Captain's reins and led him back to where Waco held the dead woman.

Waco looked for a long moment at Callie's still face then carefully laid her down. He rose and stepped into the saddle, then said, "Hand her up to me, Heck."

At once Heck bent and picked up the limp body of Callie and lifted her up. Waco took the body and placed her in front of him, and with his left arm, he held her close to his chest. He touched Captain with his heels, and the big stallion moved forward at a slow place. Waco did not look back nor did he speak.

As Waco rode away, Sabrina said, "Marshal, I know I should be rejoicing. My sister and I are both safe and LeBeau and his outlaws are gone—but I feel like crying."

Heck turned and said softly, "Know what you mean, Miss Sabrina. I never saw a man take anything so hard. It's like that bullet that killed that woman hit him right in the heart. I just don't understand it. Waco is a pretty tough man, but this has brought him down. He must have loved her a lot."

"No, he didn't love her," Sabrina whispered. She watched as Captain bore his burden out of the tree line then added, "He didn't love her enough." *He'll never forget her,* she thought, *not after this.*

She turned quickly and went back to stand beside her family. They seemed mystified by what had happened, but no one questioned her.

"Well, we've got to get the bodies and the prisoners back to Fort Smith." Heck walked to his horse, mounted, and moved forward slowly. The others all got into the saddle, and as they left the clearing, both Sabrina and Marianne turned and gave the cabin a last glance. Sabrina knew that this day would not be easily forgotten—if ever.

❧

As the procession reached the train, Heck waited until Waco halted. Then when the big man simply sat there silently holding the limp form of Callie, he knew what he must do. He dismounted and said, "I'll be right back, Waco."

Heck moved quickly to the car that ordinarily would have carried mail and gold. He stepped inside and found three of his men sitting around laughing. Heck said roughly, "You fellows clear out." His words were sharp, and the three left without waiting for any other word.

Heck had remembered that the car held a cot for the use of the mail clerk who traveled for the railroad. He found a clean blanket, laid it carefully over the cot, then moved to the sliding door and opened it. He saw Waco still holding the woman and called, "You can put her in here, son."

He saw Waco move his shoulders and give him a strange look.

"Hand her up to me," Heck said, and at this word, Waco spoke

SABRINA'S MAN

to the big stallion, who came to stand at the sliding door. "I can take her," Heck said, and for a moment he thought that Waco would refuse, but then he nodded and lifted the lifeless woman. Heck took her and said, "Come on in, and I'll put your horse in the cattle car with the other mounts."

"All right, Heck." Waco simply stood up in the stirrups, then with an agile move rose and, catching the side of the opening, lifted himself into the car.

"You can put her on that cot," Heck said. When Waco lifted his arms and took the woman, he said, "I'll take care of your horse, and then we'll be on our way."

"Thanks, Heck," Waco said woodenly.

Heck left the car and shut the door. Taking Captain's reins, he walked down the track and loaded the big stallion into the cattle car.

As soon as he closed the door, Sabrina came to ask, "Where did you put her, Marshal?"

"The railroad furnishes a cot for the man who handles the mail. I expect Waco will put her on there."

"Did he say anything?"

"Not much. Reckon I'll go back and see if everything is all right."

He moved back, mounted the steps, and entered the mail car. He saw at once that Waco had laid the body of Callie on the cot, had folded her hands over her breast, and was smoothing her hair.

"This okay, Waco?"

"Sure." Waco finished arranging Callie's hair, then turned suddenly and asked, "Did you ever do a friend a bad turn, Heck?"

Heck Thomas was caught off guard but nodded slowly. "I'm grieved to say that I let my partner down. Ain't ever been about to put it out of my mind, and that was over twenty years ago."

"What happened?"

"I was in the Texas Rangers then, and my partner was Sollie Bacus. We got jumped by a Kiowa war party. We lit out, but Sollie caught an arrow in his back. He hollered at me to keep going, said he was a goner."

Heck fell silent then said, "The Kiowas swarmed all over him. I was about to stop and help, but he called out, 'Get out of here, Heck!' " A sad expression came into Heck's face, and he said, "I should have gone to him, Waco. I know the hostiles would have gotten both of us, but I've grieved over what I done for twenty years."

Both men were silent, lost in a deep sadness, and finally Heck said, "No going back, Waco. We both of us got regrets, but all we can do is go on livin' and make sure we never let anybody else down."

Waco sat beside the body of Callie. Heck came and sat beside him and tried to make him feel better, but Waco would not be comforted.

Finally Heck said, "Well son, one person in this world loved you enough to die for you. That's one more than most folks have."

As soon as the train pulled to a stop at the station in Fort Smith, Charles Warren stepped down and gave Sabrina and Marianne a helping hand. Caroline had been waiting and rushed forward to embrace both her daughters. She was weeping for joy and could not speak.

Heck saw Judge Parker standing to watch the train and went at once to him. "Well, Judge, we got the whole bunch. All but two of them are dead."

"What about LeBeau?"

"Dead as a hammer."

"Who got him, Heck?"

"Well, it's a right sad story, Judge." He told Parker the story of how the woman Callie had taken a bullet for Waco and how Waco had killed him.

"I'm sorry it didn't work out for Waco, but LeBeau was the kingpin. I'd say we owe Waco Smith something. I hope he'll join up with us."

Heck shook his head, saying, "Doubt that will happen, Judge. The bullet that killed the woman—it was like Waco took a bullet right in his heart but didn't die."

"He'll have to get over it."

"I ain't sure he can ever do that."

⤳

Judge Parker stood before Waco. "I'm sorry for all this Waco, but let me say we have a place for you on the force."

"Judge, I'm through with all this."

Parker nodded and said, "Let me take care of your friend."

"No, I have to do it all, Judge. Who takes care of things like this?"

"I thought so. You need Caleb Felton. His place is right across from the courthouse. He's a good man, and he'll take good care of your friend."

Waco picked up Callie's body and carried her down the street. He was aware that people were watching but could only think of the loss her death had caused him.

He was met at the door by a tall man with dark blue eyes who said, "I'm Caleb Felton. I heard about your loss."

"My name is Smith. This is Calandra Montevado. Do your best for her."

"I'll do my best for the lady. Bring her this way."

Waco followed Felton down a hall and placed her body on a padded table. He took one look at Callie then walked rapidly away.

CHAPTER 24

"Marianne, I've got to talk to you."

The sound of Frank Morgan's voice had caught Marianne off guard. She had been overwhelmed by the almost hysterical happiness of her mother, and her father seemed unwilling to let her out of his sight. She knew they had been terribly hurt by what had happened to her.

She had been standing in the twilight of the afternoon watching the sun drop beneath the horizon. It made a golden glow, but her emotions were anything but cheerful. Over and over again she went over how foolish she had been to ignore her parents' advice about LeBeau, and then following that was the utter misery thinking how he had used her and abused her. She turned quickly and said, "I can't talk to you now, Frank."

Morgan moved closer and saw that tears stained her cheeks. "I know you're all upset," he said, "but I've got some things I need to say to you."

"Not now, Frank, please!"

Morgan almost turned and walked away, but he set his jaw

and shook his head. "I know it's not a good time, but probably it will never be a good time, or at least a better time than right now." He reached out tentatively, for she had turned away. He turned her around until she was looking up at him.

She studied him with an odd intensity, and then her lips began to tremble and she knew that there was nothing he or anyone else could do to change what had happened.

"We're going to have to talk about this, Marianne." His voice was gentle, and suddenly she began to sob. Reaching out, Morgan pulled her in and held her. She put her head against his shoulder and for a long time could do nothing but give great gasping sobs. Slowly she began to grow calm, and Frank waited until she was. Taking out his handkerchief, he wiped the tears from her face and said, "I know it's going to take some time, Marianne. What happened to you was terrible, but it's over now."

"No, it will never be over." Her voice was tense, and she looked up at him and whispered, "No man could ever forget what's happened to me."

"Don't be foolish. A good man wouldn't think twice about that. It's not your fault, Marianne. It was against your will."

"Doesn't matter."

"It matters to me. You know I've cared for you a long time, and when you were in such trouble, my love seemed to grow. What I want us to do, Marianne, just as quickly as you can do it, both of us together, we'll shut the door on this. I want you to marry me. I know it's too early to talk of that, but we'll spend time together. We'll be going home soon. I'll go back to work, and you'll live in your house. We'll begin doing things together. We'll take rides in the park. We'll go to the zoo. We'll read books together, and all the time God will be giving us both peace."

"You think that could happen, Frank?" Marianne's tone was wistful, and she felt like a small child as she stood in the encirclement of his arms.

"Of course it can, and it's going to."

Sighing suddenly, she put her cheek against his chest and savored for a brief moment the strength she felt there. "I'll never forget how you came to fight for me, Frank. That was something I didn't expect."

"Well, I'm hoping you'll see a lot of things in me you didn't expect."

The two stood there until the sun suddenly dropped and they were standing in the shadows.

As the sunlight faded, Marianne felt another light begin to dispel some of the darkness in her heart.

Judge Parker looked over at Heck Thomas, who was sitting in his chair tilted back against the wall. "Waco is still acting like he's a dead man."

Heck shrugged his shoulders. "I did some askin' around. Found out a few things. He and that woman had quite an affair goin' a few years ago. Sweethearts, you know. The way I get it, he was gonna use her to make his getaway, and then when she got killed, well. . ."

"You're right about that. He stays in the saloon all night and hides out in the daytime where nobody can get at him. I've tried to talk to him, but he just won't listen."

"Well, he's too good a man to waste. I never thought we'd bust up LeBeau's bunch, but he did the job. As you know, I wanted him to become a marshal, but he declined my offer." Parker sighed.

"He just seems so lost."

"Well, that's what a woman can do to a man. When I was talkin' to Miss Sabrina, though, somethin' came out. I could tell she feels somethin' for Waco."

Parker looked up with surprise. "Why, she's rich and comes from a fine family. Waco hasn't got anything but the clothes he's standing in."

"I don't think that's the whole story. I'll keep an eye on him, Judge."

"You do that. He's too good a man to waste."

"Sabrina, I need to talk to you."

Turning quickly, Sabrina gave her father a quick look and saw that he was in deep thought. She had learned to read him fairly well and saw that he was troubled. "What is it, Dad?"

"Something I have to ask you about."

Sabrina sighed. "I'm tired of talking about it. I thank God He got us out of that by His grace. Just a miracle that Waco wasn't killed, and I think LeBeau pretty well decided to kill me and Marianne, too. He just kept us alive to trap Waco."

"Sit down a minute and let's talk." They were on the front porch of the hotel, and the walkway was empty. It was midday, and the sun was beating down on Fort Smith, bringing with it the intolerable heat.

Sabrina shrugged but followed his request and sat down in one of the rockers.

He pulled his chair around to where he could see her face and said, "I've got to know something, daughter."

"What's that, Dad?"

"Well, you can tell me if it's none of my business. I'm used to that. But I've had some long thoughts since all this happened with Marianne and then almost losing you. It shook me up some."

"You never were much shaken by anything," Sabrina remarked. She studied her father's face and saw that there were lines that she had never noticed before. "What is it that's bothering you?"

"Well, I may be all wrong," Charles Warren said slowly and rather reluctantly. "But I've got the feeling that you feel something for this man Smith. Your mother feels the same way. Now, I don't know about a father poking into his children's private lives, but this thing has made me love my family more. I don't want to miss any signs. What do you think of this man?"

Sabrina dropped her head and was silent for a while. When she looked up, Charles Warren saw that her face was tense. "It's hard to say. He's not what I thought he was."

"What do you mean by that?"

"Well, he was in prison, and to tell the truth I was a real snob. I just used him, but we were together alone quite a bit, and I got to know him. He's had a terrible life. Betrayed by his best friend and a woman that he loved. He's never gotten over it."

"That can cut a man pretty bad."

"Well, it almost destroyed him. He just gave up and became an outlaw. But he's got more to him than that. I know he has."

"So you love the man?"

"I—I feel something for him."

"What about him? Does he care for you?"

"It's hard to say. I think he does, but since Callie died, he's been sunk in some sort of deep depression. He drinks all the time, and from what I hear that's not like him."

"Well, I can kind of understand that. She took a bullet for

303

him. From what you told me, it would have killed him if she hadn't jumped to save him."

"I know. He's very bitter, and I don't know anything to bring him out of it."

"Well, we've got the woman's funeral to go to."

"Are you going?"

"Yes, we'll all go. She wasn't a good woman, but she did a good thing there at the last, and I want to honor her for it."

Waco did not want to attend the funeral of Callie. More than anything else he longed to just get on his horse and ride away and try to put all the thoughts of her and everything else about this sorry affair behind him. He knew, however, that he would be a long time, maybe forever, trying to forget her.

Pastor Mordecai Jones read a long list of scriptures, but they meant little to Waco. Finally he heard the pastor say, "One thing I may conclude my remarks with. Most of us live for ourselves. We take care of ourselves, we're worried about our problems, and very rarely do we find a human being who steps outside of that pattern." Jones hesitated for a moment then said, "But this woman, who had struggled with a hard life, at the last moment gave the gift, the greatest gift. The Bible says that Jesus came to die for the sins of all of us, and we are eternally grateful for that. Now every time I think of this woman, I will have the thought she had her problems but at the end she gave the most precious thing she had, her life, for her friend."

At these words Waco bowed his head and closed his eyes. He wanted to get up and leave but could not. He stayed until the service was over and then followed the funeral procession. When they reached the cemetery, they surrounded the open grave. The pastor read a few scriptures and then dismissed.

Finally Waco turned and stumbled away. He heard Sabrina calling him, but he did not hesitate.

Sabrina followed him, saying, "I have to talk to you, Waco."

Waco stopped, turned, and saw that the crowd was dispersing. "I've got to get away from here." He turned back and began walking.

"Then I'll go with you."

Waco gritted his teeth and said harshly, "Go away and leave me alone!"

"I can't do that."

Finally they reached the edge of town. There were few people stirring that afternoon.

Sabrina said, "Waco, I know you're sad and grieved over Callie's death, and you should be. It was the bravest thing I ever saw anybody ever do. She loved you very much indeed."

"Don't say that!"

Sabrina's eyes opened with surprise. "Why shouldn't I? It's true enough."

"Don't you understand, Sabrina? I was using her. I let her think I loved her. That after the robbery she and I would run away together. I knew all the time that was a lie. I'd give anything if I could do it all over again."

Sabrina knew she was standing on precarious ground. She said quietly after a long pause, "You were trying to do a good thing in the best way you could. Think about what it means to my family, especially to Marianne. I think she'll marry Frank and they'll have a family. That never would have happened if it hadn't been for you. I think LeBeau would have killed me. I saw it in his eyes, and it didn't happen because you were there."

Waco stood with his head bowed, listening as Sabrina spoke on. Finally he said, "I can't live with this thing."

"You can have a good life, Waco."

"How can I live a good life? God can't use me."

"God doesn't need to use any of us. You know what the Bible says God wants of us?"

"I guess to work hard for Him."

"He doesn't need anybody to work for Him. He's almighty. He can do what He pleases. But there's one thing we can give Him, and I'm just now finding out what it is."

Waco lifted his head and saw that there was a tremendously sober look on her features. "What's that?"

"God created us to do one thing. To worship Him. To love Him. If we do that, we've satisfied Him. Anything we could do for Him, that's fine, but to love God, that's what Jesus said. 'Thou shall love the Lord thy God with all thy heart, with all thy soul, and with all thy might.' That's what I'm going to try to do for the rest of my life—and I would like it very much if you would do the same thing."

Waco did not answer. He heaved a deep sigh and said, "I'm not sure I could do a thing like that."

"I would like to see you try, and I'll help you all I can. You've made so many friends here. Judge Parker and Heck and my family. We all care for you. But we don't care for you as much as God cares for you."

Waco stood stock still, and he whispered, "I just don't know, Sabrina. Let me alone." He turned and walked quickly away and was relieved when she did not follow him. He walked to the stable and was surprised to see Gray Wolf standing in the shadows.

"Hello, Gray Wolf."

He said in his direct manner, "God's giving you another chance. If that woman hadn't got in the way, you would have been dead, and you wouldn't have any way to make it right with God. But she bought you some time. Now act like it. Don't act like a fool."

Waco felt a flash of anger, but then it passed. He shook his head slightly. "I'm not worth saving."

"Yes, you are as much as any of us. Climb out of that whiskey bottle and act like a man."

Gray Wolf suddenly faded back in the shadows, and Waco stood there silently, thinking of Sabrina's words and then of Gray Wolf's warning. He got his horse and went for a long ride, but he could not ride far enough to avoid the thoughts that came to him. He thought of Callie's face as she lay dying in his arms, and it was a razor cutting him to pieces on the inside.

Finally, when darkness came, he went back and for a moment thought of going to talk to Sabrina. But instead he turned and walked into the Lone Eagle Saloon. He began to drink and knew that he was a lost cause.

Time passed, and he knew he was so drunk he could barely walk. Suddenly he felt something on his side. He turned to see that Heck Thomas had pulled his gun loose. "Don't take my gun, Heck."

"Come along with me. You're under arrest."

Waco had trouble speaking his tongue was so thick. "For what?"

"For being a fool. Now come on." Heck hauled Waco out of the saloon, and Waco could barely walk. When he got to the jail, he hardly knew it when Heck shoved him into a cell and down onto a cot. "Stay there for a while."

Waco wanted to protest, but he was so drunk he fell into a stupor.

"Well, are you sober enough for me to turn you loose?"

Waco looked up, and his head was throbbing. "Let me out of this place."

"I'll let you out, but first you've got to talk to a man."

"What man?"

Thomas did not answer. He led Waco out of the cell and took him to a small office.

Waco saw that Charles Warren was sitting there. "Hello, Waco," Warren said. "Sit down. I've got to talk to you."

"You can pick up your gun when you leave, Waco," Heck said. "You listen to this man. He's got sense."

Charles Warren said nothing but watched as Waco sat down in a chair. Waco's hands were trembling, and Warren said, "I know you feel awful. Hangovers are no fun."

"No, they're not. What do you want to talk about?"

"What are you going to do with yourself, Smith?"

"I got no idea."

"Are you going to become one of Judge Parker's marshals? He told me he'd be glad to have you."

"No, I'll never do that again. I've had enough of that sort of thing."

"Then you'll have to have a job."

"I can get a job somewhere takin' care of stock or on a ranch. I can handle cattle."

Warren fell silent, and Waco blinked. "What else do you want to talk about besides my future?"

"I want to find out how you feel about my daughter."

"Your daughter?"

"Yes. Sabrina. You remember her?"

"What do you mean how I feel about her?"

"I think she cares for you."

"Well, that's impossible. We're too different."

"Women choose men who are different sometimes. My wife did. I was no good when I met her, but she saw something in me. If it hadn't been for her, I'd be in the poorhouse or worse. I was no good for her. Maybe you're no good for my daughter, but I need to know how you feel about her."

"It doesn't matter," Waco said quietly. "She'd never care for me."

"I think she does."

Waco said, "You're a smart man, Mr. Warren, but you're wrong this time."

"You'll have to talk to her. If she cares for you, and you walk away from her, you'll hurt her terribly. I think she's been hurt enough, and I'm asking you to overlook some things in her. I know she's proud, she's spoiled, but she's got good stuff in her. She's a good woman."

"No question about that. The question is me."

"I guess I know more about men than most, and I see something in you that needs to come out."

Waco laughed. "I don't know what that would be."

"You talk to her, and you two decide which way you're going. If you decide to tell her you love her and you'll share each other the rest of your life and she tells you the same thing, we'll talk some more."

"I'll talk to her, but it seems a waste to me." Waco got up and left the room. He picked up his gun, strapped it on, and looked at it with disgust. "I hope I never have to shoot you again," he said.

He made his way toward the hotel where he knew the Warrens were staying. When he walked up on the porch, he saw that Sabrina was sitting there.

"Did you talk to Dad?"

Surprised, Waco said, "Yes, I did. How did you know?"

"Because I told him to talk to you. Sit down, Waco."

Waco sat down feeling as uncomfortable as he ever had in his life. "Your dad's got some funny ideas."

"Funny like what?"

"He thinks—" Waco could barely say the words. "He thinks we're in love."

"What's funny about that?"

Waco suddenly grinned. He felt miserable, but this woman always had something to throw at him when he wasn't ready. "Nothing much except you're rich, from a fine family, and used to good things. I'm nothing but a bum, never done anything really good in my life. Why shouldn't we fall in love?"

Sabrina suddenly rose and said, "Stand up."

Waco stood up at once and stood to face her.

She suddenly reached up, put her arms around his neck, pulled his head down, and kissed him.

Waco felt something turn over in him. He knew that he had had some feeling for this woman, but the tragedy of Callie had driven it all away. When she released him, he looked down at her and said, "I guess I'll have to tell you, Sabrina, I love you. Never thought I'd say that."

"Well, I love you, too, Waco. I know we're different. I know there's going to be hard times. I'm a spoiled brat, and some of that's still in me, but I ask you to help me to become a godly woman and a good wife."

"Well, who's going to help me?"

"Everybody. My father will help you and my mother. Marianne, too. She worships you almost. You know you saved her from death. And I care for you, too. I love you, Waco."

Suddenly Waco Smith found himself unable to speak. "One thing, Sabrina. . .I've been thinking about God for some time now. I don't know how to go about it, but I'm going to become a servant of the Lord."

"Waco, I'm so glad. Come on. Let's go tell my family that we're engaged."

"Why, we can't just bust in and tell them that."

"I can. Come along."

The two walked into the hotel. "I saw Father come in a minute ago. He'll be with Mother." Sabrina smiled. "They'll be waiting on a report of our matrimonial expectations."

"It'll be mighty poor doings if we get married. No honeymoon."

"As long as we have each other, Waco, that's all I ask."

The two walked upstairs and paused in front of a door. Sabrina knocked on the door, and Charles Warren's voice said, "Come in, daughter. Bring him with you."

As soon as they stepped inside, Waco felt that he was trapped. He saw the whole family was there, including Marianne and Frank Morgan.

"Well, what's the status? Did he say he loved you, daughter?"

"He said so."

"And Sabrina, do you love him?" her mother asked anxiously.

"Yes, I do."

"Oh, that's wonderful!" Marianne said. She was standing

beside Frank Morgan, and her eyes now glowed. "You saved my life, Waco, and I'll never forget it."

"Neither one of us will. This is good news," Frank added.

"Not very good news," Waco said. "I never heard of a more unlikely pair. I don't even have a job."

Charles said, "You sure this is what you want to do? You love my daughter?"

"Yes, I do, Mr. Warren. That's the one thing that's sure."

"Well, let me tell you something. I've been investing in fine horses for a couple of years. I bought some land and hired three louts to take care of the horses. They don't know one end of a horse from the other. You think you got sense enough to make it pay?"

Waco laughed. "It's the only thing I did growing up, take care of horses. It's the only thing I'm good at."

Mrs. Warren came over and put her hand on Waco's cheek. "Do you *really* love Sabrina?"

"Yes, I do, Mrs. Warren, with all my heart. She'll never know anything but love from me."

"Well, I'll have to have a little bit more than that," Sabrina said loudly.

Waco's eyes opened wide. "What do you mean?"

"We're going back to our home. You're going to show us you know something about horses, and you've got to come courting me. You've got to buy some nice clothes and learn how to say sweet and lovely things. Say something sweet to me now just to get into practice."

Waco suddenly laughed. He winked at Charles Warren and said, "Marshmallow."

Sabrina laughed. "Well, that's sweeter than anything you've

ever said. Come on, let's go have our engagement party."

"Judge Parker will be sad," Warren said. "He's losing a marshal."

"Yes, but you're gaining a good son-in-law," Sabrina said. She took Waco's arm and said, "Come on, husband-to-be, let's start our courting."

ABOUT THE AUTHOR

Award-winning, bestselling author Gilbert Morris is well known for penning numerous Christian novels for adults and children since 1984 with 6.5 million books in print. He is probably best known for the forty-book House of Winslow series, and his Edge of Honor was a 2001 Christy Award winner. He lives with his wife in Gulf Shores, Alabama.

The Old West Adventure Continues with. . .

RAINA'S CHOICE

Coming June 2014